Praise f

"This book is such a savvy, deadpan, moving meditation-unto-absurdity on obsession and trauma and throwaway television and the ways that our hobbies can hurt us and heal us and sometimes overwhelm us. I absolutely loved it."

—**Amber Sparks,** author of *And I Do Not Forgive You*

"Like some uncanny hybrid of Tom McCarthy, Ottessa Moshfegh, and *Mulholland Drive*, Ashley Hutson's high-concept black comedy, *One's Company*, packs deranged laughs against deep trauma in a no-holds-barred debut. Surreal, ambitious, and page-turning, the painful memory performance of Bonnie Lincoln's wish to live forever in a sitcom might be more realistic than the realism we think we know."

—**Blake Butler,** author of *Alice Knott*

"Ashley Hutson's novel fearlessly takes on trauma, loneliness, madness, and desire in wholly unexpected ways. The dazzling imagination of the novel's formidable protagonist, Bonnie Lincoln, is rivaled only by that of her brilliant creator: *One's Company* is a totally original, bitterly funny, and emotionally complex tale about the power of fantasy to both save and destroy the things we cherish."

—**Maryse Meijer,** author of *The Seventh Mansion*

One's Company

One's Company

a novel

Ashley Hutson

W. W. NORTON & COMPANY
Independent Publishers Since 1923

For information about permission to reproduce selections from this book,
write to Permissions, W. W. Norton & Company, Inc.,
500 Fifth Avenue, New York, NY 10110

For information about special discounts for bulk purchases, please contact
W. W. Norton Special Sales at specialsales@wwnorton.com or 800-233-4830

Manufacturing by Lakeside Book Company
Book design by Beth Steidle
Production manager: Beth Steidle

ISBN 978-0-393-86664-3 (pbk.)

W. W. Norton & Company, Inc., 500 Fifth Avenue, New York, N.Y. 10110
www.wwnorton.com

W. W. Norton & Company Ltd., 15 Carlisle Street, London W1D 3BS

1 2 3 4 5 6 7 8 9 0

For Brian George Hose,
my oldest and dearest

The dream that I see makes me what I am.

—Walter Marks, "I've Gotta Be Me"

One

After I won the lottery, a lot of strangers showed up to tell me what a piece of trash I was. Then they would ask me for money. Neighbors known and unknown to me, people I used to see at the market, old high school classmates who'd never given me the time of day—they all felt compelled to "just say hi."

I knew they hated me because most people hate unglamorous luck. That's what winning money with a mindless number is, unearned and uninherited wealth, and each new arrival acted like something had been stolen from them. "It's so nice that someone like *you* won the lottery, Bonnie," they'd say in a half-joking tone verging on a sneer. "Want to take me out to dinner?" They knew how to keep it subtle. Some of them even called me Bon Bon, an overfamiliar nickname I hadn't heard since childhood, which told me their hatred had ripened into the sourest grape on the vine.

These strangers swarmed onto my tiny porch, undeterred by the sunken corner that had rotted through, and knocked on my door one by one, jerking me out of the deep planning and dreaming I was absorbed in. For this, I wished them dead. But I tried to be polite. Each time I opened the door I told myself that this was the sacrifice that was required. One of many to come, I suspected.

Even when the cameras and news teams came to gawk and rut up the scabby grass in front of my trailer, I stayed cool. *What does it feel like to win so much money?* they'd say. *What will you be doing with it all?* Reporters loved asking those types of questions when they caught me coming out my front door. One of them even asked, *Are you planning on investing in your community?* They'd looked around at my shit neighborhood and expected me to soak in it forever, I guess.

I told them that I didn't know what I would do with the money. Or I answered the way I knew I was supposed to answer—that I was planning on saving it. I'd say it in a really earnest voice, as if the mere thought of saving all that beautiful cash was turning me into a realer, wiser adult as I stood there.

But my days of scrimping and saving were over. I had big ideas, was planning big moves. My fate had been brewing long before I walked a mile to where LOTTO BEER CIGS glowed in neon letters on the gas station door, long before I handed over my money to the pimply cashier and my future was handed back.

I didn't dare tell that story to another human being, though. Let alone a reporter. Back then I never shared my plans or preferences, my ambitions or desires. I never gave away the things I loved.

I knew better. Other people can ruin a dream just by knowing it.

•••••••••••••

My brain had been feeling ragged for weeks by the time I bought the lottery tickets, it's true, sick of everything around me, and I longed for something more, something extraordinary. But on the afternoon I walked to the gas station, I received the mission of my life, the plan, and it was channeled through the television show *Three's Company*.

It had been a Saturday, my day off from work, and I had just finished watching "The Root of All Evil," wherein Jack Tripper goes to the racetrack, bets on the horses chosen by his roommates Chrissy Snow and Janet Wood, wins, and returns to Apartment 201 with fistfuls of money. I'd already seen the episode dozens of times, and it wasn't even one of my favorites, but on that afternoon in late August, as the credits rolled, I sweated and dreamed inside my trailer that never seemed to get cool, yearning for a different time and place, a different identity—and I was wishing, as usual, that I could crawl into *Three's Company* and live there, curled up on the trio's living room carpet, willing to eat scraps and suck vinegar from a sponge if that's what it took to have the honor—when a voice emerged from the dulling cloud that had been hanging over my life for the past five of my thirty-six years and whispered, *Now. Your turn.*

And I knew then and there that it was my turn, and my power, my own life, that I was the grand master puppeteer, running this show, up onstage and in charge. My winning horse would be myself.

The idea was like an electric shock that reset my brain. The details still vague, I marched out of my house and started toward the gas station, keeping to one side of the narrow, shoulderless road. Cars whooshed by me in the heat, sometimes coming so close that I had to hop into the thin strip of tick-infested grass separating the road from the forest beyond, the uneven terrain threatening to break my ankles.

Some cars honked angrily; there were several blind curves on this stretch and all the locals drove like maniacs. The road was a test of speed and mortality—could you round the bend at 55 mph and not die? 60? It was a game we all played. Indeed, at the halfway point of my trek a car rounded the curve directly ahead of me and hit the brakes so hard it fishtailed and went over the center line, nearly flipping off the road and into the trees before steadying itself. Had another car come the other way at that moment, everyone involved, including me, would have died spectacularly.

I owned a pickup truck that worked fine, and I knew how dangerous walking on the road was, but it seemed important that I risk death in my journey. I was on my way to a blessing, and every blessing required sacrifice. If I died, well, that would be another kind of blessing. Either way, my fortune would be arranged.

Obviously I made it back fine. I bought those tickets. I admit, I was much more careful on my return journey. My future was in my pocket, after all.

My plan, my dream, the thing I feared saying aloud in the presence of another human, was this: I would buy property somewhere remote, on a mountain or deep in forested country, and on it I would build a replica of the *Three's Company* apartment building. I would live in an identical re-creation of Jack, Janet, and Chrissy's apartment where I would wake and eat, and bathe and sleep, and around the apartment building I would build the world seen on the show—the Regal Beagle bar, the Arcade Florists flower shop, Jack's Bistro, Nurse Terri's hospital waiting room, secretary Chrissy's office building. It would be a small city. And I planned on living the lives of each character in succession, one after another, until the years ran out.

I would start my life over in the year 1977, when Season 1 began, and the décor of the apartment and everything around it would also start in Season 1, and it would be Season 1 for me, Bonnie Lincoln, a fresh start, the pilot season, for however long I wished. As the show progressed, I would, too, as would the surroundings, to reflect the series' later seasons. This would all be thanks to the indecent amount of money I won. It was the largest amount ever won in a single national lottery, and I was the only claimant.

Jack, Janet, Chrissy, the Ropers, Ralph Furley, neighbors Larry and Lana, later roommates Terri and Cindy—they were my surrogate family by that time, impervious to death or harm, preserved forever in an eight-season arc. I wanted only to live among them, to breach the seam between sick reality and my favorite fiction, step through, and sew up the hole behind me. Oh, I had yet to work out the specifics, and there were many—how I'd maintain food or supplies, how I'd go about replicating the characters' lives down to the minutest detail—but in my hungry fantasy these questions were inviting and juicy, beckoning me forward like a banquet table receding into the distance, laden with an endless feast.

The planning itself was its own odyssey, its own cocooning world. I spent days in my trailer making notes and gazing into the middle distance where, on the dingy twelve inches of my kitchen countertop, the last two bananas sat rotting on the stem. My dreams seemed crucial, urgent. Risky. I planned to manipulate time itself, to escape it and warp it, bend it to my will.

I had no intention of allowing any audience to see my creation. No tourists, no tickets. No, my escape would be real and total, fully lived and experienced by me, a lone human, and shared with as few people as I could get away with. Mine would not be a soundstage, or have any reference to cameras or lights, or acknowledge an audience or fandom; nor would it hint that it was a fictional show: *I would live inside the show.* I would burrow past plotlines or jokes, I would bury myself in it. I would figure out everything I needed to survive, alone, and then I could dismiss every other person on earth, living and dead, with one triumphant wave goodbye.

Before the lottery, before I discovered *Three's Company*, I had worked at Scheele's Market for twelve years, starting when I was twenty. Before that I worked at a shoe store at the mall in town, but when Krystal, my best friend since the second grade, told me that her dad was hiring at the local market that was only three minutes from my house by car, fifteen by foot, I applied and was hired.

The market was small. More like a convenience store, really, than a proper market. It was the nearest place to get any type of groceries or sundries without driving to the supermarket in town, and because of that it offered everything from coffee to hot deli food to lottery tickets and basic groceries, plus state-themed souvenirs and postcards for any passing tourist. It even rented out videos before the internet took over. Geannie and Jim had owned it for twenty years. There were three long aisles, mostly stacked with canned and boxed goods, and the store had been robbed only once before I started working there. That robber had been a local kid who pretended to have a gun by pointing his finger inside his coat pocket. Jim had almost laughed at him, the story went, but handed him a few twenties from the till, anyway. The few customers who had witnessed it always found a way to bring it up. It was probably the most exciting thing they'd ever lived through.

Mostly the market did business on cigarettes and chewing tobacco, plus the deli subs and soups I helped prepare. On Fridays and Saturdays we were open later than usual, until 10 p.m., for the beer sales, and I knew most of the customers by name and brand. In the mornings retired men would come in and buy a coffee and hang around, shooting the breeze for hours, trying to flirt with me or one of the summer helpers—usually a cute kid on summer break from community college who turned red and mute at the attention. When the old men tried out lines on me, though, I would play along and answer with something slightly bitchy, but in a clever way that they delighted in rejoining; I probably reminded them of some long-ago missed conquest they were never smart enough to deal with when they were younger and only now could fully appreciate. I admired them. Well, I admired the *idea* of being an old man. Now that they were old and nothing was at stake, they were freer, looser. They could get away with anything.

Hernan, Krystal's brother, worked part time as a cashier on the weekends. During the week he worked construction and would occasionally come in after his shift was over, smelling like asphalt and sweating like a god. He was older than me, and sometimes, when we closed the market together, he walked me home as the days grew shorter. I lived for those times. The weather was always cold or getting cold on those nights, and he was taller than me but not by much, and thin, and his eyes were so brown they almost seemed red, and his voice was deep and resonant, a butter-in-a-barrel kind of voice. Unlike with the old men who hung around the store, I was quiet around Hernan, stricken with a crush that rendered me hot and wordless. I wanted to be his lover, his sister, his buddy, whatever would get me closest to him. Krystal would talk about him like he was a pesky little brother, though he was two years older than her, and I think it had something to do with the fact that he'd been adopted when he was five or six, when Krystal was three. Krystal always felt older than him, or that she had one up on him, I guess, having known her parents for three extra years. Even as adults she was always complaining about him. *Hernan keeps doing this*, she'd say, or *Hernan won't leave me alone about this*, and I'd be sick with jealousy, longing to be someone Hernan would not leave alone.

Midway through the second year I worked there, my mother died after a long, liver-related illness, and Geannie invited me to stay at their house for a few weeks after the funeral. Krystal had recently moved out, eager to get away, and her bed was free. "Just come over so you won't be alone," is how Geannie put it, and, curious, I took her up on it. In this way I was welcomed into her and Jim's lives in earnest. She felt so sorry for me, I could tell, though my mother's tight-lipped, distant parenting style wasn't something I exactly missed. In fact, it was quickly over-shadowed by how Geannie and Jim treated me, which involved a lot of talking and affection, and making me feel like I was an individual human with opinions and feelings and an observable personality. Throughout my years of childhood friendship with Krystal I had always savored whatever crumbs of attention they had paid me between their hectic work schedules and hurried hellos and goodbyes, but only as an orphaned adult was I fully immersed in their love. The image of my mother hardly had time to fade before Geannie stepped in, and the handoff from mother to mother figure was so seamless that sometimes, in the years that followed, I had to remind myself that Geannie was not actually my mother.

On several occasions after I sold my mother's house and got my own place, usually around Christmas, the Scheeles invited me to come stay overnight for a few days. I would lie in the dark in Krystal's old bed, awaiting Christmas morning like a child, and

as I listened to the lazy holiday music Jim had put on the downstairs stereo while they finished their glass of wine before bed—a
habit that seemed impossibly fancy—I tried to brainwash myself
into believing that I had grown up in that house, with both of
them as my parents, and that I was very young, maybe eight or
nine, and that the rest of my life was still a happy mystery.

Christmases with them were like a dream within which I
could suspend myself, where time and reality would pause, and
the air itself moved in a kinder, gentler way. They had annual
routines that fascinated me: searching for and cutting down the
perfect pine tree at their favorite local nursery; decorating it in a
particular order (lights, then tinsel, then homemade ornaments
that held significance, then the more elegant but less meaningful
icicles and colored balls); shopping for sensible gifts with what
seemed like endless money; Geannie taking a whole afternoon
to make six kinds of cookies and two types of brownies. Each
year when I first arrived she would invite me in, flushed and
smiling, and I'd find the kitchen floured and happily shimmering, the air full of hot sugar and cinnamon. Elvis crooned in the
background, keeping at bay the cold, fading December outside
the window. The scene almost makes me cringe now, the sentimental perfection of it.

Perhaps the most fantastical thing was the snow village.
Every December, Jim would drag out five long wooden pallets
and set the miniature, lit-from-within ceramic buildings up in
front of the Christmas tree. He arranged them in a way that
mimicked hills and valleys, or perhaps suggested different neighborhoods, and covered them with rolls of wispy white batting.
First he laid the small, figure-eight train track, making sure the
train ran smoothly before he did anything else, in true methodi-
cal Jim form, and then began building the town around it.

The buildings were nothing like anything I had ever seen, and the town they formed was out of a Hollywood fever dream of no particular century or style, a hodgepodge of architecture and economic status, from a small fishing shack to a set of city row houses to a grand mansion or courthouse (I could never tell which), to a gothic stone castle that always sat near the back, as if it were bashful about its foreboding aura. Each small building would be placed on the fake snow in a similar pattern to the year before, though something always had to shift to make room for a new addition; the final Christmas I spent with them, the newest piece had been an ice pond. A mechanized magnet moved a small skater across the clear acrylic sheet of ice in figure eights, but it never traveled the same path twice. I found it utterly mesmerizing.

Somehow Jim would always make the buildings fit together in a pleasing way, and when he finished he would turn all the lights off in the living room and kitchen except for the Christmas tree, and call us in—Geannie, me, Krystal, Hernan, any of their other relatives who were in town, and the summer part-timers at the market were invited, too—and without much flourish but with much pride he would flip a switch, and they'd all light up, all at once, and the skater went round the pond, and the train went round its track, and the Scheele living room was turned into a place of surreal wonder and comfort, the glowing ideal of Christmas.

A subterranean longing would pass through me at those moments, a sharp, wrenching desire for wholeness, for the correct way of living. When I saw it up close it didn't seem funny, or lame, or maudlin. It wasn't anything but beautiful. Whenever I witnessed these moments of domestic perfection, the things that good people were born into, I had an odd feeling that I was floating somewhere beyond myself, in a far corner, watching my heart grasp at the scene like a drowning person inches away from a life jacket, clutching at the water of love, ecstatic and terrified. Until this time in my life, with the exceptions of my parents' deaths, library books, and a brief high school association I'd had with a boy more concerned with professional wrestling than romance, I had little understanding of how the larger world worked. Death and the wisdom of Bret "the Hitman" Hart were the extent of my lived experience. In many ways I was like a child, and I experienced Christmas at the Scheeles' as a child: it was brand new to me, imitative of nothing, and it imprinted upon my heart the sincerest wish of any happy child who knows she is happy—that nothing would ever change.

But then the holiday would end, and life would resume. After I sold my mother's house I had more money than I knew what to do with, and when I mentioned that I was looking for an apartment at work one day, Jim suggested buying a trailer, and offered to help me figure out the financing. I could have figured it out myself, but I let him help me. I loved sitting at their kitchen table, or standing around in the market during a lull, looking at paperwork and listening to him talk like he was the expert. I liked how his advice was quiet and simple, yet carried total authority, and that his creased forehead and deep *hmm*'s signaled hard and earnest concentration. He liked being useful, and I liked making him feel useful.

When I finished signing all the papers for the trailer, and after he and Geannie helped me repaint it and move some spare furniture in, the toilet stopped flushing on my second night there. And after he took me into town the next day to get a new toilet, and after he installed it and checked the pipes before finally declaring that everything was fine, he left, and I missed him. I sometimes sat in my living room and considered breaking something on purpose. I wanted to give him the opportunity to come over, exert his masculine know-how upon it.

Occasionally I did that, but not too often. Once, when I was feeling particularly lonely, I unscrewed a pipe under the kitchen sink so that it leaked slightly, and another time I cut the outside wire to my telephone. I enjoyed watching him stand around and quietly assess a problem, putting a name to it and sorting it out. I liked giving him that gift.

At night I would sometimes lie in my bed and dream about living with Geannie and Jim, dream of them adopting me. It was a strange dream, I admit, for a twenty-something, thirty-something woman to have. But they had become so dear to me, and, most mysterious of all, they seemed to *like* me. For a time I even dressed like Geannie in an effort to understand her, or maybe I wanted to pay homage to her, or perhaps it was simply the result of being around her most days at the store; the motives of my earlier self are hard to pin down. I think I wished to be subsumed by her, by their whole life and way of living, in the way I'd always wished to be subsumed by a book. I wanted to disappear into a new, unexpected version of myself.

My own identity had always seemed suspect to me. Though I believed a shadowy, hidden kernel of personal essence lay within the heart of every individual—a certain absolute truth that determines one's identity—I had never found mine. I felt I could change in an instant depending on the situation or the people around me. It all seemed so real in the moment, and so completely fake upon reflection. Recalling my own memories felt like remembering a stranger's dreams. I had no true idea of myself. Life with Geannie and Jim offered a way out completely, an off-ramp into another story altogether. I could start over. The witnesses would be different. And isn't that what decides a life?

The witnesses? Whatever I really was, the promise of this other self always beckoned.

There seemed to be a background noise to life, I had always noticed, a frequency that hummed continuously and held a certain color and mood. It changed with each season of the year though it was beyond weather, beyond any change of light. It was felt in my bones, the waves creating a wall of safety, of certainty. Geannie and Jim kept the frequency going. Oh, I would do other things and see other people—Krystal and I went clubbing in town once, disastrously, and a few times we went to parties at her friends' or coworkers' houses, which ended in puke or blackout or both, and sometimes we explored abandoned houses together, wandering bored through the rot, or sometimes I took walks and went to the library, and I read books, and I consumed movies and food, and I paid bills, and once I went to the DMV to get something sorted out with my truck—but the background hum, the thing that reassured me that the world was real and solid, seemed to be always traceable to the Scheeles, their presence, their unspoken support, the surety that they would always be there.

When Geannie and Jim left, the background noise stopped. The silence felt like a warning. Of what, though, I had no idea.

My first phone call after winning the lottery was to Elmo Larwin, who ran a legal empire named Larwin, Morris & Hawkes. Their claims to fame were estate planning and financial affairs, and their offices took up an entire floor of a flashy, ten-story office building in the city's downtown district.

Not wanting to settle for any second bananas, I went straight to Larwin himself. "I'm Bonnie Lincoln," I said when I called to make an appointment, "and I recently won the lottery." I mentioned the amount I had won.

"How about next Tuesday," Larwin's secretary said. Her voice was cordial but otherwise expressionless at the figure I quoted; like a nurse or doctor, she had seen all shapes, all sizes. Her aloof attitude was how I knew I was getting the best.

Tuesday came, and I drove an hour and a half into the city. Everyone on the highway seemed to have a death wish they had resigned themselves to. Not used to driving in such traffic, I was terrified, certain I would die, my fortune and life snatched away. A tractor-trailer almost mowed me down while I merged onto the highway.

Larwin's building was easy to find. It was one of the taller ones downtown, its glass front scattering the afternoon sun into a thousand golden coins. The elevator up to the seventh floor glided skyward with barely a whisper, and his office was cool and dark and brown the way everything old-rich is. Nothing like the gaudy dazzle of the building's exterior. Ornate, titleless books sat between potted ferns on wood-paneled bookcases and lent the space an air of haughtiness, as if the room itself were resisting the passage of time. Even the secretary's desk, which was unattended for the duration of my visit, was immaculate, not a fingerprint or paper clip in sight. A single ivory tusk mounted on brass, presumably a paperweight, was the only sign of personality.

I sucked in the circulated, chemical air quietly. So. This was real money.

"Come in, come in," Mr. Larwin said, appearing at the doorway of an inner room, and I rose and went into his office. I was surprised to see that he was much older than I expected. His hair was thick and almost blue-white, with a beard to match, and his face was a mass of smoker wrinkles. He had to be at least seventy-five years old, though who could tell age with smokers. When he stood to shake my hand he looked like a small T.rex, with short arms and elegant, bird-like hands.

"I've seen your name all over the news and am so glad you came to us," he began.

"Well, I came to you, specifically, Mr. Larwin. I don't want to deal with anyone else."

He told me a client of his had just died, so I had reached him at a good time. "Do you have anything in particular in mind?"

I handed him a piece of paper I had brought with me. On the paper I had written some ideas for investments. I had done some rudimentary research. My face burned as I watched him read my scrawl, realizing how childish I must have seemed. But, to his credit, Mr. Larwin only nodded his head, as blank as his invisible secretary had been on the phone, and made suggestions.

Toward the end of my appointment, there was a pause in the conversation. The afternoon light had lowered and now streamed through the wooden venetian blinds that adorned the windows behind Larwin's desk. Its pattern was mesmerizing.

"There's one stipulation I want to be understood," I said. He had been writing something on his blotter, but my tone made him look up. He folded his delicate hands and leaned in, giving me his full attention.

"I want full privacy. There will come a point where I will only be reachable by landline telephone, and even then I will be the one to reach out to you. I will let you know when this time begins. Hopefully we will be able to solidify everything by then.

"But I want to prepare you. After that point, when I tell you to stop contacting me, you must stop, or else I will cut off all communication and take my business elsewhere." I slid forward to the edge of the leather chair I'd sunk into and leaned toward him. My fingers rested on the edge of his high-polish desk. I spoke rapidly, just above a whisper, as if I were uttering a rosary. "I have a project in mind. It's a major project. I'm not going to tell you about it unless absolutely necessary, because I want to keep it to myself. But once it's completed I want to be left completely alone. It's not anything illegal, so don't worry about that." I licked my lips. "If I need to, I can make this part of our business contract. I'm going to trust you with my finances, and I want to know they'll be in good hands. I want you to make sensible choices. But most of all, when the time comes, I want to make sure that I will not be disturbed. Is that acceptable to you?"

Mr. Larwin didn't blink an eyelash. He was probably used to dealing with rich brats, old eccentrics, perverted barons of industry with their velvet-walled abattoirs—secrets darker and more tawdry than whatever he imagined mine was, if he bothered imagining it at all.

He said, "When the time comes, just say the word."

We wrapped up our business with promises to speak by phone to tie up loose ends, but by the end of my visit my finances were in order, and several solid investments promised to multiply my money, and, most importantly, I was reassured that preparations for my project could go forward. I walked out of the glass building and into the waning afternoon feeling like a queen. The world felt different. It was full of possibility for the first time in a long while. A future was visible. Even the cold air seemed cheerful. And Mr. Larwin had been so patient and diplomatic toward me, like a real professional. He had even been kind.

That's when I realized what money can really get a person: respect they didn't earn. I briefly felt disgusting, then free.

At the time I won the lottery I had been in love with *Three's Company* for five years, and the show was forty-six years old. That seemed significant at the time, because my father was forty-six when he died. My father smoked a pack a day and drank, killing himself slowly, then got impatient and killed himself all at once. I was twelve when it happened. He was an unpredictable man prone to loud, drunken outbursts or cold, distant stretches of sobriety, but then he'd come home from work and meet me in the doorway, gather me in his arms, and say, *How's my girl!* Or, when I was smaller, he'd put me atop his shoulders and walk me around, holding onto my hands—moments of love so shining and stunning I could never think too poorly of him. And then he did the best thing an uneven parent can do: he died. And he did it himself, with a shotgun, which always struck me as a little glamorous. A little gutsy. Perhaps because of his largeness of mood and method of death he seemed mythical to me as I got older, and I often wondered if he had watched *Three's Company* when it first aired. I liked to imagine him as a young man sitting in his mother's living room, drinking a beer and watching her floor-model television, my grandmoo young again and napping in her armchair.

The image gave me such pleasure, my TV and biological families made one. It made time, the idea of time, sing in my blood. Whenever I'd wake up strangling in the dark, or was caught unawares by an unpleasant memory, or whenever someone at the warehouse where I worked tried to tell me about their divorce or dumb kid or money troubles, or whatever small item had crawled up their ass and died that day, I would sometimes picture my father, young again, sitting and watching my favorite show, laughing at all the corny jokes. The nature of death, of history, of decay and molecular aging became one intersecting and beautiful pattern in those seconds, and I could believe that life was more than the meaningless misery it had become.

But even more than my dead dad, I dreamed about *Three's Company* itself. How can a person explain their love of something inanimate? Or worse, a television show that belongs to everyone? It's so personal. My father would take us to church sometimes during one of his stretches of sobriety, and sometimes my love of *Three's Company* reminded me of prayer. I remembered sitting quietly in the hushed sanctuary, every head around me bowed with eyes closed, like they'd gone to sleep. I would pinch my arm to resist laughing. After I started collecting the DVDs, though, and after I had watched every episode three or four times all the way through, back-to-back, and then started collecting the *TV Guides* and other clipped articles with the cast and crew, and sometimes even a reproduction episode script, I understood the concept of religion, the one-sided relationship with the intangible. Like God, the show never talked back to me. It felt familiar and reassuring, yet I could find something new to love every time. It took place in a time period I would never truly understand, having never lived in it, and for all its relatability, there would always be something unreachable about it. I kept returning, returning, wanting terribly to be let in, looking forward to the day I might achieve full enlightenment. I finally knew what it was like to love something sacred and deep, to own an appreciation so big that its gravity felt like returned love.

I dared not say anything to anyone else about my growing

obsession. Oh, if someone asked me what my favorite TV show was, I might have told them the truth. But that information alone, obviously, was not the whole truth. Most people figured I meant that I enjoyed the show ironically, anyway, with a wry hipster's appreciation. I did nothing to dissuade them. I was only aware that I needed to protect the one pure thing inside me from the judging eyes of the world. After my recent history had gone so wrong, I was desperate to hold something intact.

Collecting *Three's Company*-related things became my main pastime. Tickets to particular tapings that sold for a few bucks on auction sites, small trinkets that may have appeared on the set at some point. I didn't have a lot of money back then, so most of these things were small and dinky, with dubious certificates of authentication, but I was happy enough. The searches alone were enjoyable. I trawled through *Three's Company* hashtags, old memorabilia auction listings, image databases. I found fan websites, T-shirts, coffee mugs, even an assortment of hand towels emblazoned with the title or photos of the show. I looked and looked at these things, and took notes, and longed in my heart.

Geannie Scheele had been a collector of sorts. One time, when I was staying over she led me upstairs, unlocked Hernan's old room they had recently remodeled, and swept her arm out solemnly, as if showing me her kingdom.

Floor to ceiling, the room throbbed with Beanie Babies. Staggered shelves spanned every wall, and small stools and display tables were arranged tea-party style in two corners. I hadn't known what to say, but she looked so proud. So pleased. *I even snarfed up the Betty Blues!* she told me, taking a small blue dog-rabbit thing off one of the shelves and smoothing its ears lovingly. Apparently the Betty Blues had a seam defect and were really rare.

At the time I didn't get it, what she was so proud of, but after I first started my *Three's Company* collecting I understood the mindless pleasure in hoarding, in finding and in keeping.

I grew obsessed with the set decoration. I started watching each episode while taking notes of where items were, and how they moved around or disappeared and reappeared around the apartment from episode to episode. I formulated theories on where shut doors led, doors the audience never saw through. I took notes about character wardrobe, how much it was repeated within a season and variously accessorized.

What was the meaning of everything moving around? Why did the décor look different week to week? Even the walls of the set looked to be set at slightly different angles from one episode to the next, and while I knew, intellectually, from my research, that the changes were due to the set being torn down and rebuilt every week, the sheer negligence of continuity ate at me. How could someone be so careless? If I were working as the person who built and tore down the sets, you could bet I'd be taking notes, making sketches. I looked up the names of the set decorators who worked on the show over the years and considered contacting them, asking them: *Where is your pride?* Wondering if that would qualify as harassment.

My trailer had one bedroom, and I started to use it for my collection. I slept in the large recliner in my living room instead. In the bedroom—which I kept locked, and only unlocked to visit reverently, as if it were a museum—I displayed my finds: a couple of posters, and some Topps playing cards that I arranged inside a large frame, the various articles and paper items either framed and hung or placed inside marked file folders that I kept on a bookshelf. Finally, in each corner of the room I hung a couple of festive T-shirts that bore the *Three's Company* logo.

I didn't dare wear any of the shirts out of the house, though. I didn't want anyone commenting on them and breaking the spell. The last thing I needed was some idiot approaching me in the middle of the hardware store or wherever and hee-hawing at me, *Hey, I love that show, too!* I didn't want to meet anyone like me. I needed to believe that my peculiar fixation was mine and mine alone. Over the years I'd come to understand that my interests lay beyond a secret, private window in my brain, and when someone else came to know them they put fingerprints on the glass, smearing and spoiling the view forever. Immediately I'd want to smash the window, murder everything beyond it, then annihilate myself for such carelessness. So many ideas and dreams had died this way, by becoming known by others. I was determined to keep this one alive.

People who research anything, who deep-dive anything, understand that solitude is never loneliness when you have your subject. The subject looms before you like a bright city on the horizon, beckoning you forward. And you're forever living in it, or going toward it.

About a year before I won the lottery, I discovered, accidentally, that Krystal was squatting at Geannie and Jim's house on and off. For the past few years a FOR SALE sign had sat in the front yard, but like most of the houses in the area, it had never found a buyer. One of Jim's estranged sisters whom I'd never seen had inherited it due to a will he had drawn up years ago and, in a surprising twist for such a meticulous man, never updated. Yet, for the past five years Krystal kept intercepting the power bills in the mail and paying them, and possibly the water bill, too—she had a good job as a dental hygienist in the next town over, with money to blow.

The house was on my way to work, and one night while driving in on the late shift I'd noticed Krystal's car parked in the driveway. It was almost 9:30 p.m. on an October night, and I could see a light on in the living room and in an upstairs room, the one where Geannie had kept her Beanie Babies. When I passed it on my way home, Krystal's car was still there.

Arriving home at my own house, I called Geannie's old number. I had deleted it, but the muscle memory of dialing it hadn't left me. My fingers passing over the old numbers felt faintly occult, as if a ghost was two rooms over and I could detect just the edges of it. But the number was disconnected.

I set my phone down and looked at my hands, which were shaking. Why were they shaking? For days after, whenever I thought about Krystal in the house, my hands shook. Until then I had avoided looking at Geannie and Jim's house on my way to work, had even taken an alternate, longer route to work for a time, but since I saw her car there it was all I could think about. And I was curious, too. What could she be doing in there? Who gave her the right? She'd always disliked it. Called it names, insulted its style, the overwhelming potpourri her mother used, the fact that Jim was so particular about how things were arranged. Krystal had no appreciation for that house. I imagined her in there trashing it, taking out her petty furies on it, and my insides turned to acid. These thoughts disturbed the delicate mental biosphere I had cultivated by that time, clouding up my head where total blankness, the state of being I strove for in those days, could have been.

The next time I saw Krystal after that, we were sitting at the small kitchen table in her apartment on a Friday night. Her place was small and kind of dingy, and everything had the ground-in smell of cooking grease and ancient cigarette smoke from past tenants, but her kitchen was cozy—yellow checked curtains at the window and blue and green plates in the cupboard. Since the robbery we'd fallen into a habit of eating dinner together on Fridays at her place, after which we'd wash the dishes or watch television together in silence. Or sometimes, in warm weather, we took a walk around her neighborhood before it got dark. Both of us seemed to have lost the interest or the ability to befriend other people.

She had made us TV dinners that now steamed up at us. "Saw your car at Geannie's the other night," I said, watching her.

She started spooning the grainy Salisbury steak gravy into her mouth with extra enthusiasm, not looking at me. "Oh, that," she said. At first I thought she was just going to leave it there.

Then she said, "I go over there sometimes. I go over to pack it up. That's what they would want, you know."

I nodded and took a drink. We both sat there and chewed in silence.

"I go over to pack it up," she said again, "but I always end up staying. You know?"

I knew. I let it drop and changed the subject. We finished the evening as usual, and I left without bringing it up again.

But I worked the night shift for another four months after that, and I started mentally tracking the days I saw her car at the house. Once it was there for a week straight. Once it was only two nights. Then a whole month.

One morning on my way home from work I pulled into Geannie's driveway and parked behind Krystal's car. It was shortly after dawn when I arrived, and it was a late winter day, the air hard and cold. The landscaping that Jim had taken great pains to maintain over the years had descended into wildness. Dead, scrubby bushes coiled around the front of the house, their thorny brambles shining in the frost.

At the time, I hadn't been this close to the place since before the robbery. Walking onto the porch felt so strange, as if I was reaching my arm through a secret curtain and petting another timeline. It seemed incorrect, slightly mystical. I knocked and tried not to imagine anyone else besides my friend padding toward the door. After a few more knocks the blinds on the other side of the front door rustled, and then the door heaved open and Krystal stood before me.

"What do you want?" she said.

Her eyes were puffy slits, her hair crazed. She had been sleeping, apparently.

She was wearing one of Geannie's old housecoats.

I looked at her. Looked at the housecoat. The ruffled collar.

"I saw your car," I told her. She stepped aside to let me in and shut the door. We stood in the small foyer, looking at each other for a long moment. The house felt big and silent around us. Not even a clock ticked. The air smelled the same as I remembered. I had fully stepped through the curtain.

Krystal put her hand on my shoulder. She told me it was okay. "What is okay?" I said. She didn't answer.

I walked away from her and deeper into the house. I knew it better than I knew my own body. There was nothing showy about it, a large, two-story brick farmhouse with black shutters, but it seemed like the height of luxury to me. Geannie had always kept it nice. She had decorated the inside with heavy floral curtains and sturdy furniture, a giant, puffy couch, vases and artwork from the local antique mart. The wood floors had been refinished shortly before they left. The kitchen featured a sparkly granite countertop and white cupboards with small black knobs. Copper-bottom pots. Granny décor, Krystal had once said to me, joking, and I had gone silent, freezing her out for a week.

In the living room, the picture window looked out on a wide, sweeping field and the mountain beyond, and in the winter the mountain looked brown, and in the summer, blue. *Our little heaven*, Jim used to call the house.

Krystal trailed behind me as I walked upstairs. She called my name. I reached the bedrooms. The master was immaculate. Someone had made the bed with hospital corners, pulled the blinds shut. I didn't linger long; it felt too private, like watching a man look at himself in a mirror. Krystal's old bedroom contained my old Christmastime bed and nightstand, which my eyes skipped over. The room had also been used as their office and catchall place after she moved out, with a desk in one corner and an exercise machine stashed behind the door, odds and ends that never fit anywhere else.

Then, Geannie's collection. The third bedroom, at the end of the hall. Hernan's old room, really. The door was halfway open and a rumpled sleeping bag lay in the middle of the floor. As I stared at it, trying to understand what it meant, Krystal leaned against the doorjamb behind me and folded her arms. When I turned to face her she shrugged. "I can't sleep in the beds," she said. Then, a little defensively, "I sleep on the couch downstairs, too."

I didn't know what to say. She was blocking my way out of the room, so I had to look around at all the stupid Beanie Babies, the blue carpet Hernan had chosen years ago when it was still his room. How Geannie had loved them. How much love lived in this room.

Krystal's mouth did this quivery thing and she shrugged again. "I just miss them sometimes, I can't help it."

I stared at her, wanting to slap her. Wanting to drag her to the ground and punch her nose into her throat.

"Don't you, Bonnie? Don't you ever miss them?"

I went to leave but she didn't move, so I moved her. I pushed her to one side to get through the door, and was pleased to find that it was like flicking paper, that she felt like nothing.

She might have stumbled or fallen but I wasn't sure, I was walking out of the house. I was getting into my pickup truck. I was getting the fuck out of there. I drove home and thanked god it was Friday. I didn't answer my phone when it rang. I showered, got something to eat, put on some *Three's* and let the DVD loop until I fell asleep.

December arrived. When my lottery winnings were first transferred to my accounts I stared at the number, feeling nothing. But overall my sense of an ending intensified. I had already started touring potential properties for my project. The real estate agent would meet me in the county seat, which was halfway between where I lived and the wilderness, and we'd go exploring in her car.

The final property I toured was at the top of a minor mountain that lay in less inhabited territory, miles out from the nearest large town, and about two hours away from my trailer. To get to it we had to drive up a narrow, twisting road that would be harrowing to navigate in all seasons, particularly in winter, and at the end of it was a two-mile driveway that led to the front doors of the main house.

Where the long driveway met the road the land flattened out, acres of it. Trees grew thick at the edges of the property and thinned closer to the main house, giving way to open fields. The land was surprisingly level at the top, despite the fact that my ears popped as we drove. The nearest neighbors were miles and miles away. A small village of about 150 people sat near the foot of the mountain on the other side, just as the mountain ceased its incline, but that, too, was at least five miles away from the property, and was the closest hint of civilization.

Upon arrival, we both stepped out of the car dumbstruck. Her name is lost to me now, but when I asked the real estate agent what kind of privacy I could expect, she said, "Really?"

She thought I was kidding. Then she collected herself and regained the confident, professional tone she'd been using on me the whole drive there. "The biggest threat might be hunters, but there's so much land here that you may never even see them. And you can put up signs for that." She wore a dress suit and high heels that sunk into the recently rained-on grass. When we opened the door to the main house I saw her shiver. She seemed nice, but I could tell she wanted to get back to town as soon as she could. Some people can't take isolation.

And that is what the house, the property, was built for. Isolation. The house was as large as a mansion but looked more like a giant farmhouse—big and plain, with two kitchens, giant, witchy fireplaces, and cavernous rooms. Everything was layered in dust. The house wasn't really my concern, though. My eye was on the empty clearing beyond the house, at the edge of the woods. That was it. I could see it. My city. My Apartment 201.

Oh, I suppose I could have moved to California and done it right, but that posed too many uncertainties—would I go to the beach? Wouldn't that defeat the purpose of never leaving the compound? And what about mudslides and earthquakes and drought and fire? Especially fire. It was too risky. California— the idea of California—was a shimmering dream and needed to stay that way. The California I wanted was gone, anyway. The California most people want is gone.

Behind the main house were several outbuildings. The last owner had been a hoarder of some kind, perhaps of automobiles, because each outbuilding was as large as a garage. We walked through them one by one. These would do fine, I thought, to hold all supplies or extra equipment.

"Well, there you have it," the real estate agent said as we concluded the tour. By that time she had put on her bravest face;

moments before, as we walked back toward the house, her heel had sunk into the ground and she had stumbled, sitting down hard, and mud had daubed a brown swath across her left ass cheek. As I helped her up her voice became brighter. "I think it would be great for getting away, or as a vacation home. Your very own mountain place."

From then on when I thought of the property I thought of it as "the mountain place," and never without the image of her sinking shoe. Her pratfall felt like good luck.

*T*hree's Company was sent to me by something divine, maybe a ghost or maybe God, five years before I won the lottery. On the night it first graced me I was staying at Krystal's apartment, and two nights prior to that evening I had been beaten, and raped, and Scheele's Market had been robbed, and Geannie and Jim had been gunned down in the cooler, and Hernan had been shot dead, and I had watched his blood settle into the grout lines of the brown tile near where I lay panting, facedown, trying not to taste the floor—that had been my prevailing thought in the moment, that *I must not taste the floor* for fear of being grossed out forever—and the coffeepot on the counter above me had exploded fantastically, comically, in the wake of gunfire, and a bullet grazed my neck. And then the police had come, and an ambulance and medical workers, and I was loaded onto a stretcher and taken to a hospital, and strangers examined and photographed me and took my statement, and the collective kindness of everyone witnessed me, and every sympathetic face telegraphed pity to me, and I was told the gunshot was only a flesh wound, that I was very lucky, and after I was kept overnight I was told by a doctor that it would be in my best interest if I stayed with someone while I recovered, and I was too exhausted to argue—which is how I came to dial Krystal's phone number with shaky fingers while the doctor watched, and how I came to be staying with Krystal on the night I discovered *Three's Company*.

After she picked me up from the hospital and brought me

back to her place, she cooked me stuffing and macaroni and cheese from a box, both the good, brand-name kinds, and set me up with one of her dead grandmother's crocheted blankets on the couch, and when she went to bed I lay with an ice pack on my crotch and a frozen pea bag on my left eye socket and flipped through the TV channels.

I watched a little bit of national news, and it all assured the end—grinning politicians, the nuclear threat, biohazards in the air, everything burning, everything flooding. The stakes. Then the local news came on and showed a familiar parking lot and the parrot-blue SCHEELE'S MARKET sign with a stretch of yellow police tape near it, and I zestfully pressed the channel arrow button over and over again, so hard the remote creaked.

A game show. An infomercial. A show about dead and missing children. Naked people vying for money. Movies about murder and unhappy couples and a dog and another murder.

Then, suddenly, a glow emanated from the screen. It was golden, like God. The warm air of the 1970s wafted over me, and I fell into a paralytic hypnosis. A show played on the screen but another thing was happening on a separate level, inside a secret flap of consciousness, and there was something autumnal about the feeling it generated, deep and nostalgic, regressing my heart to a past date that might have been real and might have been a mishmash of fiction or advertisements or childhood happiness, or a collection of weather: the pleasure of a rosy-lit room in a cold season, the dream of a warm ocean, the late afternoon sun. My reality cracked open, and the television spooned another one on top.

I froze under Krystal's blanket, the pea bag melting against my eye. I was bearing witness to my own salvation. Now here was a world, I thought. Now here *is* a world. The show was bright and silly, escapist pap, but the most important thing was that none of it had anything to do with me. The show didn't know where I lived or how I lived, or anything I had seen or endured; the screen showed me something blissfully ignorant. Innocent. I hadn't even been born when this episode was filmed. It was untouched by my existence and the world that hung around me, and it would forever remain that way. It was a Season 2 episode of *Three's Company*.

By the end of the week at Krystal's, I could get around without limping too much, and the diarrhea attacks and weird numbness in my face and hands had abated somewhat, and my neck only throbbed a little, and upon arriving home in my dark, chilly trailer I immediately ordered my first set of *Three's Company* DVDs. I played them so much I worried I would ruin them, so after a few weeks I bought an extra set. After that I bought another DVD player, and another set of the DVDs. After that I bought a third player just in case the first two broke (you never know), and one more set of DVDs. I rotated them diligently, in order to avoid wearing any one set out. I cleared out half of the only closet in my home to make room for my collection. Each evening I stood back and looked at my horde. It was stacked neatly on milk carton shelves, the colors of each boxed season repeating pleasantly.

I felt pretty good, having a collection of something. When I wasn't being careful I would let a memory of Geannie's Beanie Babies slip through, and I'd wish she were there with me. I wanted her to look into my closet and see herself there.

Other things went on in the year after I found the show. One funeral for three people. Court dates and sentencing. By the time everything was said and done, I was past caring. I felt I had transcended my previous self, had shed the skin of the lone survivor of the robbed market, and when a stray reporter called for an update, to get a comment on the capture of the final man, I told him he had the wrong number.

Life kept grinding onward. I got a job at the big chain grocery store in town, but in the back stockroom, away from the public. First I had tried my luck at the deli counter for a while, but kept flinching at every little thing, and hesitating at the mouth of the cooler. To bring me out of one of these spells, the shift manager would invariably clap at me, saying "Chop-chop!" I hated her. She would hand me large sandwich orders, sandwiches I had made a hundred thousand times at the market, but the olives became eyes and the ketchup was blood, or maybe my brain didn't consciously make those connections, actually, but it's easier if I write it that way. Something would happen and my stomach turned to jelly and I'd go into slow motion, or I would stop moving completely, the knife in my hand hovering over the sandwich, and one time I put my hand over my nose and mouth (a no-no in the food-prep world) and ran to the sink to puke my guts out. Then I had to bleach the sink.

I didn't understand it myself, why I couldn't do simple things the way I always had. A couple of weeks into it, the consensus was that I was freaking everyone out. When I saw a job opening in the warehouse, I went for it. The deli boss had a word with the warehouse boss, happy to be rid of me, and I was allowed to transfer, even though most of the workers back there were large men who could throw around large flats of cans in one go.

The warehouse was darker and less cheerful than out front, but I didn't mind. I was the only woman back there but I liked it that way; everyone left me alone. My favorite task was refilling the dairy section from the back room, pushing the gallons of milk onto their refrigerated shelves from a hidden, private perch.

Every now and then a little kid would be standing on the other side when I did this, and I liked to imagine the world through their eyes, watching the cartons appear like magic, glimpsing disembodied hands ushering them through a distant window. Most children froze in wonder when they realized what was happening. Sometimes they screamed. I also counted cans and took inventory and wheeled giant pallets off the delivery trucks. My arms and legs grew strong; after half a year even the most skeptical of the warehouse guys started nodding hello, and the more senior workers slowly began offering me more choice on what shifts I could work, which I figured meant they had decided to respect me.

Around this time was when one of them, Patrick, tried to ask me out. I had been there for a year by the time he worked up the nerve. At first I was flattered, but when I politely declined, the prospect of involving myself with another human too frightening and exhausting to comprehend, he asked me what I did all night after I left work. He said it was probably best if I wasn't alone, a woman in this town. I could get into trouble. After all— and here his voice lowered slightly, just us chums, I guess—he had heard about *what happened* to me.

It was the first time someone had said something like that to me. Not even the horrid deli boss had ever said anything, too embarrassed to acknowledge a stranger's troubles. And Krystal, during the whole week I'd stayed with her, had not referred to the robbery once. In her mercy and decency she had let me crawl out of the memory.

Patrick meant well, I think. His face was concerned. He was a large guy with sandy hair, a slight beer gut, and too-big hands, farmboy handsome. If I looked stunned, he did a great job of not noticing. "C'mon, I worry about you. Just one beer," he'd said good-naturedly, and my shock switched over to a different frequency, and the rage was so vivid that pink, keloidal slashes zigzagged across my vision. I might have swayed in its wake. I stared at him, trying to focus.

Of course, it wasn't until later that I thought of all the foul things I could have said to him. I wanted to cauterize him with words or worse. *If I let you ram me like a dead pig carcass, if I yodeled on your dick until I choked, on a scale of one to ten, how worried about me would you still be?* I wanted to place my iron of fury on him, watch his face go white as a scar.

Instead, I backed away as I politely smiled and shook my head. "I'll be okay," I said.

And I was. I was okay because I had something to live for. And contrary to whatever Patrick thought, I did have something to go home to. I had 172 episodes of my favorite show, all of them familiar, all of them filmed long ago and locked safely inside their little discs.

Here was my nightly routine: I would go home, shower, and fix something to eat. While the food was heating up I'd open the closet door and stare at the DVD boxes lined up neatly on their shelves. I liked how they asked nothing of me. They reminded me of nothing but themselves. I could stand there for an hour deciding which season, which episode, what mood I was in, and they would remain inert. They were quiet, contained. Dead cardboard and plastic and ink, patiently waiting for me to make the decision.

I first toured the mountain place in the first week of December; by the middle of the month I had signed the documents, Mr. Larwin began closing the deal, and the real estate agent was able to buy a new skirt and then some. I put my trailer up for sale and took to packing up my belongings. It took a single afternoon. I decided I would take my clothes, my recliner, my collection, a bowl, a cup, and a fork. Everything but the recliner fit into a duffel bag. Though leaving most things behind seemed wasteful, it also felt necessary; everything in the trailer felt tainted, irradiated by my past life and everyone who had witnessed it.

The news crews and unexpected visitors had dropped off by then. I decided to stay on at my job for another couple of weeks as I got everything wrapped up. I wanted to continue life as normally as possible until I moved to the next phase. I suppose, for someone else, it would have felt awkward dealing with coworkers who once considered you an equal but now treated you with distrust and resentment, but I found it more amusing than anything else. It was almost fun now, going to work, portraying myself. "Bonnie Lincoln." Right after I won, my coworkers had been overly friendly, but once it was clear I was not sharing the wealth, how quickly their demeanors changed! No more hellos or smiles. Barely any acknowledgment at all. I didn't blame them. I understood the instinctual contempt toward people with money—even now that I had money I still resented rich people, because I could not think of myself as rich, only as having more to lose. And winning my wealth by way of the lottery truly irked some people. I didn't earn it, and worse, I didn't deserve it. I was a not-young single woman in a decent job, no kids, no husband, no family to share my millions with, and I wasn't even that great-looking—what sense did the world make? People didn't like it.

Another part of the coldness at work was that I'd never gone along with the flirty male coworkers the way a lot of the women in the store did, and the time had come to pay the piper. Both men and women resented me for my indifference. I suspected that the women felt betrayed—I refused to play a game they had never felt free enough to refuse, and women generally don't like being reminded that if one is willing to be unattractive, you can get away with anything. Men resented me for more obvious reasons. After I had rejected Patrick, the warehouse worker who'd asked me out a few years before, the message got around fast that I was an oddball, probably a lesbian or feminist man-hater, or was defective in some other way their brains couldn't dare to fathom. And now, though he'd behaved decently to me in the years since I'd turned him down, Patrick seemed to take special pleasure in fake-smiling at me when he passed by me, and leaning forward suddenly, wanting to see me flinch. Some men don't trust a woman who doesn't play their game, and then, if that women wins at a bigger game—one that has nothing to do with them—their hatred is complete.

It was fine. I had little care for what any of them thought of me. I was done with being liked, or admired, or trying to be understood. In fact, the more hostility I felt from others, the cockier and more self-assured I felt. *Big-feelin'*, is what my mother would have called it. I couldn't help it. Finally, I was manifesting my destiny.

("Never expect people to understand," Jim said to me once.

This was after he painted the outside trim of the market and the overall sign an electric, nearly neon blue. It was a stunning color, and tropical, like nothing else in the town, and some of the locals protested it. At town meetings detractors called the market Margaritaville, which customers gleefully related back to Jim, who happened to be a teetotaler. He'd shrug it off and play it cool. I had always admired that about him. He never allowed anyone to see what he really felt. I never did find out why he used such a fantastical color. The simplest and most radical explanation—the one I prefer to believe—was that he liked it.)

Being aware of so many opinions during my final days at the warehouse got me thinking about another issue, however. How would I create my other world without revealing the depth of it to others? By necessity many people would be coming and going from the property, doing highly specialized work, and I realized it would be easier to keep them quiet if I kept them mostly separate and uninformed, and I could even have each of them sign nondisclosure agreements to be sure they would keep my secret.

I can't claim credit for this idea. I got it from an article I read in a newspaper about a sadist who murdered women a hundred years ago. When constructing his clever little murder hotel, he never allowed any of the contractors to speak to one another. If one of them caught on to his scheme, he killed them.

After he was captured and sentenced to hang, he wrote his confession in jail. When it came to the plans he made for the hotel, his memoirs read, "Oh, the future! The future lay before me like a ribbon." I cut it out and kept it. I put that in the duffel bag, too.

fter the robbery the closeness of other people repulsed me. Especially Krystal. All I wanted to do was to escape. Even slogging through my routine was a daily expedition into mindlessness, blankness, the diligent work of allowing time to elapse. Before that final night in the market, suicide of any kind had disgusted me. But each thing that reminded me of Geannie and Jim—the house, the goddamn Christmas village, the store that now stood locked and boarded up (who owned that now? Jim's sister? I had no idea), Krystal's red, watery eyes and thinning face—was a tiny cyanide capsule between my teeth, daring me to bite down.

Love was a sickness. It had poisoned me. People lie when they say misery or loneliness kills; it's love. Love is the lethal agent. The more you have to live for, the more can be taken away.

And now, with *Three's Company*, I had a secret inside me, a romantic, fantastical vision that kept me afloat, and I cherished it so much that my spiritual survival seemed at stake. If other people came to know it, the depth of it, my end was assured. I could be killed by a skeptical eyebrow. Murdered with one look. Then I'd have to kill my body. But if I kept it to myself, I could inoculate myself against the death-urge forever. Only my own private obsession would save me. That is why I needed to resist love's hostile invasion at every turn. With love comes attention, then judgment, then annihilation.

Don't think I didn't know what was going on. I had a vague sense of my severe avoidance and its possible abnormality, but I chose to believe instead that the world was abnormal and I had only adapted to it. Like every person in denial, I believed my methods were acceptable simply because I acknowledged them. In my mind avoidance was rational, fine, even natural—animals run away from predators every day. Love, on the other hand, was transmitted through human contact, the embarrassing need to connect. A manufactured product. And, again and again, it had actively threatened me.

I had known it as a child. I had loved both of my parents foolishly, wholly. I'm ashamed of it even now. But I was a child! How else are children supposed to love. The moments my parents loved me back glow out at me. My mother, a quiet, clipped woman, teaching me to cook basic dishes when she had a couple of free hours between the three jobs she juggled after my father died, telling me in a hot kitchen that I had done well. Eating Ho Hos in front of the television every so often. "Our little treat," she'd whisper, and wink at me, the equivalent of another type of mother's luxurious cuddle. But it wasn't just heartfelt moments. There were a thousand small things, daily things that blurred together that made me understand my mother loved me, even if she didn't say it all the time, or didn't hug me as much as fiction told me mothers should, or talk to me much at all. Even my father, villain that every drunken father is supposed to be in stories like these, remained saintly—the big burly lovey daddy he was in my memory, and his stretches of cold brush-offs and rages in other rooms belonged to another daddy, maybe one who would have mellowed out in old age. I had quite the imagination, and I was a fool back then—I read a lot of books. I believed in fiction. If something unpleasant happened, I could believe it was good. I had that power.

I was delusional. When I got older, and first my father died, and then a few years later my mother, I told myself that they had gone on extended vacations. What a laugh, that people like my parents would have ever taken a vacation! But, as I said, I was delusional. The permanence of their condition never seemed possible. I watched my mother die in the hospital, silent as ever, not giving an inch, and yes, I did have some desperate moments of thinking bleak thoughts; I thought about suicide, about dying, about ending the whole family line right then and there— the world was a hard place, and no darling kitchen memories could change that. Perhaps my father had been onto something. But I kept going. I told myself: extended vacations. Mother and Daddy were somewhere together on a warm island, happy, drinking from coconuts. And before I could get too deep into that particular fantasy, Geannie and Jim came along.

After that, love had always hung over me like a sword, the moment of departure looming ahead of me in the shadowy future. Romantic love was no different. I had loved Hernan and he died. He was shot in the head, skull cleaved in two, brains spattered all over the cigarettes behind the counter. There's a metaphor in there somewhere that I used to believe—maybe his skull was my heart? Cleaved in two? And his brains were . . . love? And the stacked cigarettes that received his brain matter, and some stray hairs, and flecks of blood and plasma—were they the abyssal hole where love goes?

Maybe. Or maybe he just died, and in the numb weeks follow-ing his death my wild insomniac brain kept trying to make sense of the senseless, my skull clanging with the memory of his life streaming out of him in the color and form of blood. Hernan had not been my boyfriend. We had never kissed, had never touched beyond a brotherly hug. My feelings toward him are difficult to state even now. Since I always tended to romanticize things in the privacy of my mind, I could say it was romantic love, but it may have been a level beyond that; in my fantasies I imagined simple, silly things, too shamefully tame to utter aloud. Falling asleep together holding hands, for example, or talking earnestly over a book we both had read, or taking evening autumn walks (the weather was always cool in my fantasies; I had a severe preoccupation with fall). One of my most detailed dreams involved me cooking him dinner in my trailer, and he would sit down at first and keep me company—laughing at me, calling me Bon Bon with a familiarity that never failed to shock and delight me, doing impressions of customers we knew from the market—and then he would stand up and walk over to me, place his hand on my shoulder, and tell me he wanted to help me prepare the food.

In this dream I didn't have to instruct him, or give him directions; he knew how to do everything. He chopped vegetables while we laughed and exchanged banter, like in a commercial, and he would man the sauces (for there were always multiple sauces) like a professional chef. The dinner was perfect, nothing burned and nothing bland, and we ate together in silence. Had anyone come to know these banal domestic fantasies, I would have been deeply ashamed, more so than if they'd been the most perverse sexual desire imaginable. Their sincerity was mortifying.

In real life he actually did perform impressions of market customers to make me laugh. There was a short old guy named Spitz, for example, who had been grizzled with work and age and a two-pack-a-day habit, and who was also a regular asshole, and sometimes when there was a lull Hernan would hunch himself over and contort his face and pretend to suck lustily on a cigarette. "I just really need my smokes," he would say in a wheezing, asshole voice. "Please, I gotta have 'em! Jiminy Christmas, do I need my smokes!" He'd do it over and over again, his pleas becoming more and more absurd, until I and whoever else was around would be dying from laughter.

Other than these little interludes, and the nights when he'd walk me home, we never interacted much. Other people were always around when we worked together. All of my fantasies involved just the two of us. I didn't know how to navigate the presence of other people. Beyond the mental script I used at the store, or when I was joking with the old men, being easy with other people was exhausting. I never spoke with Hernan at length about much at all.

So Hernan was dead. What else is there to say? In that whirlwind first year after he died, I'd helped Krystal clean out his apartment, which took less than a day. There was no secret journal exposing all his hopes and fears, not even a laptop with a pervy internet history. His phone had been damaged during the robbery, and had either been thrown away or handed back to Krystal, so I never knew what the last song he listened to was, who he'd been texting recently. In death he gave me no more insight into who he was than he'd given me in life, not really. That was when I knew it was really over, that there was truly nothing left.

I could have been someone who pined, who thought about him each and every day, who listened to sad songs and mourned for all that could have been. But there had been nothing between us. There was nothing to mourn. I had known him, and now he was dead. If any feeling stronger than that cropped up and threatened to obliterate me, I circumnavigated it. I was the Magellan of misery, a master of escaping my brain's busy, killing work. At first, all I wished to do was to blunt my feelings, to head them off at the pass like I would a migraine. If I could just get away from everything, if I would be allowed that, I was confident I could extinguish them forever.

I woke each day at the mountain place in a bath of morning light. The sun climbed into my room slowly, minute by minute, and on clear mornings it seared through the windowpanes, opening my eyes all at once. People who say that money cannot buy happiness have never woken in sunlight after years of waking in dark rooms, places where the blinds are shut day and night to preserve the last scrap of privacy. Before, in the trailer park, my insomniac nights had ended in a few hours of sleep before dawn, and each morning began with a shrill alarm, distant yelling or engines revving, and schoolchildren chattering so close outside my thin walls that they might have been in the room with me. So many tiny assaults were endured in the dark, first thing, before I slid out of bed and into the world. Now sleeping and waking were like coming through a door.

My trailer hadn't sold, but I had started living at the new place full time, only returning now and then to pick up my mail. The new house felt like a hotel full of doors and hallways and secret, unseen places. It was huge, the largest house I had ever stepped foot in. I only used a few rooms—my bedroom, the living room, the kitchen in the front of the house—feeling like a small animal relocated to a vast, foreign landscape, trying to form a nest that felt familiar. It took a while to get used to the idea that the house was mine, not some in-between place that was on loan to me, or a permanent hallucination. Often I thought of rich people who are rich from birth—how they must swagger through rooms like this, how free they must feel in their natural habitat, their birthright, whereas I visited each room in my new mansion as one would visit an exotic island, standing in the doorway and gazing in, amazed at how fabulous the light was! How high the ceilings were! The closet space—my god! Everything was a marvel. The lonely sun in winter and the locusts' drone in summer drifted freely through the open windows. There was room for everything.

Despite the fresh air and good sleep, though, dread still pecked at me. For the first few weeks I spent my time walking aimlessly, getting lost in the woods for hours. After the constant hum of human noise had haunted me for so long, the quiet felt confrontational. I wandered around like a guest waiting for the host to arrive and tell me what to do.

I worried about myself. I remembered reading about astronaut training, how they strapped themselves into capsules, subjected themselves to g-force torture, to isolation chambers, all to see how much they could take. The more I thought about it, the more sense it made, and eventually I concluded that an experiment might answer my questions.

So, for a whole week, I camped out in the woods and pretended I was an intruder. What a thrill it was to look at the house from the tree line, an outsider once again! It's delicious to spy on one's self. During that week I watched the house from afar and imagined walking around in the rooms, what meals a person might cook in the giant kitchen. I fabricated an entire routine for the person who inhabited it—their fondness for certain spaces, their shitting and eating schedules, their mundane, bizarre habits done every day at the same time, thinking themselves invisible. I took notes.

In this way, I taught myself how to live there. It was the first in several new strategies that leaped up at me. My brain was plushing out again with activity where it had previously been flat, inert; it was now a fresh towel fluffy and warm and ready for soiling. When I returned to the house I truly understood the possibilities before me and was also aware of every weak entry point, every window and door and crawl space that needed to be secured. For the first time in my life, I became territorial. I looked out an upstairs window and surveyed the land spreading out before me, anger and pride rising up behind me, the need to protect and defend floating around me.

Overall, I felt new. Lobotomized. I decided I was ready for the next step.

Krystal and I didn't talk for two whole months after I stormed out of Geannie's house, until she called me out of the blue one day. "You want to come over Friday?" she asked. And things resumed as before.

I didn't bring up the house after we reconnected. After our fight, if that is what it had been, I had started taking a different route to work.

Honestly, I didn't want to know. I didn't want to see the house and I didn't want to see Krystal's car. Grief was ugly and embarrassing. The word itself, *grief*, embarrassed me, something that dated back to childhood. After my father killed himself, my teetotaler mother went from her usual quiet self to almost totally silent, but still carried on exactly the same as before, for seven months, before she went out one night, got blind drunk, and accidentally drove her car into the front window of the local pharmacy. No one was hurt in the crash and no charges were filed. (I was thirteen at the time, and for years afterward I wondered where and how my mother had gotten drunk—as far as I knew, she had never stepped foot inside a liquor store or bar, and would have died of shame to do so.) When she died years later, I found out my mother had paid for the damages in installments over several years. But at the time, the police officer who brought her home told me to put her to bed for a while. "Your mama's grieving," he'd said, making me turn scarlet. "She's had a bad time of it." Then he left.

I was overwhelmed with shame that was amplified by fear.

Your mama's grieving. The phrase frightened me the same as if
he'd told me she had cancer. Here I had figured she was fine, and
that whatever sadness I felt over my father's death was because
I was a dumb kid, and a girl, and everyone knew how girls were
prone to maudlin feelings. Adults, I wanted to believe, went
largely unaffected, and the prospect that one day I, too, could
reach a point of dignified apathy reassured me. But now all that
was ruined, and the officer's message got through: my mother's
suffering was as ugly as my own, and there was no remedy for
either of us. I could only put her to bed and let her work it out
in private until she was finished. Grief was worse than death or
crime. It was humiliation.

But Krystal wasn't my mother and I wasn't thirteen anymore, and since I had dedicated myself to my complete immersion in *Three's Company*, I had a frank disinterest in whatever
Krystal was going through, or how Geannie's house figured into
it. When she called me up again I'd hoped that she was over it,
but when I went over to her place for our first regular Friday
night dinner since our hiatus, I noticed for the first time that
she had started losing weight. And she was sullen and pale, the
picture of a suffering someone. Now, after almost five years, she
was on some kind of grief kick? I didn't comment. I watched her
pick at her food as I swallowed my rage.

Of course, my careful avoidance of the subject didn't matter. Krystal brought up the house all by herself. One Friday in
early summer, a month or two after we'd reconnected and a few
months before the lottery drawing, she started talking about
money. She didn't have enough of it, story of our lives. She had
been getting headaches and missing a lot of work, and was now
on probation.

"The dentist put you on *probation*?" I said, snorting with

laughter. For some reason I thought it was really funny. The dentist-jailer.

"It's not funny," she said. But it was.

Krystal had been one of those overachievers in school who cared a lot about what teachers and bosses thought of her. The office where she worked was one of the fancier places, where multiple dentists glued veneers on rich people. They also offered spa treatments to patients. For a regular dentist appointment. You could go in, get a hot rag on your forehead and a hand massage while Dr. So-and-so drilled your teeth. The comforts some people could afford, my god. We used to laugh about stuff like that, but now her face was serious.

"I think I might get fired."

"Well, go to the doctor. For your headaches, I mean."

Get your shit taken care of, dummy, is what I wanted to say, but I was her friend, and ever since I'd pushed her in Geannie's house (yes, she had fallen down, she told me later, showing me a blood bruise on her shin that wouldn't go away), I'd been trying to be nice.

"I went to one, but he says it's just nerves."

She got up and cleared our dishes, which is how I knew she was lying. She could never look at me when she lied.

"Are you going to throw all of that out?" I asked as I watched her carry her bowl over to the sink. She had heated up some chili and her bowl was almost full. It was the closest I ever got to acknowledging her new eating habits. She shrugged. I told her to pack it up, I would take it home. I knew better than to suggest she keep it for later; I had seen the moldy specimens lingering in her fridge.

"I think I have to sell the house." Her voice was small.

I kept my mouth shut. We had been having a nice night, no

major tiffs, none of her whiny-piney bullshit. Now the mostly full bowl of chili was irritating me. I watched her crimp foil around the bowl's edges. Like, she couldn't even put it in a Cool Whip tub or something? Now I'd have to be careful to wash and return the bowl, which would probably spill over in my truck.

She said, "My aunt wants to sell it and I can't afford to buy it, and I was wondering: Would you help me pack it up?"

I watched her put the bowl to one side on the counter. It sat there, still warm, and she did not put it in the fridge. We still had our usual routine ahead of us, watching TV on the couch or the walk. How long does it take for foodborne illness to take hold? Two hours at room temperature? An hour in more heated conditions? For the life of me, I could not understand why she was being so fucking careless.

"Come on, Bonnie," she said. She had sat down again. "You're the only person I can ask. So I'm asking." She paused and smiled. "And you have muscles now! You can throw boxes around."

In a way, I was relieved that she was going to pack up the place and be done. But I dreaded going back inside that house. When a person dies, everything they owned dies with them. I didn't want to touch dead things. Cleaning out the closets of a dead person is a sign that the grieving process has reached the later stages, experts say—you've become strong enough to murder whatever didn't die already. Keep that stuff around, and it's like the dead aren't dead. It gives you ideas. My mother never threw out anything of my father's, so it always seemed like he had taken a trip somewhere and could return at any moment. When she died, I sold the house with everything in it. The ancient Egyptians were onto something, packing the Pyramids with the deceased's belongings, sealing up the tomb, walking away.

"Fine," I said, finding the fastest route out of the conversation.

I figured I owed Krystal something. She had taken me in those first nights after the robbery. And I had a strange feeling, and had been feeling it increasingly during the years since my discovery of *Three's Company*, that I was nearing a point—an end point, it felt like, though I could not have said what it was an ending to—that required all debts to be settled.

So starting in July, a month before I bought the winning tickets, I met Krystal in the driveway of Geannie and Jim's house, and we entered the house together, and began packing up the belongings of the dead people we'd loved.

I interviewed contractors and workers in the living room of the new place. The room's main features were a sprawling expanse of hardwood and a floor-to-ceiling fireplace on one wall. Three naked windows stretched daylight across everything. In my haste to get out of my trailer and into the future, I had not bothered much with furniture, not even drapes. My old armchair sat in the middle of the room like a throne. I had to bring in folding chairs I found in one of the outbuildings for extra seating. The arrangement resembled a church basement waiting for an AA meeting.

Ray Wineholt was the fourth contractor I interviewed, and the man who won the project. He didn't raise an eyebrow at my bare living room, the first point in his favor, and I was reassured by his sturdy, flanneled presence. His voice was gentle and cigarette-rich. But I was most encouraged by his wild, mountain-man beard that hung down to his nipples. He smelled like laundry detergent, tobacco, and patchouli. Right away I could tell that he was a trustable and practical man, and that he had a glimmer of a savage artist deep within him. When he showed me hard-copy pictures of his work, they were faded and wrinkled at the edges, and exuded a faint vanilla scent I'd always associated with cheap air fresheners that dangled from rearview mirrors; I suspected they'd been forgotten in the backseat of his car for a year. Finally, here was someone who could appreciate damage.

For I wanted dents in the walls, inconvenient layouts, all the mild absurdities one could expect to encounter in a run-down, dated apartment building that had been lived in for forty years. The four other draftsmen had not understood this.

The *Three's Company* apartment building was an impossible space. Apartments and balconies disappeared and reappeared throughout the series; there were references to the building being a "house," and then other times an entire complex. Even within the individual apartments that appeared on the show there were rooms that were mentioned but never seen, and other rooms that were left mysterious as to whether they existed at all, though logic dictated they should be there. I wanted this sense of strangeness to be reflected in the construction. The only certain things were the general layouts and dimensions of Apartment 201, the trio's apartment; Apartment 101, the landlords' apartment; and Apartment 304, Larry Dallas's apartment; and that overall it would be a three-story, eighteen-unit building in the Spanish Colonial Revival style of Los Angeles in the early twentieth century—rounded edges and doorways, stuccoed walls, wrought-iron balconies, clay-tiled steps. I had memorized all these details, compiled them into a mental script, and I repeated it to Ray like a guru repeating a mantra.

He took it fine. As we sat in the living room, our legs crossed beneath our folding chairs, I could see the possibilities unfold in his head. "And above all else," I added, animating my voice a little more, "I want you to understand that whatever you build, whatever you put into this, you'll never see it again after it's finished. And neither will anyone else. Just me."

He had one of those pencils without an eraser, the sign of a true architect in my limited knowledge of what an architect should be, and when I made that declaration he placed the blunt end to his lips, gazing at the rough sketch I had handed him. He nodded. "I understand," he said solemnly. "I like it," he said, meaning, I think, that he liked that he would never see it again. I knew he was the one.

He then shook my hand and said he would get right to work, and he did. Within a month he had drawn up a blueprint we both agreed upon, the permits were acquired, ground was broken, and fifty men were on the job.

The project began.

The day I won the lottery, Krystal called me and asked if I wanted to go over to Geannie's house again.

The house had remained mostly untouched until we'd started packing it up in July. Our progress had been slow because neither of us wanted to do it. "Let's meet over there around three," she said on the phone, and I agreed. It was a Saturday in October but the leaves stubbornly clung to the trees, unchanged. The sun kept going and going. My air conditioner continued to shudder on, probably on its last year of life, and my trailer still felt like an oven. The lottery drawing, announced live on television, was five hours away.

When I arrived she had already been there for hours, wading through the embarrassing amount of stuff two people collect over twenty years together and worrying over wolf spiders hiding in the basement's damp corners. Boxes were strewn everywhere, an explosion of a life. The kitchen hadn't been so bad, but the basement alone had taken four weekends to sort through and put into boxes, each one carefully labeled. We were only three-quarters of the way finished.

What was to become of it all? I did not ask. Had the house been sold? I did not ask. I did not wish to know or do anything that enhanced my consciousness above the level necessary for basic survival. My *Three's Company* obsession, also going on five years by this point, had sunk me into a waking dream, and everything else—work, my time with Krystal, packing up the house, the past and present—became hazy and unreal, a mindless ritual. My brain actually felt soft when I performed my daily work tasks, as if reality itself had become mushy, and I began incurring warnings at work for carelessness. I stocked a dairy case with sour cream too near its expiration; on another day I had not secured a pallet and several gallons of milk fell to the floor and burst. In lieu of being formally reprimanded, I agreed to pay for the damages out of my own paycheck, and cleaned up the spilled milk myself, and because I stayed meek and mild during the dressing-down portion of my punishment, the warehouse manager was merciful. I lacked attention, he told me, and he was questioning my commitment to safety. I had shaken my head and nodded at the appropriate moments, having learned long ago that the best way to communicate with him was through well-timed head movements. So far my strategy of barely being alive was working.

That Saturday in the basement was no different. I floated along and counted the hours until I'd be back in my favorite spot in front of the television, deciding between a Season 3 episode and a Season 6 one. As I taped up boxes, I silently tested myself—my new project was memorizing the script of each episode. At night I'd been dreaming of terrible apocalypses, burned-out rubble where my neighbors' trailers had been, everything turned to ash, until one night I awoke panting, my throat sore from breathing in the cindery debris, gripped with fear: What if the world ended? What if a global catastrophe happened? How would I watch *Three's Company*? So I started memorizing each episode down to the finest detail. I had to become a living library.

Which is what I was whispering to myself in Geannie's basement when I found Jim's Christmas village. Krystal was in a far corner still waging war on the spiders, the short exhalations of her aerosol can moving farther away as she moved deeper into the basement.

I stood there transfixed. Each small building was in its original box, stacked up under the stairs. Nearby were the risers he used, and I could see the cotton batting rolled up inside a garbage bag. Taped to each box was a photograph Jim had taken of what was within, and I was surprised to see that each structure had a name—English Cottage 3, Anderstown Courthouse, WELCOME TO SNOWVILLE, Castle Vermontaly—and a designation as to placement. There had to be fifty or sixty of them, neatly stacked one on top of the other in a pattern that resembled a brick wall.

"Do you want help?" Krystal asked, startling me. She had suddenly appeared behind me. A cloud of insecticide hovered around her.

"No," I said, and picked up a large empty box and started filling it with the village buildings, ignoring her. I needed to finish it once I started it, or it would never be finished.

An hour later the town was gone. The sixty-two smaller boxes fit into ten large boxes. The absurdity of life seemed contained in these ten boxes, the vanity of living at all. A spider drunk-walked across the floor, strangling and frightened, and I watched it slowly die and curl, looking five times smaller once dead.

I went upstairs for a glass of water, and looked out the window above the sink. Three crows were pecking at the grass outside. They seemed out of place, out of time. The weather felt like mid-June. Shouldn't October be cool, crisp, apple-flavored?

Nothing felt right anymore. Since the Scheeles had left, I felt like I knew less and less about the world.

I wanted to go home. The lottery drawing would be on later that night, televised as usual, and I had not told Krystal I'd bought three tickets. The subject had come up, actually, the night before at our weekly Friday dinner; the winning pot of money had become something of a national sensation over the previous couple of weeks after it broke some kind of record, and she had bought ten tickets on a lark. "Shouldn't you be paying your bills?" I had asked her. Over the past year she had let herself go somewhat, and usually this kind of snarky comment would make her flinch.

But this time she'd just shrugged and smiled. "Well, since you're such a doubting Thomas I won't give you any of my winnings." Then, being Krystal, she added, "Just kidding, Bonnie— I would buy you anything you wanted."

I had smiled back. I knew she meant it. She was my only friend, and I felt sorry for her. Also a little disgusted. She clearly lacked discipline if she was already promising other people stuff.

But on that Saturday, in the basement, she seemed jumpy and bright, excited, as if she really thought she had a shot at winning. I also may have been a tad more chipper than usual, at least before I came across the Christmas village.

As I stood at the kitchen window and watched the crows, Krystal climbed up the basement stairs. She stood at the doorway and asked if I wanted some ice cream. I said yes, thinking it was a good excuse to get away from this place. But, to my amazement, she walked over to the fridge and took a carton of ice cream out of the freezer, then fetched an ice cream scoop and bowls from the drawer and cupboard, and began spooning it out.

I had packed up the bowls and kitchen utensils the week before.

"So. Is this your house now?" After all the bug spray and old memories I was feeling punchy. She looked up at me. She seemed taken aback but smiled peacefully, dreamily. "No," she said. "But if I win tonight it will be."

"So you don't own it."

If she detected my passive aggression, she didn't let on. "No, it still belongs to Dad's sister out west," she replied. She looked out the window. "It's so unfair. I keep telling her I'd look after it. I'd pay rent and everything. But she asked me to pack it up instead. She really wants to sell it." She swirled her spoon around in her bowl in an annoying way that meant she wasn't going to eat. In the last year she had become near skeletal, for reasons I did not like to speculate upon. "I don't think the mortgage payments have been made," she said. "I don't think she really cares."

"Oh? What makes you think that?" I asked. I was cramming my mouth full of ice cream, hoping she'd take the hint and do likewise. I wanted to set a good example, and I wanted to leave.

Krystal set her bowl on the counter and shrugged. "I might have called the mortgage company," she said. She looked out the same window, out to where I was looking, but the crows had flown away. "I had to know. I told them I was an interested buyer." A stupid, glazed look came over her face. "If I win I'm going to buy it and live here."

I had had enough. I finished my ice cream. A sharp pain overtook my skull because I'd eaten it too fast, and I was a little out of breath. But I rinsed my bowl and set it in the sink. I turned toward Krystal.

"This isn't good for you," I said. I looked her in the eyes. "You know what I mean?"

The hope in her face crumpled. Her eyes got all red and I felt terrible, but as love rushed up at me, pricked at me, she said, "But it's *mine*. I grew up here." She shook her head. "It should have been mine."

My love instantly turned into an urge to shove her, to hit her.

You hated this house, I wanted to say. You couldn't wait to ditch it. To ditch them. All your wishes have come true.

I only sighed. "I want to leave," I said.

She started to cry, but that didn't stop me. I walked out the door, and two hours later I won the lottery, and by the end of the year that version of me was gone for good.

W hen potential workers arrived, I took them into my new living room, where I had added a desk to the AA setup, and where several papers waited for them.

Three's Company *premiered on the ABC network at 9 p.m. on March 15, 1977, a Tuesday. Its premise: Sensible flower-shop worker Janet Wood and naive secretary Chrissy Snow need a third roommate to make rent in their Santa Monica apartment. They find Jack Tripper, culinary student and aspiring chef, in the bathtub one morning after a party, and take him in. However, their stodgy landlord Stanley Roper will not allow unmarried heterosexual people of the opposite sex to live together, as it was against the conservative social and sexual mores of the time. Janet tells Roper that Jack is gay, and the living arrangement becomes acceptable. Helen Roper, Stanley's love-starved wife, learns Jack's true sexuality but keeps the secret—she, and all of the younger generation, are all-in on putting one over on old-fashioned Mr. Roper.*

Later in the series, cast changes occur. Chrissy Snow leaves to care for her sick mother and is replaced by her younger, country-bumpkin cousin Cindy Snow, and a year later Cindy is replaced by Terri Alden, a blonde nurse. The Ropers sell the apartment building and move out, and Ralph Furley, a middle-aged, wannabe-macho-man bachelor, moves in as the sole landlord. For a brief time in Season 4 another neighbor moves in, Lana Shields, who is hot-to-trot for young Jack, but she disappears as quickly as she came. Throughout all of these cast changes Larry Dallas, a car salesman and Jack's ne'er-do-well pal, lives upstairs and often gets the roommates into trouble in his perpetual quest for money and women.

The series begins as a bedroom farce that later transitions into more physical humor. Most plots revolve around misunderstandings due to a lack of information or unfortunate coincidences. Most episodes, in sitcom tradition, end with a moment of clarity, a coming-together of the characters, and a resetting of the universe. Though very broad story lines are sometimes resolved over a season (such as Jack eventually completing his college degree and becoming a chef), all episodes are stand-alone plots, and the series can be entered into at any point without much background.

Each person who applied for employment received a paper with this spiel written on it. Some had seen the show, but others had been unaware of its existence, and still others had seen the show and hated it, and some had only heard of it but never watched it, and there were people from every group listed above who had concluded that it had been a mess comedically, or backward according to today's politics, or they loved it because it was "anti-PC," or they loathed it for being so vapid, or they enjoyed it for its kitsch value. Only a few people were true fans like me. I was familiar with every attitude. At first, I did not require the workers to enjoy the series, only to fully dedicate themselves to whatever aspect of the series they had been assigned to. But it soon became clear that when it came to pop culture, one speck of sincere hostility could taint everything. I started holding screening sessions where candidates would watch an episode while I monitored their reactions.

Anyone who seemed particularly empathetic toward Mr. Roper being a harangued man beset by an increasingly progressive world was dismissed immediately. I didn't have time for stupidity. My judgment had no root in political correctness, though I was accused of this by one man who was angry I was running "a liberal shitshow" when he was shown the door. No, it was a matter of love. I needed people who could keep an open mind. I took in only those who appreciated the spirit of the show in the context of the era in which it was created, minus the sandbag of political beliefs. I turned away people who only liked the show because they thought it was on their side. *Three's Company* was a farce, after all. Farce punishes everyone eventually.

I kept waiting for someone to ask me why I liked it so much. "Oh, I think it's funny," I would tell them.

But that wasn't all of it. One of the main things about the show that had so completely hooked my interest was that it was rooted in the decade(s) that produced it: the late 1970s and early eighties. The seventies were a bleak time, I had no illusions about that. Bombings, terrorism, pointless war, the rise of cults, environmental alarmism, and at the end of it, Reagan. Nobody who actually lived through that decade enjoyed it. But it was gone, it was done, and it now sat safely in its little historical drawer. Nothing would change it. That's the beauty of anything set firmly in the past, especially a past time that was never one's present—you know how it ends.

And then there were the character dynamics. The roommates and landlords formed a family unit, one forged not by blood but by circumstance, by chance, and they loved one another with a purity I had never experienced in real life. The lines were clearly drawn on *Three's Company*. Everyone always knew their part, their value. And because they were not blood, they were all outsiders. That appealed to me on a soul level, that I could walk among them, be them, and experience such acceptance. *Three's Company* was a door into a new way of life, an immersion into a different decade, into lives and histories that were different from my own, into a family that could not be broken. And for all their foibles, the characters were *good*. They were good people living good, decent lives. They rarely fell into trouble or tragedy that could not be reversed in twenty minutes; they never hurt others in any permanent way.

I had been watching good people my whole life from a distance, and though I had tried—over and over I'd tried—I had never been able to excoriate the deep, deep wrongness of being that I felt ever since I was a little kid. I was always choosing the wrong thing, always making the wrong moves. Always outside. The goodness, the *rightness*, of others fascinated me, the way that things one is not born into usually do. In a way, my project was an opportunity to study it close-up. I wanted to know what it was like, even if it was only for one minute in a decade, to feel good because I *was* good, because I was born the right way.

All in all I wanted to touch the fabrics, to eat the ice cream, to feel the same afternoon sunlight a model kicking up her heels in a seventies-era Sears autumn catalog was selling. The humming safety of a packaged life. I wanted to experience a whole other timeline. Through *Three's Company* I would transcend the existence of Bonnie Lincoln. Time itself would no longer be an enemy. The filth of my own life would cease to be a threat.

Still, I would not say that I was depressed or damaged in any way. That's the conclusion most of the potential workers drew when I gave away more of these details than I should have during their interviews. I had a hard time not staring at them as each interview progressed, always trying to read myself there, their impression of me, and their faces told me all I needed to know. Eccentricity, depression, maladaptive daydreaming, trauma, etc. . . . when later describing me to one of their friends, I'm sure they used all the terminology they learned on *Dr. Phil.* Some of them stared at my neck, where I had rolled up the collar to cover the scar.

But while it was true that I still had bad dreams, it was also true that their intensity had subsided. In the new sunlight of each morning, they quickly receded from memory. For the most part, I felt renewed.

What numbers had I used to win? I suppose it would show commitment to my cause if I had used the dates that my favorite *Three's Company* episodes originally aired, or the birth dates of the show's cast members, or some other date or statistic related to the show. But the truth is that I had used the birth dates of Geannie, Jim, and Hernan, all of which I knew by heart, and also the date of the robbery.

I had prepared myself for victory in the week leading up to the readout of the lottery number. That was when I first found Larwin's name and number. I thought of Jim, what steps he would have advised me to take. When in doubt I had always called him, and just hearing his voice would calm me, make me feel more in control.

The night the lottery was drawn I felt too jangly to eat. My hands shook as I sat in my recliner clutching my ticket. For the occasion I had dragged out all of my *Three's Company* DVDs and perched them around me. There were enough to place a few on either side of my head and on the armrests, and the remaining sets I placed in a circle around the recliner, and after doing so I felt strengthened. When the television announced the winning numbers, I stared at the screen for a minute, and then back at my ticket, then back at the screen. I had done it.

Stunned, I stared at the ceiling. Was I God? It felt possible. Beside the recliner was the list I had made days before: call an attorney, call an accountant. Nothing felt real but my future. For long minutes I did not move, enjoying the air of safe harbor the DVDs wafted up at me.

My phone, which I had left sitting on my kitchen counter, rang. It startled me, making me think for a second that someone already knew I had won, or could somehow see into my trailer, into my very brain. I rose and stepped out of my shrine, panicking a little when one of the boxes nearly fell to the floor.

It was Krystal. "I didn't win," she said. "The house! Now I'll never have it." She was crying.

"Calm down," I told her. My voice surprised me by sounding thin, hoarse, as if I had swallowed something too hot.

I had just won the lottery. I had done it. I had bet on myself, and I had won.

I moved my hand in front of my face and I perceived it slowly, as if I had exited my body. Through the phone I could hear Krystal sob.

The night she picked me up from the hospital, she had greeted me with a smile. I was stuffing my soiled clothing into a bag, my back to the door, when she knocked on the doorframe of my room. My ears were still half-deaf from the gunshots, but when I heard the knock I jerked my head around and I saw her register it, my too-quick motion, as a sign of something deeply wrong.

But she had not looked at me with sympathy. She didn't look sad or unhappy or stunned. She didn't look like her parents and brother had just died. Her face was unreadable. All she said then was, "Hey, Bon Bon, you ready for the Days Inn experience?" And then she'd smiled a little, and I could have wept. The kindness of others was the worst.

On the phone now she started hiccuping on her tears. "It's all gone," she kept repeating. "It's all gone now."

"You're overreacting, Krys. Just take a breath. I'll come over."

When I arrived at her place I did what she did for me on that night five years before: I got her situated on the couch and brought her comfort food, keeping silent company with her. I turned off all the lights and we sat and watched television in the dark. Sometimes I could hear her sniffle. I said, "It doesn't matter, that old house. Probably better, anyway."

She stayed quiet, her breath evening, and eventually she drifted off.

I became drowsy and my brain started crawling the way it always did at the edge of sleep, loosely holding wonder, idly thinking about the past, or the day, or my life, or how luck unfolds. How time folds in on itself, and how so many versions of a person live and die and resurrect over the course of one life. An hour and a half earlier, when I found my friend in her living room, on the floor, her television babbling commercials, the TV screen caught my eye and I recalled discovering *Three's Company* on that very machine, and the world shifted in the same way it did on voting days, when I walked into my old, unchanged elementary school cafeteria and saw it as an adult. I'd belonged there once, but not anymore. I hadn't belonged for a while. Between the moment the announcer read the lottery numbers and the moment my brain confirmed that I'd won, the world stayed the same but I molted into my next stage. This apartment had become a relic. A museum piece. And there was Krystal, crumpled on the carpet, abject, face mottled and wet, the star of the exhibition.

A phase was ending. A new one waited. Gradually my mind fell away from the television's glowing murmur, and sank into darkness.

•••••••••••

I woke up to a crick in my neck and a cold room—Krystal, ever the penny-pincher, never turned on the heat or AC unless she absolutely had to. I decided to make my escape. Outside it was just coming up on daylight, still shadowy in the living room. I stretched and walked into the kitchen, not bothering to tiptoe. Krystal always slept heavily, a skill I envied. I put a pot of coffee on for her and left her a note—I'd been called into work for an extra shift.

It was bullshit, of course. I went home. My neighborhood looked like a movie set on Sunday mornings, the sun coming up over the trailers that sat silent and still, sleeping off the night before. As soon as I was inside the door I called the financial adviser and lawyer but got answering machines. It was Sunday morning and no one was in, but an odd feeling kept pressing at me, an urge to execute my list of preparations like a ritual. I feared that if I did not, if I slowed down to doubt for a moment, if I did not pay proper respect to the luck that had befallen me, I risked breaking the reality. Maybe I would realize I had seen the wrong numbers on the winning ticket, or maybe the numbers themselves would change. Luck was always punishing me. This time I desperately wanted to appease it. So to keep a sense of momentum I went down my to-do list that I had made long ago, in anticipation of my winning.

After a while I sat back in my recliner and stared into nothing for a little bit, sour morning light filtering in. The sky was clouding over. The quiet hummed around me.

I found myself standing before the door of my erstwhile bedroom. I didn't recall walking the short distance. Maybe I'd dozed off and sleepwalked. That happened to me sometimes, just like it happened to Chrissy in Season 1. I turned the knob and went inside.

My collection looked sad in the mean light of dawn. But I saw what it could be. What it would be. What I felt then was bigger, beyond any mere universe's gift, beyond any energy that might grace or punish me on a whim. I could see my future before me, and it was a one-road path—a labyrinth, maybe, but a single way out, a total escape from my present self. Everything was leading me there.

My phone buzzed just then. It was Krystal. I didn't pick up. And she didn't leave a message.

I woke shortly after dawn one day in March and looked out my window at the mountain place, and I saw the skeleton of my dream rising slowly, slowly, one beam at a time, out of fog. The air was chilly and deep, like autumn, and the distant sound of a hammer came at me, the lazy drone of a saw. Because it was so early the sky was still gray, and the tops of the black trees disappeared in a swirl of fog. On the ground, figures in hard hats milled about, a few empty-handed, a couple more carrying long planks of wood on their shoulders, while others knelt down, attuned to their work—a bevy of strangers moving in a weird, syncopated rhythm, the sounds of work floating in hushed, far-off tones. The outline of the building's foundation had been laid and I could see the edges rising up. Off to the side Ray stood talking in a huddle with two other workers, pointing at an unrolled blueprint.

The entire scene was muted, like a painting composed of feathery brushstrokes and a palette of grays and greens and browns, with the occasional dull orange speckles of hard hats, and I observed it as I would an ocean or a baby, the possibilities of all things past and future rolling and multiplying within it.

After several long minutes of staring, I turned away and went downstairs to the large kitchen and made myself a pot of coffee. On the counter was the thick three-ring binder I had started looking at the day before. PROGRESS REPORT was printed on the cover, as well as a bulleted list of its contents.

I had asked for all information on all branches of the ongoing project to be printed out when possible and served to me in these weekly reports. The results were delicious in their tangibility; I already had five or six of these binders stacking up, each one fatter than the last.

The one I was looking at that March morning had been left at the front door by someone named Brenda who had become my phantom assistant. I rarely saw her, but her name, Brenda Hollins, and the date were inscribed on the front pages of each of these binders, as well as any memos or emergency packets. She was my liaison to the caseworkers. I faintly remembered interviewing her and being amused by her pride in multitasking. She seemed to have little need of direction. There was something ominously efficient in the way I could provide her with a list of notes or tasks, and—poof!—she would have whatever I asked for the next morning.

As I drank my coffee I hunched over the counter and flipped through this binder, the beginning of which detailed the gathering of authentic *Los Angeles Times* newspapers dated from March 15, 1977, until September 18, 1984 (the trio and landlords had subscriptions to the *LA Times* throughout the series). In a few episodes there also appeared a few editions of the *Los Angeles Herald Examiner*, a paper that went extinct in the late 1980s and was now almost impossible to find. I desired pristine editions—no signs of yellowing or decay were allowed. I didn't want to smell any basements. I wanted them to be as fresh as they would have been on the first day they were printed. If authentic papers could not be located, I had instructed my workers to find a way to print the newspaper on era-specific printing presses and paper in order to convey the appropriate time period.

Digital materials could be used to create the necessary environment, such as re-creating the newspapers, but nothing of the modern era would be allowed in the actual experience of living in Apartment 201. That was one thing that I made sure all my workers knew. Smartphones, apps, tablets, computers—gone. The trio hadn't even owned a microwave. The most high-tech devices the apartment building had (at least starting out) were the push-button phone and old television. Chrissy's parents sent her a Canon Super 8 camera and film projector in Season 2, so that was permissible. The apartment also sported a record player and a portable radio.

But except for a small robotic device that would collect and fling the rolled-up newspapers onto the balcony before disappearing back into its tiny storage space in a nearby building, never to be seen, there was to be no anachronistic technology of any kind in the world I was building; I would be blessedly cut off from the outside world. The landline phone would be my only source of communication. During that first year of preparation, when I was technically still "in" the world, I severely cut down on all outside communication; as I did with Larwin, I eschewed phone calls or text messages. I even had built it into most of my workers' contracts that they were not allowed to contact me except in dire emergencies.

I peered at the report that concerned the vintage *Los Angeles Times* papers. The two caseworkers who had been assigned to this task had tracked down some leads in the California area. Wealthy folks of a certain age. I was finding more and more that eccentric rich people were going to be my saving grace, the key to all of this—they were the only hoarders who stored their hoard in temperature-controlled vaults, preserving the most trivial items in their original condition. They could afford an obsession with their own past. There was a lady in Agoura Hills who had decades of the *Los Angeles Times* papers stacked up in a room inside her large mansion, and from what the caseworkers said, she kept a fairly clean house. They were flying out tomorrow to meet with her and survey the collection in person. It was the only way to properly evaluate. I needed a human nose to make sure they were acceptable.

Caseworkers were allotted for each item or group of items that needed to be tracked down. For example, there were caseworkers for the indoor potted plants seen in each set throughout the series—one person who watched every episode and noted the species and receptacle of each potted plant, another person who researched the care of each plant, and yet another who was in charge of acquiring the plants, and a fourth one who tracked down each decorative pot or macramé holder that would then be matched with the appropriate plant when the time came. Janet Wood worked in a flower shop, after all, and it was the 1970s, the height of the houseplant craze. Some plants were seen in Apartment 201 throughout the series, such as a schefflera next to the telephone in the living room, and others rotated or appeared and disappeared and reappeared, such as Boston ferns, a corn plant, and several varieties of ivy and philodendron, so this level of detail was necessary. And the care and feeding of the plants were also important—the ones that only appeared in a few episodes would have to be stowed away in one of the large outbuildings on my property (converted into a large indoor/outdoor greenhouse for the purpose, a construction project in and of itself, and whose progress was also enclosed in the binder I held) until its appearance was due, and I needed to know how to take care of them.

By March I had employed nearly one hundred caseworkers, all from relatively distant places to avoid overlap with anyone I might have known, and more seemed inevitable. The binders and coffee routine became a daily necessity in order to keep up with the progress. My house and grounds became a hive of creative forces, and the energy powered me. The more efficiently the people finished their tasks, the faster I could hire new people for different tasks, or move existing workers to new or tangential projects. I strove for authenticity in every aspect, and checked each person's work accordingly, for who better to perform quality control than me, the person who had watched and internalized the show the most?

One of the biggest problems I had to solve was the issue of the television. Because cable was out of the question, I wanted to be able to turn on my 1970s-era model television in Apartment 201 at any time and see what the characters—or, really, any Santa Monica resident—might have seen during the years of 1977–84, day or night. But how to do it?

The eccentric rich came through again. There was a lady— it was usually old ladies whose sentimental preservation of the present eventually became the vital source material of the past— who lived in Burbank and had invested early on in Betamax machines. Not having a particular preference for any one program, she had taken it into her head to record every single thing that played on her television for years. She was a fellow obsessive, a woman after my own heart. She was network loyal—she only recorded ABC programming for most of the duration, but even so this find was a fabulous discovery, for it provided an authentic viewing experience, commercials and all.

Once the caseworker found this woman he also discovered a cadre of older folks who had compulsively recorded television throughout the time period I needed. It was some kind of cult. Whether they were lovers of television or of Betamax technology, or whether they were, in a more existential twist, desperate people compelled to document every hour of every day, as if to say, *I witnessed this*, I didn't know. I was only grateful. I bought all of their collections when I could, and where I couldn't, I rented the original tapes so I could copy them, all for an incredible price.

From these tapes, and using period-specific *TV Guide*s from the local Santa Monica area at the time, several other caseworkers were able to piece together authentic programming that would play around the clock from all the major networks. I would be able to change channels through some digital miracle devised by a young caseworker whose specialty was electronics and digital manipulation. I wanted a finished product that, by virtue of clicking the remote control as one would in 1977, I could change the channel at will and find appropriate programming. I required that nothing would take time to "load" or otherwise hint at its modern framework—I needed the facsimile to be seamless. Somehow they managed it.

All caseworkers signed a nondisclosure agreement. If they breathed a word of it, I would sue them into oblivion. I told everyone I had eyes and ears out in the world—and, considering the scale of my project and the attention to detail they witnessed each day upon coming onto my property, my claim seemed entirely possible. But most of all, I tried to hire people with an artistic temperament, who could appreciate the sacred nature of the project; an NDA is only as good as the person's appreciation of money or law. What I really needed to do was to instill a deeper, heart-level obligation—I needed the workers to feel like a public reveal of my project would be an abasement of their own moral fiber, a betrayal of values.

That is why I nurtured the clannishness of a hippy-dippy commune by providing several opportunities for camaraderie.

I offered food and drink in lavish fashion. I brought in picnic tables and set them around the grounds, which were already vast and park-like, and on rainy days I provided shelter inside the huge dining room in the main house and a hot meal. They were forbidden to talk about their current work, but all other subjects were open for discussion. Sometimes these rainy-day lunches began in an oddly monastic mood, with everyone sitting down together at first quietly, solemnly. Slowly the atmosphere turned jovial in the way that enjoying a meal with strangers can turn, and occasionally, when the bright, cozy, raucous interior held back the dreary day outside, I was blasted with nostalgia for Geannie and Jim, or some other part of my past life that included the love and communion of other people washing over me. When that happened I excused myself and walked around the half-finished foundation of the apartment building until the lunch was over, my feet sucking at the mud. Joy was a contagion I needn't catch at that late stage.

Many of the caseworkers were artists, carpenters, artisans— when I could not locate original art prints that hung in Apartment 201, for example, I had copies commissioned, and the same went for all the furnishings, carpet, and knickknacks. Even the doorbells, even the dish towels. I had each inanimate object in the apartment cataloged by episode number, and then the original was located or re-created when possible.

I searched for many of these things myself, because there was pleasure in doing so. Whenever I looked at the furnishings or houseplants or wall hangings while watching an episode, I imagined myself as one of the characters on the show—Janet Wood, maybe, or Chrissy Snow—idly searching for the perfect item to complement the living room as a young twenty-something in 1977. I weascled my way into the characters' heads and climbed into their reality, inside their very skin, and tried to think as they did. Sometimes, when studying a piece of art from the apartment—say, F. X. Leyendecker's *The Flapper* print that appeared in nearly every single episode in the series—I gazed at its image for long minutes, trying to figure out what, exactly, appealed to the roommate who might have chosen it, in this case probably serious Janet Wood. Was it the contrast between the joyful, brightly colored image and the sad story of the artist—a gay man in the early 1900s who, overshadowed by his brother, a much more famous and accomplished artist at the time, committed suicide by morphine at age forty-eight? Was it the composition? Was it the general theme? Did she love butterflies, or the metaphor of a butterfly? Did she have a random experience as a child watching an exotic swallowtail flit across her path one summer day, and did the ghost of its beauty subconsciously guide her down the aisle of the secondhand store and toward *The Flapper*? The artwork itself was a pun. A 1920s flapper dressed in a gauzy costume floated in front of an anise swallowtail butterfly that was huge, almost looming, and her outstretched arms mimicked the widespread wings of the butterfly. And "Life" was merely a coincidence—the illustration was used as the cover of a *Life* magazine in February 1922. But the word LIFE emblazoned above the image had a suggestive effect. Was *this* life? A bright explosion of youth and beauty? A pun? A joke?

I decided that Janet, sensible but unsentimental character that she was, probably just thought it was pretty, and maybe on a deeper level she appreciated the all-American *Life* magazine connection as well as the art nouveau influence; many of the art prints that appeared in Apartment 201 in the early seasons were of this style, and I liked imagining that most of the pieces were chosen by Janet . . . thoughtful, cohesive décor seemed like a Janet thing.

And then there was the question of origin. Where did the print come from? What was it like, that day she first saw *The Flapper*? Was it something she'd brought with her to LA from her childhood home in Speedway, Indiana? No, that didn't seem right. I reasoned that if it had been something of childhood importance, it would have been hung in a more personal space, like her bedroom.

I imagined myself as Janet, sauntering through a second-hand thrift shop in Santa Monica in the early winter months of 1977, the weather chilly and cloudy, the store dim and musty, its long aisles cluttered with tchotchkes, old appliances from the fifties and sixties, things from her parents' and her grandparents' houses, an old 1940s-era sewing machine, chipped crockery. So many earth tones of brown and dull greens, burnt oranges and the occasional burst of red. And the feeling of discovery, of wonder. For only a few weeks ago she had moved across the country! A thousand miles away from the Midwest, to the golden city of California! And here she was, Janet Wood, a few bucks in her pocket from her new job at the flower shop, choosing the art pieces for her new apartment.

Maybe, as she strolled through those dingy aisles, she thought of her parents. Her mother and father, who loved her with their midwestern stoicism, and who were from strong stock—a line of farmers, maybe, though they themselves were not farmers—who had hopes of her living a traditional life full of family and marriage and children and church on Sundays. And all she could do was dream of escape, escape! She had fled that fate, and had felt guilty, and the random items that now appeared in the thrift shop—an old washstand, a hunter's trap—reminded her of home and gave her a pang. But it lasted for only a moment before she remembered where she was, and how she was, and how she came to be in California, the land of palm trees and dreams. And then, in a corner booth, way in the back, in a poorly lit part of the store, a flash of white and yellow clanged out of a box of sundries, and walking toward it she grew excited, the promise of beauty in the midst of junk. She unwedged the framed print of *The Flapper*, its bright, obnoxiously feel-good message cutting through any nostalgia to remind her of the task at hand, of shopping for a new apartment on a new adventure in California.

So much of the characters' lives happened offscreen, and it would be these kinds of details that would occupy my mind and my life in the coming months and years. The amount of thought and emotion that went into my project was maudlin—it went beyond all art, all pretension of greatness. The depth of my feeling and the wildness of my imagination was a farce unto itself. Even I had to laugh at it. I would have been rejected by every artist working for me had they known how much personal melodrama was invested into this project.

I needn't have worried, though. Since beginning the work, I spoke with very few people. After initial interviews and screenings, I put some distance between myself and most of the workers. The lunches were the only exception, and even then I kept busy with setting out food or rattling pots and pans. The person I spoke with most regularly was Ray, and we mostly discussed the ongoing work, what cornice I preferred, if I wanted this or that shade of paint. Ray was a chain-smoker and always had a cigarette between his fingers, and he had a talent for lighting his next cigarette with the dying cherry of the one in his mouth, like an Olympic torch that never extinguished. The nail on his right middle finger was dark, almost black, from nicotine.

I felt safe with Ray. Sometimes I went out to the construction site and watched its progress, but I stayed out of the way.

If he saw me, he came over and stood beside me as if he was keeping me company. But we rarely talked. I never learned the names of his family or pets, or if he lived alone, or what health problems he might have struggled with, or what losses and triumphs he had endured in his life. Instead, we looked over plans or drawings or paint swatches, and sometimes we stood together in silence and watched the activity around us, observing the task that was unfolding, or the next task revealing itself. When I was around him there was no inkling of a past or future, only the present. I was grateful.

Rain moved in a few weeks after I submitted my winning lottery ticket, and the season turned into its chilly, dying self. The ground turned to mud, and a couple of back roads in the area flooded out. I was lucky I lived in a trailer—no basement to flood. But my place wasn't completely spared. A support beam that held up a corner of my brief front porch—a five-by-five-foot slatted platform that connected the front steps to my screen door—collapsed one morning as I left the house, putting the whole thing at a crazed angle. The beam had been looking rather dark and moldy for a few months, so I wasn't too surprised. But I couldn't have cared less. I let the collapsed beam stay where it was.

By that time, strangers had started showing up at random times to knock on my door. I liked envisioning them tripping over the collapsed porch, striking their head on the debris below, and bleeding out in the mud. I still had that strange sense of forward motion, and fixing my old porch was one of a million little signifiers of the present that threatened it, and soon I avoided anything that required daily upkeep, or that sent the subtle message to my brain that I was remaining in this place.

As it turned out, the collapsed porch was a hit with the reporters. I guess it made their rags-to-riches stories all the more juicy, really adding to the white-trash flavoring that peppered most of their articles about me. I was glad my mother was dead. She would have been horrified.

I lived in a state that required the public disclosure of lottery winners' names. That's how word got out. Before, during, and, after the reporters came to my door, every other stranger who wanted to congratulate or extort me in person kept coming.

The worst of these visitors were the old customers I remembered from the market. One afternoon Mr. Spitz himself drove by in his pickup, leaned out the window, and hollered either a congratulations or a fuck-you. It was hard to tell, knowing Spitz. He had a cigarette hanging out of his mouth and was being an asshole, so not much had changed in his life. But I noticed he looked more gray and faded than I remembered. His truck looked older, too. It gave me a shiver.

When these people showed up I hated it, turned off the lights, tried to make it look like nobody was home. Their existence rattled my sense of time, the surety of my plans. I didn't like knowing they were alive. Inside every person's head is a set of films, each a spool of memories, and one of these reels features the most trivial things a person does over the course of a lifetime, including ordering a ham sandwich from the local market's deli counter years ago and the girl who handed it to you, and I hated that the films in these other people's brains were still running, and that I was in them. The humiliation of being alive, and being seen! Oh, it wrangled me. I wanted to kill the very fact. I had known these strangers only briefly, and only by which brand of chaw they preferred, or what cut of meat to set aside, but they threatened to fan the dying ember of the past into a full, hemorrhoidal flame again, just when I was about to leave it behind forever. But there wasn't much I could do to stop it. News of my winnings made the national outlets; my front porch and I sagged in the rain across fifty states.

The market and the robbery haunted every article and video segment about my win. For those few weeks, as I went to work and home again, I was careful not to look anyone in the eye, knowing that my coworkers' and neighbors' memory of that event was being refreshed daily. I was framed as a success story, a person who had been dealt reverses and then advanced to the front of the line. According to these reports, I was a Christian dream in action—suffer now, glory later—and the words *happy ending* were used more than once, as if winning the lottery was the end of my story, my final payment, materially and spiritually, for whatever had been taken from me.

And things were taken from me—oh yes, the media wanted everyone to know exactly what had been taken from me. The sordid details of the robbery were trotted out again, and the newscasters smacked their lips recounting the facts as if tasting a favorite dish for the second time. Some reports described me as "a survivor," a term that was so ludicrous I snorted the first time I heard it, its suggestion of heroism. As if there is heroism in keeping one's body alive.

If only they knew how I wanted to shuck it off, this shell. This bag. This thing that carried me around from place to place. When I looked in a mirror, I never knew what I saw. It wasn't me.

The local paper had a field day, too. I made the front page. This happened soon after word got out. At that time I was still answering the door, foolishly thinking that if I gave them a statement they'd go away. The reporter had been some blonde pearl-and-suit lady, and when I opened my door to her she had actually stuck her foot, clad in a flashy patent-leather heel, inside the jamb. I had stood there, staring at her foot as if it were an alien probe, flabbergasted. As I stared, she asked if I thought Geannie and Jim were in heaven, sending me gifts. If I thought Hernan was blessing me. Did I believe in the afterlife? In justice, in karma?

Firmly but swiftly, without any particular malice, I kicked her foot out of the doorway, and she hopped back, as if my booted toe had burned her. The screen door she'd been holding open slammed between us. For a moment we both looked at each other in a strange moment of clarity, dazed at the things we were lowering ourselves to.

She didn't mention any of that in my profile, though. Instead, her article painted me as the "reclusive salt of the earth" of the local region, and was accompanied by a photo of me smiling thinly and radiating hostility, my one concession to civility after kicking her. This is how Krystal discovered I had won the lottery.

I n that first year, that year of my project's construction, of creation, I listened to the news over the radio. I treated those months as a farewell to civilization, and so felt an obligation to stay in touch with the current era as much as I could, barring actual communication. From the top of the mountain I masqueraded as an engaged citizen with an audience of zero.

Reports of possible nuclear war and increased global armaments, along with warnings of environmental disasters, dominated the broadcasts. Oil was a problem, getting it and keeping it. Terrorism was on the rise. Rich men bombed and shot things. Stories of a contagion ravaging a country a mere two borders away peppered the local news, flanked by cheerful season-specific bumpers and chatty announcers covering traffic jam-ups. The world felt large and doomed, yet everyone seemed destined to carry on normally. Commercials blasted in between national news reports, as did the latest music about love, love lost, love never had. Global ruin was discussed constantly but no one could imagine it. It was like any other year.

I subscribed to the local newspaper. For all the research that was being done, I also had an internet service, which I used sparingly. I didn't want to spoil myself. But occasionally I went on internet binges, the aim of which was the same as a junk-food binge: I would make myself sick and then swear it off completely. The glut of information, the hubbub of people who worked in the buildings around my property, all of it was a sickness. I could even feel it physically, like an exotic pneumonia, a pulling-down at the stomach, the chest area, a ragged feeling of need. I was determined to cure it. However, it's one thing to wish for solitude, and another thing to embrace it. I understood that for all of my misanthropy, if that's what it was, part of me still longed for the most basic connection—saying hello, or hearing someone work in another room. These thoughts disturbed me. They didn't fit with the other feeling I had in most waking hours, the one that had boiled down to a low-level resentment within me, the grating torture of knowing others and being known. When my project was finished, ready to be inhabited, I wanted to be free of human contact once and for all.

That is why, in addition to the project-related preparations, I planned for practical eventualities like food, power, and basic necessities. I made an arrangement with the local food service to have my kitchen stocked every two weeks. This would be done without my physical presence. I interviewed several people for this task and finally chose a young man named Bernie who lived in the town at the foot of the mountain. He seemed just dull enough to never ask too many questions or overstay his welcome. He also seemed highly neurotic, complete with odd tics and fixations that centered on his appearance—he had glasses and wore jaunty vests, very White Rabbit-ish—and he was especially interested in time management, for which he had a giant wristwatch he constantly checked when he wasn't rubbing his fingers along the creases of his nostrils and smelling whatever residue he found there. These eccentricities worked in my favor. As long as he was preoccupied with himself, I need not worry about his errant curiosity or unexpected visits.

We worked out a system: starting on a yet-to-be-determined date, I would leave a list of items on the left end of the big kitchen's counter inside the main house. I would prioritize these items.

PRIORITY ONE meant that he must, at all costs, get the item(s) in question by any means possible. I figured that would cover me in case I ever ran into an emergency.

Bernie signed the usual NDA agreement, and because he was a key-holder there was additional legalese ensuring that he would never bring strangers onto the property, let alone the house. I was nothing if not thorough. Or maybe I should say that Larwin was thorough on my behalf.

Larwin and I communicated over the phone often during that year. He told me he gave up two of his other clients to devote most of his time to me. Was I flattered? No. I knew it was all business to him, including the flattery. Soon he wouldn't be in touch with me at all, other than a yearly paycheck I would automatically issue him to keep him on the payroll. I knew he would say anything to remain in my good graces until then.

All of these things—the lawyer, the many workers, the construction costs, the research, the purchase of various memorabilia items—had barely put a dent in my lottery winnings. I tried not to think about it. Money was like drugs or a favorite food—as soon as I had it, all I could think about was losing it, for its purpose was to be used, so the having was never permanent. And I was convinced I would lose it, that nothing literally gold could stay. The best antidote to this worry was practiced indifference.

But, as it goes for most rich people, it wasn't long before I became consumed with what more I could have. Why stop at the *Three's Company* apartment building? Why not build a facsimile of the Regal Beagle, the local bar? Jack's Bistro? The LA technical college? Arcade Florists, where Janet worked? They had been part of my original plan, but I'd hesitated on building them. As a person who had grown up on the weekly habit of standing in a grocery store and ruminating for long minutes on whether my desire to purchase a brand-name food item was too greedy, and eventually deciding that, yes, it was, and trundling my generic-food-filled cart in a dirge to the register while feeling both triumphant and pissed at this noble yet necessary self-deprivation, I had a superstition that if I breached a certain level of financial modesty I would jinx the whole thing. Imagine my shock when, one day a few months after construction started, I woke to find this superstition had worn off, and instead I felt bold and fresh. Just like that!

The city would be small but functional, laid out like a street in Santa Monica, only more compact. I wanted every detail of every set piece re-created. Most of all, I wanted the buildings to make sense from a city-planning perspective in order to do away with the need for backdrops. For example, through a window in the Regal Beagle a Bicycle Shop and Shoe Store were visible across the street—a matte painting in the television show—but in my re-creation there would be a real facade of a bicycle and shoe store across the street. Only the places whose interiors were seen on the show would be fleshed out into real buildings, I decided. Otherwise construction would never have finished.

I gave these tasks to Ray, who perked up at the challenges of city planning. On the show, some of the places, like the bar, were within walking distance of the apartment building. Others, however, required an oft-mentioned bus ride, so I commissioned a one-of-a-kind electric-powered, self-driving bus using the skeleton of the real 1970s Los Angeles bus lifted from a junkyard. This apparatus would take me to various places that, on the show, were located farther away, such as Chrissy's office and Janet's flower shop. In the end, we created something that amounted to a small town, about a mile or two square. I was displeased that the distances between places were not realistic, but measurable distances, like the apartment building's ever-changing rooms and dimensions, remained flexible and impossible.

Around the perimeter of this city, behind the buildings, was stretched a weatherproof canvas mural, a three-dimensional matte painting of the Los Angeles area near Santa Monica similar to the backdrops seen on the show. From inside the apartment building or any other building, the main house of my property was invisible. It was "out of town." At the end of the street near my apartment building, Ray fashioned a discreet exit, a giant door that was seamlessly concealed by the matte painting. This opening would allow me to move easily in and out for deliveries.

The year ended with a flurry of activity, of last-minute details and crises that had everyone working twelve-hour shifts for astounding amounts of overtime pay in order to complete it by the deadline.

And then the day came, yes, the day came when it was ready. That golden day.

ow could you? How could you?

We were in my living room, and by this time it was November, near Thanksgiving, and instead of sweltering my trailer was damp and cold.

Krystal looked bad. Her face was gaunt and papery, her cheekbones protruding like ugly tumors. Her hair, which had been thin and mousy to begin with, looked like the stringy tufts that cling to a mummified corpse. She was one of those people who take on a marionette quality when they lose weight, the head too big for the body. Though it was only 50 degrees outside, maybe 40, she was dressed in a turtleneck and parka.

Her face was bright red and her eyes were glassy and tear-filled, and when she spoke she raved like a fever victim. We stood facing one another as she demanded to know why I had kept this from her. Was I that selfish? Did I think so little of her? She'd thought we were friends. And after she had made a fool of herself that night of the lottery drawing—she guessed I knew then. Was I gloating as I had sat on the couch with her? Did I really have to work the next day, or had I just abandoned her? Did I hate her? I had made a fool of her. That seemed to be a recurring theme.

I let her yell and resisted the impulse to cover my ears. She was so loud. And so angry! I never knew what to do with angry people. It was amazing, watching someone in real life become furious. All the social polity, all the fear, all the masks dropped away. People were so rarely nakedly fearless in normal life.

But in Krystal I saw no danger, only hurt.

"I'm sorry," I told her. I opened my mouth to say that it was simply easier not to tell her, but realized at the last moment that that was probably the wrong line to follow. I tried again.

"I just had so many things to prepare for," I said, "so many people to see and talk with. I didn't ignore you on purpose, I swear."

Right away she deflated. The color receded from her face, she slumped; I feared she would crumple to the floor. She didn't, though. She sat down on the arm of my recliner and pouted. "I just don't understand why you couldn't tell me. I thought we were friends. Family."

"We *are* friends," I told her. Sensing another teary breakdown coming, I added, "And family."

She sat there, her arms limp in her lap. Her eyes were downcast and I swear she looked like she was about to fall asleep. I stayed quiet, praying she would leave. I was bored.

"I know why you avoid me, you know." Her voice was hard and low.

I pretended I didn't hear her. Instead, I turned and walked into my kitchen. "Are you hungry?" I said. My voice was neutral, even friendly. There were certain rhythms in conversations, I knew, and I hoped to seize upon this lull to segue into something else, a benign distraction. My mother had been a pro at this, steering potentially explosive conversations back into calm, glacial waters. I opened my fridge and bent down, peering into it. "I have a leftover Lean Cuisine, some soup I made Wednesday, some iced tea."

"Bonnie," she said.

I scooted things around in the fridge like I was looking for something. But my shelves were pretty bare.

"Do you sleep here?"

My head snapped around. She was still sitting on the recliner arm but was looking down at the chair itself with interest. My pillow and blankets were tucked into a pocket that hung off the other arm, and my alarm clock was on the stand beside it.

"What?"

"Do you sleep here? Are those bedsheets?"

I was still holding the fridge door open. "Are you hungry or not?"

Suddenly she stood up, her eyes fixed on the hallway. I read her mind and, trying to play it cool, moved toward her, but she had already covered half the distance to my bedroom door.

"What are you doing?" I said, but the words came out more as an angry bark, and when she saw my alarm it drove her faster toward my bedroom door, which made me spring toward her, and I could see fright on her face but also excitement—she was excited to get a reaction out of me, finally, the bitch, and then she had her hand on the knob and was turning it (I had been visiting the room so frequently I kept forgetting to lock it), and then it was over: she was standing at the open door and looking at my collection.

I could have killed her. I could have taken an ax, or a shotgun, or a knife or cudgel, and ended her right then and there. And back then I loved Krystal. She was my friend. My family.

But when she stood at the door and looked at my secret heart, without permission, something inside me withered.

She stepped into the room, transfixed, her fright forgotten. She stared and stared at the dozens of framed articles, photographs, the T-shirts. A large macaroni art mural—a replica of one of the cast photos—hung framed on the wall, and I had used different colors of macaroni in the nature-craft style of the 1970s, which had given it a funky pop-art psychedelic effect, and it was something I had been so proud of up until this moment as her judging eyes took it in, ruining it.

Krystal turned toward me, her eyes full of wonder. A shadow of pride flickered within me, but it drowned in the rage and embarrassment of being seen. Anger was the only thing that kept me looking her in the eyes.

"*This* is what you've been up to? *This?*" she demanded.

It was not a rhetorical question, but I let her sit on it, anyway, all words gone from me, until a few meek ones slid out: " . . . none of your business."

That really got her going. "You're freaking crazy," she told me. "You know that? You win a billion dollars, and you're spending it on this dumb shit. You're really a piece of work, Bonnie. I've tried to help you—"

(and at this I almost *ha!*'d out loud. Her? Helping *me?*)

"—but now I know you're just crazy. You're just—just—" She was choking on it. "You're *pathetic.*"

Then time slowed down as I watched her pick up one of the smaller frames sitting on a shelf near the door and threw it. Threw it! It missed the bedroom window by a hair, but knocked down some of the other frames that sat near it and the glass broke in all of them.

I felt all the blood in my body go to my feet. My mind groped wildly for a gun, a knife, any killing weapon. What could I use? What could I use to kill her? But I could think of nothing, my stupid feet glued to the floor.

She stormed past me and left, slamming the front door. Then a large thump of a car door, and her car leaving soon after.

I remained in the hallway, panting. Sweat sprouted off me, and I tingled from head to toe. Slowly, I started moving. I went to the kitchen first to get a drink of water. The fridge door was still hanging open, so I shut it, and closed all the blinds.

Looking back, it was quite the soap opera scene. Silence pulsed in its aftermath. If I really listened I could hear the white noise of neighbors a hundred yards away laughing, clinking beer bottles on their porch. The walls were thin. They had probably heard everything, which only added to my shame. I collapsed into my recliner and a wave of drowsiness passed over me so powerful that I blacked out for a while. When I woke it was the middle of the night. I fired up the DVD machine, trying to forget I was a human being confined to this one life cycle, this one lousy history.

It wasn't until later that it hit me. The thump. It hadn't been a car door slamming. The shitty porch had finally done its job.

"**C**ome and see, come and see!"

It was a luminous spring day, a little over a year since the project had begun. The smell of newly sawed wood and fresh paint hung over us and gave the fresh air a pleasant, sharp edge. The three of us were standing alone outside the finished apartment building. Everyone else had gone. Above us was blue, periwinkle sky and clouds with glowing, gossamer edges. Wind. Everything was turning green and being born, blooming.

Brenda was speaking, my phantom assistant. I had met her for only the second or third time minutes prior. I was surprised to find she was dressed so well—a black suit with a tie, very striking. She held a clipboard and something digital in her hands that probably contained all of the binders of information she had printed out for me, which now rested on multiple shelves in the empty living room of the main house. "We're so excited to give you the official tour," she said in a perfectly modulated, professional tone. Ray stood beside her, silent as ever.

He looked bashful in the sunshine. Brenda looked at him and nodded, and he handed me the keys with a pleased, lopsided grin. Without a crowd it seemed silly, ridiculous, like handing keys to a child. But that is what I felt like! I felt barely contained within myself. He explained the keys one by one: the Ropers' apartment (101, first floor on the end), Apartment 201 (second floor on the end), Larry's apartment in 304 (third floor, fourth apartment). There were three other apartments in the building seen in the series only once—Lesley the ventriloquist's in "The Charming Stranger," Bob and Carol's apartment in "Bob and Carol and Larry and Terri," and Arlene the painter's apartment in "Jack Takes Off." The keys to those quarters were also on the ring; there were several other copies of this set of keys, to be hidden away by me at my leisure.

I was so giddy I might have been on nitrogen gas. I probably looked deranged, with the way I felt my face contorting. Professional Brenda refused to make full eye contact with me. She seemed like one of those people accustomed to dealing with crazies, who had made a career of tactfully ignoring the worst of other people's neuroses for a certain dollar amount. I probably would have hated her in my past life, but who cared! Not I! I snatched the keys from Ray's hand (yes, I am moderately ashamed to recall my eagerness) and walked toward the door nearest me, the Ropers' apartment.

Just as in the series, here were two small steps leading up to the brown tile porch area! And here was the door! Exclamation marks exploded inside my brain like fireworks. I unlocked the door and stepped inside.

It all was there—the gray lamp to the left of the door, the Whymper pheasant prints and Wysocki folk art on the wall off to the right, the small imitation Duncan Phyfe tables, the glass-front bookcase cabinet. The cream-colored Queen Anne's couch and coffee table, the orange carpet, the gold curtains. All the tacky knickknackery was there—quintessentially 1970s, with signs of the then-recent Bicentennial (Colonial men and women curtsying, a flag-emblazoned collector's plate), eagle-marked cups. The linen slub sheers on the windows. Oh god. I could have sobbed. It was here, and it was real.

I walked into the bedroom. It was aggressively pink, Mrs.

Roper's constant pleas for romance come to life. French provincial styles dominated the space with all the cottage-chic furniture and matching bureau and bed set, the pink carpet and pink print curtains that matched the comforter, the pink-ruffled table-side lamp. Two Robert Furber prints, one for each of their birth months, flanked the bed, and the floor-length mirror seen in Season 3's "Larry's Bride" stood by the doorway. It was all there. Even the bathroom was set up according to Season 3's "Stanley's Hotline," where Stanley eavesdropped through the sink pipe on the conversations upstairs.

The caseworkers had also added a kitchen to the Ropers' apartment, a room that was never seen on-screen, using the trio's kitchen upstairs for the layout—the apartments in the building seemed to mirror one another. It was like walking through a deleted scene.

Ray trailed behind me, occasionally pointing out things of interest. When we returned to the living room, completing the tour, he moved toward the front door and said, "And now, for the main event," beckoning Brenda and me back outside. Once the three of us were crowded together once again on the Ropers' outside stoop, he said, "A foot to the left of the door here," and pressed the exterior wall to the left of the door.

A secret panel, covered by stucco, clicked open. Inside was a large lever. "Go ahead, try it. Just pull downward like this until you hear a click"—he demonstrated in the air—"and then let go."

I did as instructed, and inside the wall I could hear gears grinding and wood heaving and protesting in a large movement, and something hummed from within. "Now, wait a full minute for the rotation to complete before opening the door again," he said. The three of us stood quiet as the hum briefly reached a different pitch.

Then all noises ceased. Ray nodded his head. "It's ready."

Reverently, slowly, I opened the front door to Apartment 101 again. And there, before me, instead of the Ropers' apartment, was electric-blue carpeting and walls, busy Hawaiian-print curtains, a plush shag rug on the floor, tacky paintings of half-naked hula girls on black velvet hanging on the walls. The apartment of Mr. Ralph Furley, bachelor-at-large.

Items were always moving around on the sets from episode to episode, which would be easy enough for me to accomplish as I saw fit, but Ray knew I was concerned about how to deal with the major renovations when the landlords changed hands in Season 4. Now one apartment could be substituted for another in seconds, eliminating the overhaul entirely. I had studied the schematics, and he had explained the theory of it to me, but it wasn't until I was standing in front of it, observing its ingenuity, that I felt its kindness. He had done this for me. And for my money, yes—I could never quite forget that contract between employer and employee, lest I start believing all these faceless workers were my buddies—but when I turned to him after the demonstration, I saw the pride on his face. And something else, too, maybe a smile, one of those rare, pure expressions of joy that people witness only so many times in a life, the joy of making something and giving it away. "You can turn it back anytime," Ray said. "In case you ever need to." I understood what he meant—if I ever wanted to relive the Roper years if I was still living here that long to start living the series over again, it would be possible. I thanked him.

We walked through Mr. Furley's apartment and everything was in its place, down to the SS *Titanic* lifesaver ring in the bedroom and leopard-print pajamas in the drawers.

Then it was time to go upstairs. I couldn't wait any longer. I wanted to see Apartment 201.

For most of this time, and as we left the Furley apartment, Ray and Brenda followed behind me, Brenda running her mouth the entire time, looking at the screen in her hand and listing out loud all of the items that we were looking at, like a docent giving a museum tour. Other than his brief moment of happy triumph with the lever, Ray had remained quiet, hands folded over his chest awkwardly. At some points he stood off to one side, as if waiting for it all to be over.

I wondered how much of this seemed ridiculous to them, impossibly eccentric. In some of my many moments of solitude over the past year, I couldn't help but put myself in my workers' shoes and speculate on their judgments of me, occasionally finding myself drifting into full-blown paranoia, but mostly I indulged in generic hatred and shame. I was ashamed not of myself but of myself as seen by others, which I sensed was happening even more than I suspected. I was born into the working class, after all, maybe where Ray had been born, and here I was, flush with money, and look at how I was spending it. I had a fleeting vision of Geannie's Beanie Babies. Did my *Three's Company* obsession appear to Ray and Brenda as the Beanie Baby collection had initially appeared to me—an utter waste? Embarrassing? A childish, luxurious squander of riches? I remembered Krystal standing at the doorway of my bedroom, her face a mask of disgust. *You win a billion dollars, and you're spending it on this dumb shit.*

The thought was small but persistent. Peck, peck, peck. We were ascending the red clay tile stairs to the second floor, to my destiny, and yet I was preoccupied with the possibility that people hated me and my dream even as I walked up to meet it. And then my internal voices started sniping in response—*They're paid! They can go fuck!* Now, looking back, I see that the sudden hostility toward Ray and Brenda was largely unwarranted; they had done nothing but help me, frequently exceeding all expectations. But in that moment an undeniable, annoying feeling continued to rise within me until it took a recognizable, sickening form: I wanted Ray to like me. Not as a boss, but as a person. I wanted his complicity in all of my shenanigans. If he judged me harshly, I would be crushed.

But as quickly as it came this new realization coolly bounced off the wall of my brain and back into the despair hole it came from. I swallowed as if to tamp it down permanently.

For we were nearing the top steps. I was about to meet God. My autonomic systems shut down all distractions.

I crested the stairs and there it was: the front door to Apartment 201. A small landing extended into a tiny balcony in front of the picture window, and a wrought-iron railing hemmed it in. Large potted plants lined the railing side of the balcony: a lemon tree, a peony bush in a large planter, several bushy ferns. All the pots were ceramic or terra-cotta, and their sizes varied in a pleasing way. The chaise lounge on which Chrissy sunbathed in early season credits was on the small balcony, too. Around the door and doorbell vines crept up the walls—Brenda checked her notes and assured me these were noninvasive vines, and also nonflowering, so bees would not be a problem; they were decorative but real, and the name she mentioned flitted right by me. I took the key ring again and Ray reminded me what key matched, and—yes!—there it was! It was even marked (they were all marked with the corresponding door number, bless him) and, with shaking hands, I turned it in the lock.

The door opened, and I stood there, breathing fast. I had arrived. I felt the apartment's air wash over me like a baptism, ushering me into a new state of being. Every molecule seemed rarefied, sacred, as in a church or ancient cave, something deep and mysterious and spiritual. Undeniably transformative. I stepped inside.

I had asked, before we started this tour, that Brenda and Ray not follow me into Apartment 201. I wanted to be the only one to touch its finished floor. As soon as I stepped inside I knew it was the right choice. Nothing would sully this moment.

It was a strange experience, seeing the apartment from this angle. The TV viewer never got a view of the apartment when entering through the front door, because it would have revealed the studio cameras. That troubling fourth wall now faced me, so I crossed the apartment, to where I, the viewer, used to be once upon a time, and I turned around and pressed my back against it, looking at the apartment in the way to which I was accustomed. There was the couch, the television, the plant stand by the window. *The Flapper*! Every plant was in its place—I had settled on the plants seen in Season 1, and figured I could swap them out as necessary—and they sat in their macramé holders or hodge-podge pottery or wicker baskets, the parlor palm sitting to the left of the doorway . . . Oh god, it was beautiful. The carpet was a limp yellowish-beige, but it was layered with a knockoff Persian area rug that sat under the couch. In front of the door was the rug with its double-diamond pattern in pinks and reds and deep blues, ragged and worn from years of use—secondhand, no doubt, as most things in the apartment must have been.

I walked through the apartment and touched everything slowly, lovingly. I was shaking, hot and cold chills raking through me as if I were sick with the flu.

I pushed through the swinging door into the kitchen. The kitchen! Jack Tripper's domain. Its walls were covered in orange plaid wallpaper that had a gaudily busy, cheerful effect, and on them hung various small planters, decorative straw or hemp baskets, old iron trivets, a note board. The round pedestal table and three bentwood chairs sat in the middle of the room, in front of the weathered Harvest Gold fridge. On the counter sat a set of cookie jars, a covered toaster, and on the stove sat a clear Pyrex stovetop coffee percolator. Crocheted curtains from Sears, that long-gone scion of department store industry, hung over the window above the sink.

The sun beamed through the window over the sink and a slice of light crawled up the wall, turning the plaid wallpaper into an even brighter, manic version of itself; everything gleamed in its humble yellow-orange-gold mix. The copper salmon-shaped molds hanging on the walls glinted so hard that my eyes watered when I stared at them—and I stared at everything, everything, sunk into the warm colors of a decade I had only ever dreamed about. Another reality had swallowed me.

I opened one of the cabinets, the one nearest the sink. I took down a box of Nabisco New Tea Time cookies, an authentic box circa 1977, and flipped it over. It was light, empty. It looked like a paper box on the outside, but inside the box was another, more durable box made from acrylic plastic, something I could fill and refill accordingly, so when I ate anything in this kitchen there would be no contemporary packaging or labels to distract from the otherwise airtight timeline.

I put the cookie box back where I found it and looked out the kitchen window. Instead of the wilderness, or the trees, or any of my property, I could only see the building next door, just like it was on the show.

There were two bedrooms—Janet and Chrissy shared a room, and Jack had his own—and these, too, were done up in the style of the first three and a half seasons. Chrissy and Janet's bedroom was on a similar mechanism as the landlords' apartment downstairs because the décor changed drastically in the fourth-season episode "And Baby Makes Four," and outside their bedroom door I felt around until I felt a panel open, and I found a lever within just like the one downstairs. I pulled it and listened to the bedroom turn itself around inside. The doors to these revolving rooms needed to be closed in order for the change to happen, so I would never be able to witness the actual transformation. When it was finished, the room had indeed changed itself—the bed frames were painted a different color, a different wallpaper, different color scheme. I was looking three years into my own future. I shut the door and pulled the lever again, reversing the change, and when I saw the original décor back in place I felt better, cleaner, as if a potential catastrophe had been handled so smoothly and instantly that it slipped from my mind.

The bathroom of the apartment was large, with a freestanding white clawfoot tub, and aqua-blue tile and toilet, flowery wallpaper to the ceiling. A white porcelain sink stood on the same wall as the door, and a mirrored pharmacy cabinet hung above it. On one wall a linen closet opened to reveal all the bath and hand towels seen throughout the series—even the dish towels had a shelf! Oh, it was marvelous.

Ray and Brenda were waiting in an awkward silence that I guessed had been stretching between them since I'd disappeared inside. When I rejoined them outside on the balcony, the look on my face must have communicated everything I was feeling, because they both appeared a tad bewildered. "I love it!" I crowed. "It's *perfect*." They both smiled nervously. Brenda kept clicking her fingernail against the screen she was holding. I couldn't wait for them to be gone.

"Ready to go upstairs? To see 304, Larry's place?" said Ray.

"And then I have something extra." He smiled, but a cloud of euphoria had engulfed me, the color of brushed gold, and I only wanted to be alone with it, in it. I motioned for them to move ahead of me, back down the stairs, and as he turned Ray unfolded his arms and looked back at me, more perplexed than ever. "You don't want to see 304?" he said. He sounded crestfallen, and for the briefest of seconds I considered it—completing the full tour, going through the checklist of items Brenda had so carefully made for me—the delivery schedules, the care and upkeep of the plants and storage units, the various fail-safes in case anything went awry unexpectedly—but I was impatient, yes, I was *manic*, desperate for them to get the hell out of there, and my previous feeling of wanting Ray's approval, his acceptance—that pesky desire to be liked by another human being—triumphantly evaporated. For the first time in over a year, my original wish loomed up at me again, clearer than it had ever been. I wanted total isolation, and I wanted it now, this very minute.

"Oh, that's all right, that's all right. I'll find it," I said, suddenly breathless. "I'll look at it myself. Everything is so magnificent, just perfect, just wonderful . . ."

My words flew out fast and shrill and I sounded like the crazed person I felt myself becoming—hysterically joyful, on the verge of a dazzling, supernoval breakdown—but I couldn't stop. "It'll be fine!" I now shouted. When I looked at their faces I raised my voice even louder, as if to drown out the disapproving drone of their expressions. "I will find everything myself! I can manage! And thank you! Thank you for coming! Thank you so much for being here, for doing this, your checks will be in the mail!" And at this Ray's face fell; he looked confused and dismayed, looking back at me sharply, trying not to trip and fall to a broken neck as I practically pushed them down the stairs. I was definitely ready to get them the hell off my property, these people whom I had paid, these workers, these *paid employees* I had assigned tasks and to whom I'd given good work for more than a fair wage—why did he look so dashed?

Love, friendship, affection—all the old familial, familiar devils reared their heads. A sword dangled somewhere. But before it crept any closer the three of us were walking quickly away from the apartment building, running almost, yes, I was practically jogging as I herded them through the city's camouflaged exit door and out onto the grass of the open field, toward their vehicles, which they had parked earlier that day near the main house. "But what about—" Brenda puffed as she led the way, having a little trouble trotting gracefully in her business-formal heels. "What about the details, the schedules, all the checklists and—"

"It will be fine! You leave it to me!" I was yelling then. "DID YOU SEND ME COPIES OF ALL THE CHECKLISTS?" I bellowed, and she gasped out, "Y-yes," as if she were on her last lung, and a little afraid, maybe, and then we were at their cars and they each scrambled into them, and as they started their engines they both looked at me like I was quite insane, which maybe I was at the time, but I didn't care, not one bit, all I wanted to do was to get back into that building and start living my lives.

Ray wound down his window and motioned for me to come closer, momentarily breaking the spell. I went toward him. He said, "There was something else—I had a surprise for you." I didn't reply other than to smile urgently. "It's in Apartment 205. It's really important you unlock 205." I nodded hard and said "Okay! Okay!" over and over.

"Bonnie," he said, "it's really important you check on Apartment 205." And as he said this he actually *reached out of the window* and touched my arm, and I was astonished, not only at his touch but at the use of my name, which I had not heard anyone speak for a long time.

I jerked away and stood back. I said, "Okay! Apartment 205! I'll check it!" He didn't say anything after that, just solemnly rolled up his window again, staring at me, and put his car in gear. I could hear Brenda's car idling and shifting into gear, too. She'd been waiting for him to leave first, probably worried about leaving him alone with me.

But as soon as I was assured their exit was imminent, the threat ebbing away, I suddenly felt large and fanciful, full of gregarious jollity, the kind of feeling a host gets at the end of a long, complicated party when the last guest is leaving and seems, in that moment, like the dearest, most wonderful friend in the world, and whose soon-to-be-gone presence reminds the host that they're all human, and in this soup together, battling this fleeting timeline as one, and the thanks and smiles and sentimental goodbyes are laid on extra thick, all because freedom is in sight. As they pulled away I said, "Thank you! Have a great trip! Thank you for all you've done!" and I waved at them, my whole arm getting in on the action.

A stone lifted up, out, off of me as they disappeared past the tree line, the last live human beings I would see for three years. Then they were gone, the sound of their engines fading into silence. I fell to my knees and wept.

Nearly a month after my last encounter with Krystal, the one where she tripped on my porch, I decided to go see her.

Two months had passed since I'd won the lottery. I had just bought the new place, and my packed duffel sat on the floor of my truck. It would have been easier had I simply left for the mountain at that time without seeing her again, and the possibility of doing so had crossed my mind. But then Geannie and Jim would creep into my head, and I didn't like them there, or the implication of them being there, and I didn't like the idea that they might always give me trouble if I left things badly. While packing up my stuff I discovered some dishes she had lent me over the years that I never returned, including the damn chili bowl from our dinner months ago when I first confronted her about the house. I figured returning dishes was as good an excuse as any to visit her.

It was halfway through December, exactly ten days before Christmas. Bad weather had come on early—that white, deep-winter cold that usually saves itself for January—and snow flurries wisped at my windshield as I pulled up to her apartment.

I noticed her parking space was empty, but I got out of my truck and knocked on her door anyway. No answer. There was no sign of life anywhere. I noticed the curtains in her kitchen windows were gone, and when I looked in, the room was bare.

I turned around. The sun had set, though it wasn't yet five o'clock. For a whole minute I stood there with my back to her door, looking up at the sky.

I knew where she was. I didn't want to go. For the past few weeks I had enjoyed a clear head—almost the way I used to feel before the robbery, before the insomnia and bad dreams, before the occasional car backfiring or loud noise from someone dropping a pallet would elicit a short, shrill cry from my throat, after which I'd shake for a good five minutes. That still happened every now and then. When it did I got embarrassed and pretended I was not myself, and that whatever was happening was happening to someone else, some weak bitch I didn't even *know*, and a lot of times that worked and a lot of times it didn't.

There hadn't been any of that, though, for nearly a month. Mostly I avoided thinking about the before-times, but sometimes it couldn't be helped. On nights like that one, when I was looking for Krystal—a clawing, cloying nostalgia overtook me. There's something about being outside as the sun sets on a winter night, the weird magic of it that makes a person want to watch Charlie Brown trim his dumb Christmas tree and eat cookies while tucked under a plaid blanket. That kind of shit. I hated getting sad over stuff like that. I don't think I even had an experience like that as a kid, it was just something my brain stole from a holiday commercial. But these weak moments crept in nevertheless, and I knew going to Geannie's house would make it worse.

After knocking on her apartment door one more time, I got back in my truck and headed out toward the house. The town was halfheartedly decorated for the holidays. The lights and tinsel hung crooked from the streetlights. After the robbery I hated Christmas, but when Krystal and I started our Friday night meals together it had been unavoidable. She was the only person I ever bought a gift for. I'd go over to her apartment early on Christmas Day, or the nearest Saturday to it, even if we'd seen each other the night before, and we'd open each other's presents. She always put up a small, scraggly, fake pre-lit tree on her kitchen table, which looked like it had been hauled out of a trash can. Half of the lights didn't light up, but she just hung more gaudy ornaments on it to cover up the dark spots. Those mornings were nice, I guess, but nice things destroyed me. Krystal's dumb happy face was a little too much of a portal to the before-times. And what did she have to be happy about, anyway? Suctioning spit and blood out of some rich asshole's mouth?

Every year, right after we finished exchanging gifts, I said goodbye and took myself to the nearest fast-food joint to stuff burgers into my face, trying to regain footing in the real world with fat and salt and the anonymity of plastic booths. It usually worked.

By the time I arrived at the house, the watery indigo horizon was giving way to black. Exiting my truck, I looked up and saw all the stars, every one; out here it was almost annoying how many stars there were. The sky looked so busy. A few cloud patches hovered, though the snow flurries had almost abated. Krystal's car was in the driveway, as I knew it would be.

I could tell she had all the lights on from the glow behind the curtains, but I couldn't actually see in the windows. The brush was so overgrown that it had overtaken part of the porch and obscured the first-floor windows. In a few more years the vines would take over the second story, too; the house would be nearly invisible. I turned off my truck and sat for a second, listening to the engine click, then walked to the front door.

As I climbed the porch steps, I heard music. It was the ending of "Blue Christmas." A beat of silence, then "Santa, Bring My Baby Back to Me" started. It was Jim's Elvis record. He'd put it on every Christmas as we decorated the house.

I had packed it up three months ago.

Before I had time to raise my hand to knock I saw the blinds move, and then the door opened. Krystal leaned on the doorjamb. "Well, well, well," she said.

I was silent for a moment, judging whether she was still pissed. I determined that she was not.

"Hi there. Can I come in?" I held out the bowls I had kept by accident.

At first I thought I had miscalculated, and that she was going to refuse, but Krystal, always the relenter, relaxed her shoulders. She took the dishes from me and said, "Sure."

The smell is what hit me first—the smell of something sweet baking, plus the apple-scented candle Geannie always had burning throughout the season. And fresh pine, too—boughs of it hung from the banister and on the sills, and on the front door itself. The foyer was dark but soft lights were on in other rooms and the music played, and the heater made the air warm and wavy, just like in the before-times, and it was a trap, always a trap. The past was always so close and dangerous.

I stood still, my heart speeding up. My mind was trying to grab hold of something that was running away from me. But what was it, exactly? The air? A smell? A rogue moment that had broken out of the timeline?

Krystal had already shut the door and was walking away from me, not looking back. Suddenly I was alone in the foyer, and I hadn't seen where she'd gone. I felt small. The house was like a mouth waiting to consume me. I called her name. Nothing. Then I heard her call to me. She sounded so far away. We were floating in a void for a moment, a cloudy, dark place where people call to one another forever and ever.

Something fell on the floor with a large thud. The sound

broke me out of the spell and, relieved to have a purpose, I went toward it, into the living room. "Are you okay?" I said as I walked, thinking she had tripped.

But no. It was only one of the village buildings that had fallen over.

The village. The fucking Christmas village. There it was, all forty or sixty or however many buildings, plus the magnetic lake, plus the fake snow, all laid out under the Christmas tree, which was also decked out like it used to be, full of light and color. She had re-created Geannie and Jim's Christmas experience in total. The only things missing were Geannie and Jim. And Hernan.

"I don't get it," I said.

"Come sit," Krystal said, not hearing me. She had righted the building and was now sitting on one end of the couch. Gingerly I sat down on the other end, taking all of this in. The song I'd heard playing when I first knocked had finished; she had flipped the record and now "O Little Town of Bethlehem" washed over us with assaultive force. "Hold on," she said, getting up to turn it down.

"I don't understand," I said again as she sat back down. "I thought we had packed this up?" It came out like a scratchy, high-pitched question. I was sweating inside my coat. The thermostat must have been cranked up to 80 degrees.

Krystal looked like she needed the warmth, as thin as she was. She was wearing Geannie's housecoat again. In fact, now that I was really looking at her, I noticed that she had cut her hair into a bob just like Geannie's, plus she was wearing Geannie's bedroom slippers and Geannie's wedding band. That last detail made me feel sick; Geannie had been wearing it the night of the robbery. Where had Krystal retrieved that from? Police evidence?

She caught me looking and said, "Oh, that. She had laid it next to the sink to wash her hands. Remember Ronnie from school? He was on the cleanup crew and returned it to me—wasn't that nice? I think he wanted to do me." She tittered. "He's married now, though."

I couldn't look at her. Instead I stared at anything else.

"Bonnie, I know what you're thinking. Or not thinking. You think I've gone crazy. And maybe I have, a little." She let out another little titter. "But just look!" She spread her arms for emphasis. "Isn't it great? I'm paying homage."

I gave her a look. "Homage?" I said. My laugh came out mean, like a sneer. "You think this is *homage?*" I leaned toward her. "They're dead, Krystal. Get a grip." I said it loud and slow, as if I were speaking to an old, deaf man.

Her smile faded. She looked like she'd been slapped. But the smile returned just as fast as it disappeared. "I-I know, Bonnie. I know they're dead." She sounded congested. Her nose was running and she swiped at it. "Look. I want to ask you something now." She paused. "I want to ask you something now, and I don't want you to think too poorly of me. I know we left things kind of bad last time and, well, I'm sorry about the picture I threw and—the glass. Breaking it. I really am. I don't know what came over me. I was just so—I was surprised. You understand." She was half giggling now between almost every sentence. Her eyes were huge, those starved-out fever eyes. "I wanted to ask you about money."

"Krystal," I said. She put a hand up to stop me.

"Before you say anything, Bonnie, I just want to say something. I wanted to ask you—well, first I wanted to tell you that I'm sorry. For breaking the picture but also because I know—I know I haven't been in the best way for the past year or so. But

I'm getting better. And I just thought, well, I just thought that with all your money now, maybe you could help me buy this house. It's being foreclosed now, my aunt stopped making the payments . . . I mean what a bitch, right? She still hasn't come around." She shook her head. "But anyway, what I'm saying is, maybe you could loan it to me. The money. And I would pay you back, I really would. You probably wouldn't even miss it, anyway." She smiled that creepy smile.

The record kept going and for a minute we listened to Elvis's velvety voice and looked at each other. "No, Krystal," I said. "I don't think so."

She smiled harder. "Okay, but listen. I want to live here! I could make it nice again. Like it was. And hey—so could you. Live here, I mean. We could move in together. I wanted to ask you that. If you wanted to be roommates. I mean it makes sense, doesn't it? Remember our Friday dinners?"

I sat forward on my end of the couch and rubbed my face with both hands, my elbows on my knees. "Krystal, look at yourself. I don't think this is good for you."

"What do you mean?" She kept looking toward the tree. "Look at everything I did! I put all this together!"

"I know, that's what I mean. None of this is good for you. This house isn't good for you. And look at yourself," I said again, gesturing toward her shoes and housecoat. "Those are Geannie's things. You should sell them, like you were going to. All of this stuff, you should sell it."

"Come on, Bonnie." She wouldn't look at me. "You have so much money now. I'm not even asking for that much. I know how much you won. I *know* how much." Her smile twisted around and she started tearing up. When she started speaking again her voice came out broken. "You won so much money.

And that's all I'm asking for! Money!" She exhaled the words between sobs. Her eyes bulged out of her head. "It's just *money!* And you can't say"—she paused to get her breath—"you can't say that I ever asked for you for anything, right? I've never asked you for anything, ever!"

I couldn't look at her. "And if you needed money for anything else, I would give it to you. But I can't buy this house for you, Krystal. I can't move in with you, I don't even like being here. It's not right. Geannie and Jim are dead. They're gone. You need to move on with your life. Get out of town, or maybe—"

"Oh, go fuck yourself, Bonnie."

I'd been looking toward the tree, avoiding her face, wildly embarrassed by this entire exchange, but at this outburst my eyes darted back to her.

Her face had contorted. "Miss High-and-Mighty, Miss I-Don't-Need-Shit. Now you're giving *me* advice? Don't you remember? That week after the shooting, you were all fucked up, and you came to me. To *me.* My house. And I was happy to have you!"

I felt myself flush deeply. "Okay, well. It wasn't like that—"

"Oh fuck you, yes it was, you were *fucked up*, Bonnie. Lying on the couch in some kind of trance, whimpering in your sleep and crying like a titty-baby, and I held your hand and let you do it, do you remember *that*? Hernan was my *brother.* And Geannie and Jim . . ." She paused, as if thoughts were swarming inside her, and her voice changed, imitating me. "*Geannie and Jim, Geannie and Jim,*" she mocked. "That's all you ever say. They were my *parents*, Bonnie. Why don't you ever call them that? Geannie was my *mother*, Jim was my *father*," she said, her voice cracking. "They were *my* parents but you were there crying like they'd been *your* parents. And why? Because you were there when it happened? You walked out of there fine. A few cuts and bruises, a graze, so the fuck what. You didn't even try to stop them. Why didn't you stop them?"

"What?" I said, astonished by this sudden turn. The lights were so bright. My sweating accelerated. "What? Krystal, I was—I was—" I couldn't finish the sentence. I didn't know how to finish it.

"Oh yeah, I forgot. You were 'assaulted,' raped, whatever. Yeah I know all about it. Everybody knows all about it. Wah, wah, wah, let's-feel-sorry-for-Bonnie time." Her voice ratcheted upward. "But why didn't you *stop* them? The robbers!"

Krystal was yelling now, and looked crazed, her face flushed and sweaty, her voice at a register I had never heard before. We were both standing now, too, though I didn't recall standing up. "I know the market and where you were standing when they first came in, you could've taken a hammer or knife, or a fucking jar of pickles, I don't know, and hit one of them from behind. You could have stopped them! Some hero. Why did you just let it happen!"

"Shut up, now." I was very calm. "Shut up now, Krystal."

"Walking around with your stupid dead face, acting all holier-than-thou like nothing touches you, well let me tell you something, *Bonnie*." She moved toward me like a snake, slithery, her finger pointing at me like a knife. Her nails were long and yellow and raggedy, her hair a greasy mess. Briefly I wondered if the dentists she worked for noticed her stink, if they allowed her to get close to the patients.

Then she got right up close to me and said: "Geannie and Jim hated you."

The Elvis record ended and clicked off. We stood facing each other in silence, my surprise at her statement so large that, for a wild second, I thought the force of it had turned off the music.

"Yeah. That's right." Her posture puffed up like an inflating raft. She saw my expression, I guess. I could see it register in her face. The power. "They fucking *hated* you. Couldn't get rid of you fast enough whenever you came around. Ever wonder why you never had a key to their house? But Mom felt sorry for you. Poor little Bonnie, her dead mommy and daddy. Daughter of the town drunk. Everyone knew that, did you realize? You were the daughter of the town drunk, and I don't mean your dad." The hits kept on coming. My ears thrummed.

She must have seen my shock because she softened a little, but then I saw her remember the money. My win and her loss. I could read her thoughts by translating the rises and falls in her face like a radio waveform. "Your mother crashing into that window, I heard all about it. And my parents felt *sorry* for you. Mooning over Hernan, weirding him out. Everyone knew you were hot for him. He was always begging to change the schedule so he could avoid walking you home. You were a mute, he said! You *embarrassed* yourself. He caught secondhand *embarrassment* from you."

Standing in silence, I could only look at her, amazed. The words coming out of her mouth were alien filth, a torrent of black bilgewater. The scar on my neck throbbed.

"You think they wanted you around? 'Always hanging around,' Mom would say. 'She won't stay away.' 'Nosing into our business.' Calling Dad for favors—Christ, like he was your on-call plumber or some shit. Staying over on Christmas like you were a fucking baby. Who does that? None of us did that." She looked at me. "Yeah. Didn't you ever wonder why I never stayed overnight for Christmas? Because they didn't feel sorry for me. I had my life *together*." Her face clenched up again and she started crying. "I had my shit together, not you. And they felt *sorry* for you. And then you loved them so much you just stood there and watched—you *let* them die!"

Woodenly I turned away from her. My ears roared. Vomit edged at my throat and the lights were ripping at me, leaving tracers in my vision. The house was a nightmare I couldn't escape. I needed to exit immediately. I wanted air like water. I headed toward the door. "You're a bunch of shit," I hissed at her over my shoulder. I could barely say it, my throat was so tight.

"Keep tellin' yourself that!" she called after me, sucking back snot. Then I heard her footsteps behind me, following. "Bonnie," she said.

Her voice had changed. Just that quick. "Bonnie. Wait."

I reached the front door. I was breathing hard and seeing flashes like stars, an annoying number of stars, bursting red and white at the edges of my vision, a deep headache blooming. "What," I said to her, my hand on the doorknob.

"Bonnie, wait. I'm—I'm sorry I said those things." Using the sleeve of the housecoat now to wipe her nose. "And—I lost my job. And my apartment. They kicked me out. I need some money, just a little. If not for the house, then for something, somewhere to live. I sunk all my money into taking care of this place, can you give me, like, a couple hundred? Please?"

My voice felt like it was a long way off, quiet, flat. "Eat shit and die, Krystal."

"Please, Bonnie." She was weeping now, sobbing. "Please, Bonnie, I'm sorry for all those things I said, and you won't even miss it, please just a few—"

I swung the door open. "If you come near me again, I'll kill you," I said.

I walked out to my truck on stick legs, but I made it, thank god. I made it. The frigid air blessed me.

And then she was screaming after me, running outside after me in her bare feet, telling me to go fuck myself, and that she hated me, too, even more than Geannie and Jim and Hernan hated me, because she had loved me. Because we were family. But I was already blasting the radio and starting the engine, peeling out of there, driving away.

In the mirror I saw Krystal's wasted shell vibrating with rage, and Geannie and Jim's house lit from within.

I watched both of them shrink behind me, and then they were gone. Forever, I hoped.

A partment 205 was never mentioned in the series.

After Ray and Brenda left, I felt wiped out, as if I had run a marathon, and as I lay in the gravel driveway, listening to silence bloom in the trees, I considered ignoring Ray's last words out of spite. *It's really important you unlock 205.* His touch on my arm still tingled. His earnest face kept wafting up at me, as well as my curiosity. Perhaps it was food or something else that might spoil, or maybe it was another fantastical mechanical device—a Jack Tripper robot that needed to be oiled or powered on right away. Whatever it was, I decided to get it over with so I could stop thinking about it.

I walked back to the apartment building and climbed the stairs to 205. I pressed my ear to the door, preparing myself for anything. I heard nothing. I turned the key and twisted the knob, listening to the creak of new hinges.

The open doorway was a dark mouth carved into the bright day, the sun nearing its highest point overhead. I stepped inside and listened. Still nothing. The cool air collected around me. When my eyes adjusted I saw that this unit had a similar layout and furnishings to the other apartments in the building, though it was blander, blanker. The walls were bare.

Suddenly I heard a scrabbling noise and an odd tune. It was coming from the bathroom. Light emanated from the crack beneath the closed door, and as I walked toward it my stomach tightened. Fleetingly I had the thought that Ray had hated me all along, perhaps homicidally so, and as I turned the doorknob and pushed open the door, the idea of the robot floated up again. I imagined murder, the perfect murder—mechanical strangulation, my corpse rotting in my grand creation, Ray's final declaration of what he really thought of me.

But no. No robot and no murder.

Instead, on the floor of the lighted bathroom, was a small puppy. A white Labrador retriever.

How could I have forgotten? It was the unnamed dog Larry gave the trio in the first-season episode "No Children, No Dogs," which they in turn anonymously gifted to the Ropers to avoid eviction. Then the dog disappeared. It was never seen before or after that episode, one of those vanishing plot devices. Now here it was, whimpering at my feet.

The other sound came from slightly above me. A low chirping noise. In a cage hanging from the ceiling sat a yellow bird. The Ropers' parakeet! It had sat in a cage in their living room, another plot device. The bird was luckier than the puppy, though. It made recurring appearances throughout the Ropers' time on the show.

I was pleased that Ray had remembered. These were his gifts, I understood, even more than the carousel-like rooms. The closer I looked at the bird, though, the more uneasy I became. Something seemed wrong. Then I realized.

It wasn't a parakeet. It was a canary.

The mistake was breathtaking. Shocking. Somehow worse than a killer robot. The smallness of the error, its pointed and targeted detail more of a needle than a hammer—it seemed personal.

The floor was covered with newspaper and the room stank from where the puppy had done its business. The bottom of the birdcage was already covered in tiny, desiccated turds. I wondered how long these animals had been left in here. More and more it read like a deliberate message from Ray, one that had no goodwill in it at all.

As I looked at both of these creatures, breathing and looking back at me, all of us at the beginning of our life cycles, a veil of dread lowered over me. The three of us stood silent as if players on a stage, waiting for a cue. Even the puppy was still. I didn't feel fully seated inside myself. I felt like I used to during Christmas at Jim and Geannie's, as if I were watching myself exist while others did the actual living, struggling to hear a deeper message in a murmurous, alien tongue, forever out of my grasp.

The bird tweeted and moved time forward. The dog yipped again and nuzzled my ankle. It seemed so happy to see me. Even the bird seemed excited at my presence, as if the life of the party had just arrived. They both gazed at me, the newcomer.

Ray's "gifts." Involuntarily my heart stabbed at my throat, my stupid eyes.

All these living things. It felt like sabotage.

Two

For the first year I was Janet Wood, my first love. I needed her sensible brain to ground me, to fully settle me into my new world. In the morning I woke as Janet Wood, and I stretched in my bed as Janet Wood, wearing the same navy-blue nightgown emblazoned with the number zero that Janet Wood wore, and my alarm clock was set for 7 a.m., Janet Wood's wake time, the light barely penetrating the ugly curtains that shrouded Janet Wood's bedroom window, and when I turned off my alarm I was Janet Wood, and when I clicked on the lamp I was Janet Wood, and when I looked in the mirror I saw Janet Wood's dark and shiny hair, and my eyes were newly brown.

I'd rise from bed and put on my robe and bedroom shoes, and I'd say hello to ghost Chrissy, who, within days of beginning this routine, became real Chrissy. "Get up, Chrissy!" I'd call softly as I passed her bed to exit the room. And Chrissy would wake with the groan of a child and stretch and yawn, and I'd go to the bathroom and splash my face with cold water before shuffling into the kitchen. The dog followed me everywhere but I ignored it. In the kitchen I might find Jack standing in front of the stove. The overhead light would be on, plus the morning light coming through the window at full glare. Rainy days were best, gloomy and dark outside, the orange-yellow kitchen happily glowing inside. And if Jack was already there I would make coffee, do my part, and if he hadn't arrived yet I would make toast for myself, maybe pour a glass of orange juice. I'd also set the table for my roommates if they were behind schedule, and I'd wait until they bustled in, sleepy but bright, friendly. "Good morning!" each of them called to me. "Oh, morning!" I'd reply back.

On the days Jack cooked breakfast, I was his sous chef—I fried eggs or whipped together simple mixtures I knew by heart. Eggs and bacon, or gourmet oatmeal, toast, coffee, orange juice, milk. Wanting to get the dog away from me, I threw scraps of bacon or rubbery scrambled eggs across the kitchen, where they splatted in a far corner. Together Jack and I created a serviceable meal, usually finishing up just as Chrissy breezed in, still sleepy-eyed. Afterward we washed the dishes, each of us taking turns according to the day. We were responsible adults, always doing the dishes immediately following a meal and rarely later, though on the days it was not my turn I often found dirty dishes lingering in the sink hours after eating, the egg residue drying into an implacable scum, but instead of complaining I washed them myself, enjoying harmless, catty thoughts.

In the living room, in its cage, the canary chirped. I fed it or cleaned up after it while keeping my mind blank.

After a leisurely breakfast I brushed my hair and dressed for work. The dog nipped at my heels and I ignored it. I had a wide collection of pantyhose I rolled on day after day, sometimes taking them down from where I'd draped them over the shower rod after washing them the night before, and my closet and bureau were stocked full of bohemian jumpers and bell-bottom jeans, modest skirts and turtlenecks, though the longer I was Janet the sleeker my wardrobe became—tailored jeans and blouses, professional midi dresses. After dressing and doing my makeup I left the apartment and caught the bus on the corner.

Every day, the dog followed me outside. Then, as soon as the bus doors hissed shut, it would turn toward the woods and disappear. Watching it flee from my bus seat, I would close my eyes, relieved.

The bus began its daily trek, stopping with a hiss at several places as I patiently waited. Sometimes I observed the buildings and road; sometimes I looked at the sky, noticing the weather; sometimes I stared into space and thought of the workday ahead, anxious to get the day started, or of the news I had read that morning over breakfast. My head was pleasantly calm. When the bus stopped a block away from Arcade Florists, my workplace, I disembarked and walked the remaining distance, happy to be out in the fresh air, moving my body. This was forward motion, this was progress. My penchant for industrious, righteous movement infected every one of my waking Janet moments, the anxiety of sloth, of idleness, always pricking at the edge of my mind, prodding me forward.

At first I was merely a full-time associate who worked the register and fed and watered the plants, and who sometimes assisted in flower arranging, but six months in, during Season 2's "Janet's Promotion," I was promoted to shop manager. Readying the shop for opening became one of my many new duties, which included counting the money, spritzing the ferns, getting the merchandise in order, looking over yesterday's figures, preparing for the day ahead. I checked the paperwork—was today the Benson wedding, that fateful event in Season 2's "Jack in the Flower Shop"? No, nothing major today, just a few phone pickup orders made last night before closing, and I got right on them, efficiently and expertly gathering the materials needed. Then I unlocked the doors and turned the sign over to say OPEN.

Days in the shop often passed in meditative quiet. I tended to the flowering plants and nursed the dying ones, breathing in the earthy scent of all the fauna and counting myself lucky to be surrounded by so much life, a tiny oasis in the middle of a city. I created and rotated window displays. I made phone calls, I processed new plants that appeared in the back room, getting them ready for sale. I did and redid the price sheets. Customers came in and browsed but rarely bought.

Around 6:30 p.m. I closed up the shop, double- and triple-checking the door, and I waited for and caught the bus back to the apartment building. The ride home was filled with the light of sunset as the year waned, and I leaned my head against the window, occasionally dozing off until my stop. Upon exiting the bus I often met Chrissy at the curb, who'd just hopped off another bus coming from Westwood, and we walked the remaining block and entered the building together, trudging up the stairs to 201. Then we opened the door and threw ourselves on the couch, flopping our purses and jackets lavishly on whatever furniture was closest, the joy of being home and free exhaling from every pore, the whole evening ahead of us.

The dog would return around this time and paw at the door. Reluctantly I'd let it in. Tucked away, in the farthest corner of the fourth wall in the apartment, was an auto-feeder and water bowl Ray had left.

And what did I do in the evening? Jack arrived home from cooking school before us and often had supper on the stove waiting to be served or in its final stages. After eating we sometimes watched television together, depending on the night and whether we could agree on the channel (I liked *Police Woman* until it ended its run in March of 1978, and *The ABC Friday Night Movie*), and sometimes I read or took the bus to the library, and sometimes I went on dates with men who turned out to be cartoonishly evil. *How do I end up with such men?* I'd ask Chrissy later, speculating that I'd been cosmically cursed with bad luck in romance, and she sympathized—being blonde, and more naive, she attracted men twice as terrible.

At night the apartment glowed, and I sometimes had the rooms to myself, and on the cozy occasions I was in the living room alone, I'd lie on the couch with a bowl of popcorn on my chest, drowsing, listening to the drone of the television in front of me and Jack clacking in the kitchen as he tested a new recipe, filling the air with new and wonderful smells, and Chrissy was in the bathroom showering, the patter of the water adding to the white noise, and I ignored the bird, and the night was at the window but the rooms were all bright and sheltered, full of warm colors, and the hum of contented happiness, of freedom, echoed back at me and allowed me to doze off, flush with the dream of a life I had always believed, in another life, as another person, was impossible.

When bedtime came Chrissy and I usually retired at the same time to avoid disturbing the other since we shared the bedroom. Each night I read a book or magazine in bed and then wrote a letter to my parents back home in Indiana. I told them about my day and gave a mini weather report. I always told them it was sunny. I wrote about the flower shop and what I ate for dinner. My letters were reassuring and detailed, full of exclamation marks and hearts. I would have been ashamed to show them to another person, it's true, but these letters were to people who'd known me as a child and still thought of me as a child, and with these small flourishes I answered the questions every parent had: Was I happy? Yes. Was I safe? Yes. Was I still their good girl? Yes.

Afterward I switched off the light by my bed, turned over, and fell into a heavy, uninterrupted sleep.

On the couch, the dog snored.

The dog, the dog. The bird. They kept growing bigger and required care and feeding and watering, and though the dog did her business somewhere in the wild during the day, the bird's cage was forever being filled up with shit and debris. Food in, food out, everyone getting older, the obscene proof of time.

The animals weren't the only flaws in my world. The other large one was that my reality was manufactured and required continual maintenance. For those tasks I needed to retain some thread of the self I had been saddled with at birth. I called these the off days.

Once every two weeks I, as my old self, delivered new plants from the greenhouse to the storeroom of Arcade Florists to replace any dying ones. If needed, I also restocked the small market on the corner with food and supplies I fetched from the main house's kitchen, where Bernie the delivery boy had deposited them, always checking first to make sure he was not around. (I'd memorized his delivery schedule, but part of me always feared an unpleasant surprise that would result in an accidental meeting—a sick day of his, perhaps, and a resulting off-schedule delivery.) To restock the market I had to transfer all of the food from the twenty-first-century boxes into the 1970s packaging, in addition to stocking the shelves, which took time. Shopping trips to the market occurred on the alternate week, letting a week elapse between the distasteful task of stocking the shelves as my old self and the enjoyable task of shopping for food as Janet.

Those seven interim days allowed any scarring of the illusion to heal back over.

I cleaned the apartment building inside out, too, on the off days—this wasn't too disturbing a task inside the apartment, as Janet and her roommates were tidy, clean people, but I also checked in on the other apartments (and buildings) just to make sure the toilets and sinks were running smoothly, and for this grim reality there was no part to play. Until I was Mr. Roper, or Mr. Furley, I was just plain old Bonnie for that.

After I finished my duties on these days I trudged up to Apartment 205, the one never mentioned on the show. I unlocked the door and sat on the nondescript gray couch. In front of me was a modern television, along with a DVD player and modern amenities. I switched it on and proceeded to binge *Three's Company*, as Bonnie Lincoln, to console myself.

These guilty occasions sometimes lasted for hours—one time, I'm ashamed to admit, an entire day. In that featureless living room I watched the show on my DVDs as I used to in my trailer, and I kept a stash of Bonnie clothes there in the closet, right above Bonnie's old milk-carton shelves that held the DVDs and DVD players. Visiting 205 was like being inside a waiting room—somewhere not belonging to my past but not to the current era, either, or to the show, though it carried faint echoes of all three places.

After my little marathon watch sessions I'd return to Apartment 201 and resume life as Janet. After a few months of this routine, the missing time started eating at me. Where had I been during the off days?

I stopped falling asleep instantly after turning out the light. I lay awake in the single bed. What had I, Janet, been doing while Bonnie Lincoln was puttering around, restocking the meat freezer? My head buzzed with Bonnie thoughts, with off-day thoughts. Was I tainting my new world with my old habits? Should I have kept on a few people to restock shelves, maintain the plumbing? And then I considered calling a few of the trustiest caseworkers, asking them to check on things that I'd been checking on, but after mulling it over a few minutes I stopped myself short, sick at my own betrayal. Was merely considering this possibility jeopardizing my complete immersion, threatening the world I had worked so hard to achieve? I sat up and kicked away the covers, put on my robe and slippers, and went out into the living room late at night, where a light from somewhere outside cast a bluish hue into the darkness. I turned on the television, only to find static.

On the end of the couch the dog lay sleeping and grunting, making everything worse. The bird, thankfully, remained silent.

On these nights I considered sneaking off to Apartment 205 and watching the DVDs. In the before-times when I had suffered insomnia, *Three's Company* had been my narcotic. Through several sleepless nights in the trailer park I had consoled myself with the show—"taking the cure" was the way I'd thought of it. But what was the cure now? Now I was living in it, and I was still wide awake at 3 a.m.

And there could be no shortcuts. I had made that rule for myself a long time ago. There was a library a few blocks away, stocked with era-specific books and magazines, first editions when I could find them, and I often thought about its inviting aisles during these endless, elliptical nights, longing to distract myself. What was stopping me from walking there, after all?

But I steeled myself against it. The library would not be open at this hour, not in Janet's world. I reminded myself of this world's purity, how necessary it was to maintain it. One slip and all could crumble. And I wouldn't be able to undo it. That was the danger of setting routines, of transgressing one time—once an idea turned into action there was no undoing it. It was written in permanent ink.

I tried to get back into character. Janet Wood. I was Janet Wood. I picked up a magazine lying on the small wicker coffee table and flipped through it. Then I went into the kitchen and rummaged around, drank a glass of water. I looked out the window but saw nothing, only shadows. At times like these, I often considered going for a walk—surely Janet would do that, such a simple thing. But then I started thinking: Would a young woman as cautious as Janet have walked the Santa Monica streets in the wee hours of the morning? In the late seventies, early eighties? I decided against it. I settled for going out on the balcony, looking at the sky and imagining smog. That was one detail I couldn't fake. The sky was always so clear and the stars blared above me, threatening me with my native timeline. They wouldn't let me stay out there long. Those were hours of desperation.

Anxious nights were okay, though, I told myself. In the morning I tried to start fresh. Just a bad night, I told myself as I brushed my hair in front of the mirror and looked into my brown eyes. Janet was only human, after all.

●●●●●●●●●●●●

How to explain it? I was myself *and* Janet Wood. I was a vessel and she inhabited it, took up space; this was true of all the characters. When I went multiple days in character I lulled myself into thinking I was her, and as her I conjured up Jack and Chrissy, squinting until I could see them fully fleshed in front of me, down to their shoelaces, and in this way I also conjured the occasional customer at the flower shop, and sometimes my visiting boss, Mr. Compton. I pictured my boorish dates. My imagination was wild and deep; I had entire conversations, arguments, laughing fits . . . to an outsider I would have looked insane. But I had never felt more occupied, more *employed*, than I did when offering myself up to these ghosts.

There were so many things I had never fully enjoyed as my old self that I was now discovering. The spiritual ecstasy of walking into an anonymous building like the market, or an office, or the community center—of walking in and feeling my insignificance wash over me. The smallness of being here! In this timeline! How wonderful it felt to be a guest. These petty epiphanies felt large.

My timeline transplant was an endless wonder. Technically, I did not belong in the 1970s. I had not been born there, and I had not arrived there the usual way, growing up stuffed full of fear, with the unknown looming ahead of me; I lacked the prejudices one's parents and their parents' parents had handed down to a 1977 native; I was free from the vague weight of societal ills peculiar to recent history that accumulate in the average person's psyche and seem so crucial in the moment. Politics, culture, fashion, social upheaval, the latest gadgets, global crises . . . they remained at a remove, and therefore they seemed charmed and special when I read about them in my 1977 *LA Times* every morning.

In my former waking life, back when I was working in the supermarket warehouse and living in my trailer, the daily news of current events had been tiresome and upsetting, a white-noise villain that occasionally reached enough volume to gouge the few moments of peace I'd grabbed from the day. I had avoided it. I never liked being reminded that far beyond the grand drama of my own sorry life, a larger play was taking place, one that didn't consult me but could obliterate me at any moment.

However, in my newly made reality even the bleakest headlines and TV news reports were something of interest. I was like Scrooge on Christmas morning, pleased with everything. A true historian would no doubt be appalled to know how diverting I found world events. And this glee was despite my efforts to have Janet-type reactions to the oil crisis, or random terrorism, or news of another rapist or serial killer rampaging through local neighborhoods—I attempted disgust, disbelief, outrage. I even tried to affect the casual fear a person engages with every day just to get along—the anxiety of a concerned citizen—but the enjoyment of my surroundings was all-consuming. I was sick with contentedness.

Best of all, time moved in a sludgy pattern. Aside from the weather, and the dates on the newspapers and TV Guides, nothing alerted me to the moving days. The theory of timekeeping—of days and weeks, of holidays and birthdays and age—became an abstraction. The days were best when they passed like one long, silky strand, with no anger or despair, no insomnia, no traumatic past or anxious future, just the idle annoyances of laundry or something equally small and meaningless and gentle.

Time was happening, surely, but not to me.

•••••••••••••

I'd be lying if I said I was completely free, though. During the first few months, as I settled in alone, visions of my past life (what I thought of as my "past life") did bubble up every now and then—a vision of Krystal standing in the middle of darkness, her ravaged face wailing at me, and Geannie's house behind her, its malevolent Christmas cheer blazing from every window. Or, more disturbing, a fond memory would surface—the two of us eating together in silence, maybe, or taking drives together out to random deserted places the way we used to in our sister years, before the robbery—and the images washed over me in waves of longing, of nostalgia for my own life. Those were weak, ugly moments. Like rotten floorboards in my current reality, they threatened to send me crashing through to the dark basement of the past. At those times I wondered what became of Krystal after I left for good, and occasionally I even considered finding out. But the day after we last saw each other I had disconnected my phone number, quit my job over the phone, and got the hell out of town. I left the sale of my trailer to Larwin and whatever company he used to make such transactions, gave no one but him a forwarding address, and instructed him to keep my new address under wraps in case anyone came sniffing around.

I had never told Krystal I'd been house-hunting, let alone the location of my new place. Now I was a hundred miles from my place of origin, and whenever I felt anxious on off days, I visualized myself crawling on hands and knees across each mile, just to reassure myself of the distance. When I had gone to see her that final night, I had planned on giving her the address in case of emergency, of even (horrifying, the secret memory of it!) inviting her to live with me, maybe, in a room inside the main house for a limited period of time, until she got on her feet again. We never got to that, obviously—sometimes there was a God. There was very little chance of her finding me now, and if I went back to find her it would ruin everything. She would be back in my life, bringing with her the zombie glaze of my old self, along with all its ghosts.

I told myself that I needed to keep my new place pure. I had done the right thing, anyway, forcing her to get on with things. I had shown her what was best for her, even if she hated me for the rest of her life. I took solace in that fact, and if I felt any guilt or love I only had to conjure up the image of Krystal kneeling over the Santa village in Geannie and Jim's living room, smiling up at me with her ghoul face, to cure myself.

All that was behind me. Geannie and Jim, Hernan, the robbery, the aftermath, Krystal, the grocery store, the fucking walk-in cooler, the shakes and sweats, all the peering neighbors, news reporters, everything. All my mistakes and misfortunes, left in another town! Just that easy. The things money and an asshole temperament could buy.

I would not chalk up my new life to mental illness. It wasn't, either, that my previous, pre-lottery life had been so terrible. Aside from the robbery, which had been incidental, my life had been fairly boring but pleasant. I had held a job, and I'd known people on a friend and acquaintance level, and I had taken myself out to eat once in a while, taken myself to the occasional movie, read some good books, paid bills on time or close to it. And I had enjoyed the outdoors and lived in my own place—basic but mine, and it had been relatively clean and free of pests or infestations, and reasonably heated and cooled for comfort—and my health had been decent, and I had stayed out of legal and criminal trouble. I had possessed all of the things that a traditionally good life were conditional upon. I was functionally human. Why, then, had that life always felt like a pastime, just something I was doing while waiting for my other self, the actualized, better version of myself, to come along and make it real?

In my heart of hearts, I had wanted to be exceptional. I wanted to believe I had a higher purpose than staggering from one day to the next in fear or exhaustion, death always hanging out up ahead. The people I knew or met, especially after the robbery—Krystal, people at work and at all the places I went, from cashiers to moneybags like Mr. Larwin—they all seemed dead, or happily dying, dug into their own little foxhole of existence, enjoying the dirt of their particular ditch. And until the robbery I might have been fine with that life. Perhaps I even would have actively chosen my reassuring routine, mortified by merely *wanting* more and all the selfish implications that came with the wanting.

After the worst happened, however, my attitude changed. I became nihilistic and full of rage. There was no point to anything. And that supreme desolation—that realization that I had been abandoned by my own certainty of how the world worked—gave me the reckless freedom to do something truly wild. I started believing in myself. I believed everything I thought. I couldn't fail. My newfound narcissism felt like revenge. I figured that if the world was going to wreak its random cruelty on me, I might as well aspire to greatness in the meantime. Once I discovered *Three's Company*, I understood I could take the chaos of the universe and put a recognizable, finite face on it, the ultimate pareidolia.

I'm just glad I had the money to do it. Such a discovery would have been endlessly painful had I not been able to afford to make it happen. Big dreams are shameful when survival is on the line. Had I remained in my trailer, broke but dreaming, I might have eventually anesthetized myself with booze or drugs. There were a lot of good role models in the town I lived in, that's for sure, so many people who'd become accidentally-on-purpose dead. But the lottery money had bought me another life. Another nine lives, counting all the main *Three's Company* cast throughout the years. I would dedicate a year or more to living as each character as the spirit moved me. I was happy to shuffle off the coil that had trapped me for so long, my identity, and try a few new ones. So many people wanted to solve their problem of self; I wanted to trash it entirely. The world was so haphazard and frightening, why not arrange it the way I wanted it? Why not?

Krystal would have laughed at all this. Or sneered. During that final visit she had accused me of being in denial—she probably wanted me to *confront my trauma*, to wallow in misery with her, just like those reporters had wanted me to put money back into my trailer park forever, pumping blood into a dead corpse. But look where wallowing got her. Confronting trauma indeed. In my mind those kinds of phrases belonged to weaker specimens, a lower order of person who believed in living the worst day of their life over and over again, in perpetuity, an eternal pity party disguised as healing.

Sometimes, in the quiet of the off days, in between restocking the shelves, I pretended Krystal was there with me, if only to verbally lambaste her into oblivion. I wanted to tell her: *You're* the one in the wrong. *You're* the one making excuses, using your life's events as a reason to quit, to fall into grief, to fail. Not me, though. Maybe that works for you, but it won't work for me.

I said a lot of things to invisible Krystal. I made my case. I never failed to be eloquent, persuasive, maybe a little verbose. And in my imagination she never failed to be impressed. Completely awed by my wit and correctness. She was silent, craving my words, on the verge of tears. Sometimes I envisioned slapping her in the face.

Admittedly, this habit was an indulgence. It was always easier, talking to someone who wasn't there. Who was dead. I tried not to do it too often, but funny things happen sometimes, when a person is alone.

•••••••••••••

There was one other disconcerting thing in those early days. As part of the authentic television programming, *Three's Company* aired every Tuesday night at 9 p.m. So I was Janet, a character in the show, sitting inside the living room, and each Tuesday I'd watch the Janet on the screen sit in an identical room.

The first time it happened, that first Tuesday evening, I was lazing on one end of the couch, my bare feet tucked up under me. Chrissy sat on the other end. Jack was in the kitchen. Dinner had been heavy that night—coq au vin—and my eyes were heavy, pleasantly drowsing. Then the opening notes of the show's theme played, a song I knew like my own soul. I awoke instantly, my brain filling with horror.

There, on the screen, was us. Janet sat on the couch, and Chrissy sat on the other end like a mirror image. On the screen, Jack entered from the kitchen wearing an apron, stirring cake batter in a bowl. The trio exchanged jokes. The audience laughed.

I was sitting up straight now. I looked over to my left. Chrissy had vanished. I was alone on the couch, and the kitchen noises had ceased. No light was coming from under any of the doorways.

My insides sagged. I stood and walked into the other rooms. Empty! I opened the front door, walked out on the balcony, looked around. No one was there. I could only hear the crickets softly chirping, no city sounds at all.

Behind me, familiar voices floated. I looked back at the TV screen. This refraction of myself I had not anticipated. The dog, who sensed my distress, bounded toward me from its food corner and sat at my feet. Waiting.

I ignored it. Quickly I closed the door and sat down on the couch again. I called Jack and Chrissy into the room. I needed to feel them close to me, and I willed them to breathe and speak.

They came. Slowly at first, like a pale wind, but bit by bit they coalesced into their fleshly selves until they were fully alive, Jack emerging bleary-eyed from his room dressed in a T-shirt and sweats, holding a book, Chrissy from the kitchen licking ice cream off a spoon, clad in her housecoat.

As the three of us crowded onto the couch, I pointed at the TV and murmured, "Who is that?" My voice was timid, a tiny squeak. I cleared my throat and stared at the screen. There they were, my friends, my family. My self.

"Is that us?" I whispered.

No one replied.

A note about the dog.

The dog, it's true, was not getting any younger. Nor the bird. But the bird was so small to begin with, and required much less attention and care, and it was not trotting up to me when I got home from work, or when I got up in the morning, or relaxed on the couch, or walked outside in the evenings . . . the bird was not a knife, constantly jabbing at me.

The dog, on the other hand. Always trying to lick me. Always growing, eating more, its puppyish yips turning into adult, full-throated barks. Everything it did mocked what I had made here, and any attempt the dog made to cozy up to me I rejected with disgust. "I don't like needy people!" I yelled at it once after she nearly tripped me in the kitchen, trying to catch a falling morsel from whatever I was making, and it whimpered as if I had hit it. Then it did that cutesy TV dog thing where it crouched down and put its paws over its eyes, making me hate her even more.

I'd read where dogs can sometimes resemble their master's face, and I began to think I could see Ray's face, his shaggy, solemn face, in this dog's snout. And one day as I got off the bus the dog ran up to me with a partially smoked cigarette in its mouth, no lie. It wasn't lit, nothing as fantastic as that, but I sprinted up the steps, anyway, before the dog could follow too closely, and shut the door before it could enter. It whimpered and whined on the balcony all night. Hungry, I guessed. "You're an animal!" I had yelled through the door. "Go kill something!"

The next morning when I opened the door slowly, it was

nowhere to be seen. But outside, on the doormat, was the half-smashed cigarette butt, soggy with doggy spit.

What could I do? I couldn't shoot the dog—I didn't have a gun, and felt that might be taking things too far. More and more, though, the bird and the dog made their collective presence known. Whenever I left the apartment for a few minutes, breathed fresh air, and then came back inside, I could smell the animals, a scent I detested. No matter how much I cleaned—and it felt like I cleaned a lot more than any 1977 young person living in Santa Monica ever did, let me tell you—I could not eradicate the smell. Something was underneath it, too, probably the bird shit, the musty stench of animal bodies and their relentless emissions of sweat and piss and shit and fear and pleasure and sex. Some of my smell was probably in there, too, though I always had trouble distinguishing my own offensive odors.

The bird I could keep, I figured, for my Roper years, if it lived that long. It wasn't a parakeet but it was yellow and better than nothing. Whenever it wouldn't stop its barrage of tweets, and the weather was decent, I put the cage outside on the balcony.

But the dog, the dog. It was not a puppy anymore. By the time I got to my Roper years, the dog would be useless.

What had Ray been thinking? As the second year passed and then the third, I decided that Ray, like everyone else I left behind, had probably despised me. Nothing else could explain the animals. What a fool I had been, to ever think he was a friend. Hadn't I learned anything, first with Krystal, and then with. . . . everyone else I'd ever known? I was always learning things and forgetting how to apply the lesson.

The only good thing I could see in keeping the dog was security, but it was so capricious and near wild at times that I doubted its instinct to protect or alert me of danger. The dog wasn't an idiot. I knew it sensed my distrust. After the night with the cigarette, it never slept indoors again.

And when, late into the third year, after a night of desperate insomnia, the night before the storm, I got lonely and wooed it with soup bones and dinner scraps, and petted its ears and tried to name it, it ran away from me.

As the day turned into night, I called and called for it, but it never came. It disappeared into the woods and that was that.

It was a Thursday afternoon in October and the light was just beginning to fade, and outside the sky was masked with clouds and a chilly breeze picked up, but my name was Jack Tripper and I was tucked away safe in the kitchen of Apartment 201, cutting up vegetables, when the knock came.

Nearly three years had passed since the workers left and Ray and Brenda had fled the premises—almost three years since I had seen another human in the flesh. After my first year as Janet, I'd lived as Chrissy, bleaching my hair and piling on clownish eyeliner and blush, and trading Janet's brown eyes for blue ones. That was a year of purity, like a freshly laundered blanket fluttering in the wind. Of all of the characters, Chrissy was the least bothered, the emptiest. And what beautiful emptiness it was. Information glided over her brain like water into a reservoir, a perpetual daydream. Time moved even further away from consciousness. During my Chrissy year I graduated from my old life into my new one, moving fully into a near-astral state, getting lost in blue skies or a blade of sun, the colors and intangible fabric of the decade cushioning me, and I thought no further than the next outfit, the shape of hair, walking the aisles of the local department store in a peaceful trance, the Muzak humming above me, the joys of holiday trimmings, a soft dream of love. It was a time of childhood.

But in the final hours of my second New Year's Eve I moved into the next iteration, and since then I'd been waking and sleeping as Jack Tripper, and I dressed in Player shirts and blue boxer shorts, my hair cropped close and dyed a medium brown. My eyes remained bright blue. I had an entire bedroom to myself, and it felt luxurious having my own desk and closet, even a funky patchwork chair near the window.

There was such unexpected freedom in being a man. As Jack I could come and go as I pleased, at any hour of the day or night. I jogged around the neighborhood, regardless of the hour, at least twice a week, I walked home alone after dark. I could order a straight whiskey at the Regal Beagle, throw it over my tongue, and wipe my mouth roughly with the back of my hand, and no one looked at me twice. Most flattering of all, I was seen and judged by others as a protector, as someone strong—others naturally looked to me for help in a practical, physical way. Helping a friend move? They asked me. Shepherding my female roommates home after dark? They looked to me. Someone needed backup in the face of an enemy? I was there. These foregone expectations alone gave me a huge amount of satisfaction I never fully realized I'd been missing. For it had never been enough to merely *feel* powerful—I'd learned long ago that nobody gives a shit how a person lives in their head. To truly exist in the external world, others must judge you worthy. Like Tinkerbell being clapped into reality, my strength required others to will it into existence with their faith, and by just *presenting* as male I felt like I'd gained a new respect, a strange sense of invincibility. Of invisibility, to a degree. For the first time in my entire life, my future had a map with endless destinations, and the whole world cheered as they shoved me into the driver's seat, telling me to go, go, go.

The best part was that this confidence wasn't a conscious realization, but was assimilated into the wallpaper of my psyche, into the marrow of my bones, until I didn't give it a second thought. Everything could be done without so much as a second thought, it seemed. Beyond the most basic rituals of hygiene, for example—combed hair, clean and relatively unwrinkled clothes, deodorant, the occasional dollop of cologne—I rarely contemplated myself in the mirror as Chrissy and Janet had, fussing with my face and hair and wondering, *Good enough?* None of that. And it was effortless—I was not arrogant or an asshole, I was not crazed with masculine power. I was simply myself. I walked with swagger because the world was mine.

Being Jack Tripper solved a lot of problems I hadn't known I had, and during this time I took pleasure in eradicating almost every feminine thing about myself. Femininity had always been a conundrum for me, and throwing it off brought the greatest freedom. During the first few months of the year I changed my walk, my mannerisms, anything that felt inauthentic to being Jack. That included my period, which unfortunately I couldn't get rid of completely—I took a pill that regulated this function to every three months. Even so, I hated being reminded of my biology, and when it finally came round it was sick-inducing, a week of near-prostrate hemorrhaging and intense, punishing migraines. The pill was the only one of its kind I had been able to tolerate, and it still didn't agree with me, but there wasn't much I could do about it—changing it would have required a doctor's visit, a grave interruption of the routine. I simply had to live with it. Whenever I felt the telltale cramps coming on, dread would pull at me, then anger. I regarded it as a hostile takeover. During those days I resigned myself to a bitter depression, the only time (besides those sleepless nights that occasionally plagued me, and Ray's animals) that any inkling of discontent slipped into my world. To prevent polluting the sacred space of my usual living quarters with my nausea and dark mood, I'd retreat to Apartment 205 for the duration of my bodily revolt. Oh, if I could muster the energy I tried to use on those days to perform the maintenance tasks to kill two birds with one stone, but most of the time I lay on the couch of the neutral apartment, watching my DVDs with an ice pack on my head, eating and drinking myself into a sugary, fat-filled stupor until I either slept or vomited, or both.

By the middle of the year I had achieved Jackness to the nth degree, reading the sports page of the *LA Times* and going to Lakers games with Larry, who lived upstairs. I shamelessly flirted with my roommates, annoying and delighting them with my playful advances, whims they sometimes indulged and some-times rejected all in equal fun, the clear boundaries of our friend-ship allowing such dancing to take place. On weekends I took part-time work when I could get it, a waiter at the Pizza Paradise here, a short-order cook there. Mostly, though, my typical daily routine included catching the bus to my technical college where I trained to be a chef, and in the afternoon and evenings I moved around the kitchen of Apartment 201 with ease, whipping and frying and tasting. I wore an apron with frilly lingerie drawings at the chest and crotch level that amused me. Dinners were lav-ish, multicourse meals when the budget allowed, and the ghosts of my past selves—Janet and Chrissy—danced around me.

This was all in my recent history when the knock on the front door broke through the gauze of my new life. My knife stopped in mid-chop. At first I thought it was the dog at the door, paw-ing like it used to paw to be let in. Something inside me lurched a little. This was the day after the dog had run away, seemingly for good. For nearly twenty-four hours I had been building up resentment toward the dog for fleeing in my hour of need, such blatant disrespect. However, since I'd woken from a long nap an

hour earlier, and felt restored to the best self the sleepless night
had robbed me of, I felt open to diplomatic relations.

All of this was moot, however, because the longer I paused
in mid-chop, the more I pondered whether the knock sounded
like the dog's rough pawing or like a hard, knuckled rap.

It came again.

I hadn't heard the sound in real life in a long time, and hearing it clearly, a second time, felt like a hand reaching out and
tearing away a body-sized scab. In a moment I was no longer
Jack, but Bonnie. Small, weakling Bonnie. The speed of it was
bewildering.

Setting down the knife, I made my way to the front door. For
a brief moment I reverted to Jack Tripper and excitement spiked
through me. Answering the door! Like in the show! People were
always knocking and answering doors in the show. But when I
placed my hand on the doorknob I paused. My old self rose up
again and I jerked my hand away.

The knock came once more, more insistent. Then a whee-
dling voice: "Miss Lincoln? Miss Lincoln! Hello? Miss Lincoln,
this is Bernie. The delivery guy? Are you in there?"

The delivery boy. The first one I hired.

My anger pitched forward. I remembered his rabbity little
face, his odd tics, that way he compulsively rubbed and smelled
his own nostril creases.

How dare he come in here and try to ruin things. *He signed
a contract.*

"What do you want?" I barked. I was not opening that god-
damned door. My skin flashed hot and my armpits prickled. I
understood I was afraid. "Go away, Bernie! Go away." I licked
my lips, my mouth dry. The quiet stretched forever, and for a

moment I really believed he had walked away, had never even been there. *If he leaves now, I can pretend nothing happened.*

Another knock.

I was shattered.

"You promised you would stay away!" I shouted. "You promised! *You signed a contract!*"

There was a moment of silence on the other side of the door. When he spoke again his voice was agitated, hurried. "Listen, I know I shouldn't be here but I came to warn you."

"What?" I said. "What?"

"A big storm," he said through the door, his distress increasing as he spoke. "It's all over the news, but I didn't know if you'd seen it so I wanted to tell you. They say it's headed this way. They're warning people to get prepared, just in case." He paused again. "Listen, I gotta go, I'm gonna leave, and there may not be any deliveries for a while if trees are down on the road. So no deliveries for a while," he repeated.

My heart thumped and flop sweat was rolling off me now. "So the fuck *what*, Bernie?" I finally said. My voice was tight. "A storm? They're always saying that shit."

I heard him let out some air. *Screw this crazy bitch*, I could hear him think. And his tone changed, too. "Okay, well, it's not for sure, not *one hundred percent*, but they keep talking about it. It sounds serious this time. A superstorm, they're calling it. Look, maybe you should get out, too. Or stay inside, whatever. I just thought you'd want to know, and I didn't want to leave a note in case . . ."

When I remained silent I heard him mutter "whatever." From his footsteps I could tell he was turning around and starting down the stairs.

"Bernie!" I yelled.

"Yeah," he yelled back.

"Thanks," I said.

And he left.

•••••••••••••

I went to the bathroom and dry-heaved. I sat next to the toilet for a few minutes, thrown back into my raw Bonnie self, that bear trap I could not seem to escape completely.

I had to get hold of myself. I splashed my face with cold water and looked at myself in the mirror, and was reassured by what I saw there. I was blue-eyed Jack Tripper. I was strong.

Bernie had said a storm, but he might as well have told me a bomb was coming. Hearing his voice felt like an explosive intrusion all by itself, but a storm could do large-scale damage, knock out windows, fuck the plumbing, do things that were beyond my power to fix. Though I hated Bernie in that moment, and wanted to believe that he was an overreacting, contract-breaching twat, a more practical part of me remembered the small radio I had in my bedroom, and reluctantly I sought it out. Prerecorded programs specific to the seventies and eighties had been inserted into it via a microchip, but it still worked as a regular radio. At first there was only static, even on the emergency broadcast channel. However, as I flipped stations I heard the barest hint of a cheerful commercial jingle. Music followed, and then a DJ came on with obnoxious chatter about the latest disgraced celebrity, interspersed with audio clips of a cooing woman getting spanked.

Aha! Everything was fine. Nothing championed the status quo like smug, shock-jock comedians. I turned off the radio and returned it to its shelf, idly pondering whether Jack, Janet, or

Chrissy feared thunderstorms. My mother had always enjoyed them. She would stand at the window and watch while they rolled in, smiling to herself, as if she and the clouds shared a secret.

I shook my head as if to shake the memory away. *Still thinking like Bonnie, I see*, I scolded myself. I straightened my shoulders and returned to the kitchen. Determined to put the end of my world out of my mind, I resumed chopping vegetables, my hand quivering only slightly. Outside, the sky turned a sick gray.

Two hours later I was feeling better and making a roux. The sun had set, and the kitchen was shining its warmth around me, the heat from the stove shimmering the air. Fifteen minutes earlier Chrissy and Janet had arrived home and called hello to me through the kitchen door, and I was now half listening to the domestic sounds of a Thursday evening—the distant chatter of my roommates, a toilet flush, a bedroom door opening and closing, a gentle rumble of thunder outside, the low buzz of the television sputtering to life—when a terrific BOOM split the air, and something flashed faintly in the sky, and the lights around me flickered and then died, and the refrigerator shut off with a hard thump, and the stove was gone, too, and with this sudden change the sounds of my roommates ceased as if they were pinched into nothingness, and I was utterly alone.

Everything—even the lights outside, beaming in from the street, or from nearby buildings—blanked out. I went rigid as if I had been switched off, too. The darkness and silence engulfed me. I waited for a flicker, sure the backup generator would kick on any minute, but there was nothing.

Time passed, maybe whole minutes. There is something about sudden, utter darkness that renders a person temporarily senseless, disoriented. However, after some moments the sound of the refrigerator's motor ticking off penetrated the silence, returning me to this room, this reality. I could smell the roux again, the only tangible signal that I was still alive, and in the blackness the smell seemed like a sinister, wordless taunt, the one thread left of the world that had been ripped away. I let go of the whisk, letting it sink in the pan, and I turned left, then right. In the living room, the canary screamed.

How I depended on the light! I hadn't realized how much electricity reassured me at all hours that the world was far larger than me, and always would be. And the hum of everything, my daily background noise, was now gone. In the dark, Geannie and Jim's faces appeared to me, flashing up with such force I actually gasped aloud—"*Oh!*"—as if they'd materialized and shanked me in the liver. It was just my memory at work, that background noise thing, my Bonnie brain making connections, something I thought I had mostly freed myself from. But their images refused to fade, and they disturbed me so much I recoiled and staggered backward, turning around, frantically feeling the wall for the kitchen door, any exit.

I found it and fell into the living room, but it was dark there, too, and I kept waiting for the lights to stutter back on, maybe weaker than before but still on, alive, and then I was Chrissy, frantically praying to a personal God, and then I veered into Janet, trying to calm myself, control myself, forcing myself to consider logical solutions, and finally I returned to Jack, who decided to take action.

After fishing a flashlight from one of my bedroom desk drawers, I left the apartment, but before I closed the door behind me I heard the canary panicking. In a moment of softhearted-ness, I decided to take it with me. It seemed too scared to be left behind, and I still felt guilty about the dog. I went back in and unhooked its domed cage from the stand and carried it at my side like a briefcase.

Outside, the darkness was immense. An inky black well to

fall into. My brain swiped back into the past, remembering the exact landscape that surrounded me beyond the small city I'd built, the woods and mountaintop I was on where night falls fast. I raced down the stairs, trying not to trip, and went toward the mechanical room at the far end of the building, which housed the breakers. My hands shook so badly that I couldn't find the right key as I walked; when I reached the door I put the flashlight on the ground and knelt down in its beam to steady myself. I set the cage down, too. The canary kept chirping in alarm, its cries growing to a deafening crescendo, until I said through clenched teeth, "Shut *up.*" Like magic, the chirping stopped.

I got the right key and entered the room but it was no use—I threw the breakers inside over and over again, to no avail, and even the buttons that were supposedly hooked up to the backup generator for emergencies like this one wouldn't work. It was a total blackout.

What was I to do? I left the room and locked it again, taking my time, hoping that something would happen to save me from further action. But nothing came.

I picked up the cage and walked back toward the steps that led me to 201, but then I decided to go to the main house. I could check the breakers there.

As I walked, rain began to fall. Faster, faster. Sheeting. The wind picked up, and the combined force made the air feel solid, as if I were moving through an endless, wet curtain. I picked up my pace.

Following the sidewalk in front of the apartment building, I made my way to the disguised door where I could exit the city. I passed the electric bus stopped in the middle of the road, mid-trip. Looking behind me, I tried to catch sight of Arcade Florists, Mr. Angelino's, the Regal Beagle—I couldn't make them out.

The rain and darkness made everything invisible. The city had fallen away.

The rain still pouring, I found the door in the wall and put the canary cage down. With one hand I held the flashlight, while with the other I searched for the door handle. I found it, but as the hinges creaked open, I thought I heard something over the rain—a car pulling into the driveway.

Peeking through the opening, I looked toward the main house.

There, in the driveway, sat an SUV. It was parked directly in front of the main house, its headlights shining through the rain. Thinking it was Bernie again, I was about to shout at him to leave, when a figure passed in front of the headlights.

Was that—Krystal?

Behind me, the canary weakly chirped. I barely heard it. I stared through the rain, unbelieving, and watched her run up on the porch of the main house, knock on the door. The SUV's headlights spotlighted her as she waited. It looked like she was calling my name, although I couldn't hear her above the rain and wind. Not receiving an answer, she moved to the nearest window and looked in. Looked into my windows! Cupping her hands around her eyes against the glass like we used to do as kids at the abandoned houses at the edge of town, peering through dirty windows, trying to see what we could see.

She knocked on the front door again. *She tried the doorknob.* She struggled with it, rattling it side to side. She was trying to break in! Looking at the knob closer now, maybe thinking of picking the lock? She walked off the porch and stood in the rain, in the headlights, looking back up at the house. Probably thinking of picking up a rock, breaking a window.

A memory from long ago: us exploring abandoned houses

together on summer nights, creeping around the thresholds, shouldering open stuck doors. Wrapping a stray brick in a jacket, something we'd seen in a movie, tapping at a window until it spiderwebbed. The empty rooms inside echoed our excited laughter. We used to hold hands as we walked through those places. I would always go first, cautioning her where to step.

I stood there, waiting for her to turn around. Somehow I believed she would see me. Even through the darkness, even through the whipping rain.

But suddenly, to my surprise, she stepped out of the light and vanished.

I went very still. I waited a moment to see if she had simply stepped around to get into her car again. But the car stood alone, still running, untouched. The wind, which had quieted in the last few seconds, picked up again. Thunder rumbled overhead. I sensed something worse, something more sinister, was happening.

Krystal hated me now. All the nasty things she had said to me returned unbidden. Picking up the canary cage, I ran through the exit door and toward the main house. By this time the rain was pooling on the ground, and I struggled to keep my footing. My pants and shoes were soaked, pulling me down as if rocks were tied to me, but I kept going, trudging toward the headlights, feeling as if I were running in a dream, in slow motion. I believed she had gone around the back, was maybe trying the doors and windows there. My fear multiplied the closer I came to the house, picturing her breaking into the back of the house, lying in wait, springing upon me as I entered. Holding me hostage in my own house. That was Krystal's way. She would have liked nothing better than to hold on to me, to tether me to her pathetic version of the world.

But halfway across the lawn, I heard the car door slam, and

the car started moving again. I stopped abruptly, the canary cage bouncing against my thigh and falling out of my hands, the canary tweeting in protest. The rain had blurred my vision; the car was now turning around, its headlights aiming away from me, and it slowly moved back down the driveway the way it had come. As soon as its red lights disappeared into the rain, I started running again for the house, forgetting the poor canary, desperate to face whatever booby trap she had left for me there.

Walking in the front door, I adjusted to the shocking stillness, flicking on the flashlight. Rain drummed on the windows. I searched the entire house, front to back, but saw nothing amiss. The back door was still locked. No windows were broken. While I was there I checked the basement, which miraculously had not flooded yet, and tested the breakers there. Nothing worked. Nothing looked disturbed, either.

Still, I could not shake the unpleasant feeling that Krystal had done something to bring on this misfortune. I left the basement behind and made my way back through the kitchen. I got a plastic garbage bag and filled it up with cans of food, candles, an emergency lamp I had stashed in a cupboard years ago. My movements were mechanical, numb. I only wanted to return to my true home, Apartment 201, and get out of this night.

I returned to the front porch and stood there for a few minutes. In the pitch dark the rain sounded like it was slacking a little, but it went on and on, and I couldn't stop it. I suddenly remembered the bird. The poor bird. I had left it behind in the yard. And the whole point of this mission had been to not leave it alone, to assuage its fear.

As I stood there, about to step off the porch, lightning struck. A sound like high-tension wire snapping cracked through the air, and everything lit up like daylight, brighter than daylight, and in the flash I saw its target, my eyes widening.

The brass canary cage.

A shower of sparks exploded but immediately died in the downpour, the darkness all-enveloping once again, the lavender afterimage flashing in my vision. Damp smoke reached me, an electrical smell of something ruined. By this time my flashlight was flickering, but I jumped off the porch and ventured toward the smell until I reached the birdcage. In the beam of my flashlight I saw that the lightning had split the cage open and curled the bars back in a wicked, uneven pattern, blackening them, and somehow it was sitting upright. The canary lay on the bottom, perfect and dead. It looked like it was sleeping.

For a few minutes I stood in the rain, not knowing what to do. Finally, slinging the garbage bag of supplies over my shoulder, I picked up the cage, which was still warm, and continued on my way. I couldn't tell if I was crying for all the rain.

I returned to Apartment 201 and locked the door behind me. Immediately I stripped down and changed into dry clothes. Afterward I lit some of the candles, trying to find some coziness in riding out the storm or feel somewhat festive about it, and I put them throughout the apartment, ending up in the kitchen. Outside the window, the rain and wind picked up again.

I had left the cage on the balcony, setting it as far away from the front door as possible. I was relieved, I told myself. I'd never been too attached to the bird, anyway.

Feebly I made lewd shadow puppets on the wall, desperate to regain some of my Jack Tripper humor. When I tried to summon Janet and Chrissy to tell them what was happening, though, I didn't get a response. I called and called for them. I looked everywhere—the bathroom, the kitchen, their bedroom.

But there was no answer. They were gone, their beds empty. I envisioned them out in the darkness, running with the dog.

A deep and sudden frailty swept through my legs, my knees, but I stayed strong. Carefully I lowered myself into a chair at the kitchen table. If I weakened now, I might die. The thought numbed me. It almost reassured me. From my chair I reached for the pan that held the now-gummy roux I had made an hour earlier. It had gone cold. I scraped it into my mouth, anyway, and waited for daylight.

When I convulsed into consciousness I nearly fell off the edge of the couch. I forgot where I was and then remembered in two incestuous seconds, the sickest part of waking up. The zooming sound of aircraft had shocked me awake. Helicopters.

Sleeping in my own bed had felt like a form of denial—that would have been too normal, too routine, for what was currently happening, so I'd dozed on the sofa. Part of me, the part housed inside a box in my brain that I never opened, held a hazy impression of another violation that felt similar to the current one in scope and in terror, and from that experience I knew that if I obeyed the law of whatever action was in motion, if I let the chaos wash over me, and if I did not call its attention to the things I cherished, or associate it in my own head with anything familiar, I might be allowed to return to the life I knew. I might be spared its full wrath.

I went outside and looked up. The rain had stopped, at least. The sky was still roiling with dense, gray clouds that shrouded the day in gloom, and the wind was up. One helicopter flew west, toward the town at the foot of the mountain, and another helicopter passed it, heading east.

Stepping farther out, leaning over the balcony, I looked around and saw some broken windows. Debris everywhere, water pooling. And Chrissy and Janet were still missing, I could feel it. Where had they gone?

The emergency lights were still out. In the distance, the bus was still stopped in its tracks.

Oh god. Disaster.

Weakness overwhelmed me. Vertigo threatened. I went back inside and sat on the floor, dragging the nearest flowerpot toward me in case I was sick. For the first time, Apartment 201 looked like any other place on a morning full of tragedy—dreary plaster walls and faded furniture, dated wallpaper belonging to a bygone time. There was no comfort here. The image of Krystal from the night before came back to me. She was standing in the driving rain, looking up at the house, waiting for me to answer the door.

My chest tightened. The world I had escaped had returned to crush me in its fist. My nostalgic dream was disintegrating in front of my eyes.

I felt deranged. I wanted my roommates, I wanted the dog. I wanted people who could never be brought back. The bird had spent the night rigor-mortis-ing on the balcony inside its charred cage. And sleep had not calmed me. I had not, as I'd pep-talked myself into believing the night before, "collected my thoughts." Jack had abandoned me. I was Bonnie again, a scabless wound.

I stood up slowly, still feeling ill, and walked out again. The helicopters were beyond my line of sight but I could hear their rotors. I clung to the balcony railing and shrieked. It felt like progress, like I was doing something. Then I leaned over and puked for real, and watched it land on the concrete below. It was a curious brown, the color of the roux I had eaten the night before.

Vomiting was my least favorite bodily function. The gagging went on and on like a hurtling, brakeless train, and I felt trapped inside myself, inside this bug-eyed act, forever.

When it finally subsided and I got hold of myself, I slunk down to a sitting position, leaning against the railing. I cried like a bitch. Everything seemed at an end. For a moment I felt like sleeping, right there on the stucco floor of the balcony, but then a crazed energy surged through me, the urge to do something. Anything! A call to action! The need to go against everything I knew, everything I loved, to behave in a way that would redirect the apocalyptic, chaotic forces away from my own concerns, my own life, rose up.

I stumbled down the steps. Morning light, the bleakest light. I wanted Janet, Chrissy. For god's sake, Terri! Cindy! Mr. or Mrs. Roper! Furley! Lana, save me! Jumbled thoughts. I'd reached the street now, went down a fake alley and crawled under the backdrop of a sunny Los Angeles afternoon, running away from my city and toward the woods.

At the tree line I didn't slow down and before long I tripped. I fell hard, scraping up my wrists and forearms and momentarily stunning myself into clarity. The dog had run away the night before. That was the sign, the secret to all of it. Ray's revenge. I envisioned the dog running a hundred miles just to drag Krystal to where I was, just to teach me a lesson in humility. Like a vindictive, shorter-haired Lassie. If I could find the dog, appease it, I would find Chrissy, Janet, possibly the solution to the destruction behind me. Possibly I could reverse the whole thing! This was all a misunderstanding, I was convinced.

I could feel my own Bonnie-ness in my veins, poisoning me. My breath came ragged and the cloudy day became darker, darker the farther I ran. Soon I was deep in the woods where the treetops grew so dense they simulated a cave. When I looked back I could not distinguish any buildings, or see the edge of the forest. I had no idea how to return to where I'd started. This only renewed my despair. It started to rain.

I had succumbed to the chaos, lived inside it for only a minute, and that was where I would die.

A white flash appeared to my right. The dog! The dog, the dog, the dog! I almost barked. In my mania I wondered: Would the dog prefer barking? Over my human language? It seemed reasonable. I barked at it, yelled unintelligible things. I scrabbled through the bushes where I thought I'd seen it, but found nothing but dirt and leaves.

I lay on the ground and wondered how long it would take to starve in the woods, already giving up on finding my way back. During my time living as the characters, my thinking had become somewhat one-dimensional. My problem-solving skills had dulled down. Because of my commitment to my project, my capacity to reason well in terms of *the real world* had diminished, like an atrophied muscle.

The dog, or what I thought was the dog, moved again. It was a dirty white, low to the ground, and I stood up and kept barking. When I wasn't barking I was yelling for Janet and Chrissy. I spoke to them like I'd speak to them back home, as if they were standing in front of me. But they were nowhere. And I, as Jack, felt gone, too.

The white thing flashed again, closer, much closer. Within lunging distance. The next time it appeared I catapulted myself at it, arms wide, meaning to grab it in a bear hug. Time slowed as I flew through the air, toward the thing I thought was the dog, the reality-healer, whatever, and I could see each nanosecond crawl by in a scarlet suspension, my own blood.

I missed. I landed facedown, arms empty. For a moment I just lay there, panting. Then I heard a sharp crack, and the bark of a nearby tree jumped off its trunk.

I knew a gunshot when I heard it.

Brown tile floor. Hernan's blood in the grout.

I stood up this time. Turned around. But it was always too late.

I heard another crack, and the lights blinked out.

The world was gone. Now there was only pain, and my skull was full of it, a sack of fire ants climbing in and out of it. When I came awake I could see nothing but a gray mass with a rough texture. Cotton. Someone had wrapped cotton around my eyes.

"Hey now," a voice said, frightening me. It was not Chrissy's or Janet's voice. A stranger. I grabbed at my eyes, tore off the covering.

I was in the main house, on the living room floor near the wall. Dull afternoon light blurred across the bare floor. I'd never gotten around to furnishing it. The folding chairs I used years ago were still propped up next to the fireplace, collecting spiderwebs that glinted in the light.

"Do you live here?" the voice said. I could tell she was tall by the way she knelt down beside me. I gaped at her, the fact of her. An intruder. Her head was buzzed except for a long hank of hair on top that was slicked back and twisted into a knot at the crown of her head. From head to toe she was clad in camouflage, the hunting uniform I remembered my father wearing every fall. Her face was smudged with greasepaint or dirt. She nudged my shoulder. "Hey. Are you okay? Can you talk?"

Slowly I sat up and leaned against the wall. The bandage in my hand, which I'd ripped from my eyes, was stiff with blood. I touched my brow and my fingers came away wet and red. Seeing my stained fingers, she smiled sheepishly. "I thought you were something else. Sorry about that. Lucky you got away with just a graze."

"A dog? Did you see a dog?" I was murmuring, my voice was thick and slurred.

"No," she said. "No dog. A rabbit. One minute it was the rabbit and the next minute it was you."

"A rabbit . . . ?"

She stood up and walked around the room, inspecting every corner. She stopped at the fireplace. "The storm last night was pretty bad, huh?" She paused, dragging her heel in the soot and dust around the fireplace. Outside, I could hear rain pattering against the window. "You live here?"

"How—how are you here?" I mumbled. I touched my head again. More blood. "How did you get inside the house?"

She rubbed her thumb over the mantel. The trail she left in the thick layer of dust was visible from across the room. "Yeah, the storm was pretty bad," she continued as if she hadn't heard me. "I guess you saw all the limbs and trees down in the woods? And you have a broken window in the kitchen." She squatted down to look at the folded chairs and watched a big spider crawl over one of them. "You're lucky you're up here away from everything. In the town down there everything is flooding out." She gestured vaguely in the direction of the village at the foot of the mountain. "They are losing their *shit*."

My head ached terribly. "Yeah," I croaked. My throat was dry. "There was a blackout here. The generator." I remembered the canary and closed my eyes.

"Oh yeah?" The woman turned back toward me. "You live here?" she asked again.

"Yes," I said.

I felt under a spell. The light in the room was gray, dim, and the empty room seemed like a yawning chasm, the floorboards running away toward the windows, far away. A lunar landscape. This strange woman could ask anything and I would answer.

"Am I okay?" It was a thought but I said it aloud somehow, looking at my stained fingers.

She smiled. "Oh, that. A flesh wound, my darlin'."

I looked up at her, taken aback.

"You'll survive," she said. "I think I'll stick around, though."

The room twirled a little and I slid back down to my previous position of lying flat on the floor. All resistance drained out of me.

"I mean I can help you." She walked over to the front window and looked toward the buildings at the edge of the field. "What have you got going over there?" When I only scowled weakly in reply, she shrugged. She kept talking and talking. "I like it. Looks like a pretty strong place." She paused. "The storm is only the beginning, you know. The news is wild."

I grunted a response, my head a red haze of pain. The quiet spun out forever as she stood there looking out the window. She seemed to be looking at the city, at the tree line, performing calculations in her head or checking for intruders.

I waited for her to insist on taking me to a hospital, and I tried to formulate a response, the words slipping through my brain like oil. But she didn't. My wound seemed to matter little to her. Because of this, because of the distraction of pain, because of my desperation, I did not fear her.

Which made me afraid.

"How did you get inside this house?" I asked again.

She turned toward me. "I think I can get your generator back up and running. Maybe. If, uh, the storm didn't blow out everything. What kind of casing did it have?"

"Unnnhh," I muttered, trying to communicate that I had no clue. "How—"

"What killed it, lightning? Or the wind?"

Beyond the pain, beyond the fear, my thoughts solidified and my heart piqued—here was help, and it was only one person, not a horde. Not a total end. From her dress and demeanor I gathered that she was a signifier of nothing, a lone agent, ignorant of what I was doing here. One fringe character can recognize another without too much trouble.

"Maybe lightning," I said.

She nodded. "I'll take a look at it."

I leaned my head back against the wall. Was she a blessing? Was the pain I felt now the sacrifice? "Generator's in outbuilding three." I pointed. "That way." I swallowed, my mouth dry. "How did you get inside this house?"

She looked at me, and for a terrifying moment I thought I had misjudged the whole situation, had been tricked again, had handed the power source of this operation over to the enemy. But she only smiled.

She said, "The door was open."

Then she disappeared into the kitchen, leaving her pack on the floor. When she returned she had a sponge and a bowl full of water, a half-empty water bottle, and two Advil. "For you," she said, and after I swallowed the pills I said, "Thank you," and went back into the nothingness.

Her name was Rita. Fixing the generator was slow going. Parts had to be ordered, and because I didn't want anyone coming near the house, I gave her cash and let her use my old pickup to go fetch whatever she needed. Each time she drove away I expected her not to return, but she always came back. After parking the truck she gave me a report on the state of the outside world, though I hadn't asked, and handed me any change, though this always embarrassed me. She also brought back barrels to collect rain to flush the toilets and bathe. We mostly ate out of cans, and sometimes we built a fire in the large kitchen's fireplace and cooked rice and beans. The sky remained cloudy for a while after the storm, and the rain came and went.

I had not ventured back into my city since she arrived. Instead, I'd moved from the main house's living room floor up to the room where I'd lived during construction. Each morning she appeared at my bedroom door to play doctor. She took my temperature and believed ibuprofen was the cure for everything. I tried to wave her off, but it didn't do much good, and I was in a weakened state. When I was shot I had fallen and hit my head, and as a result I had a giant goose egg and kept having dizzy spells, which made getting around difficult. For the first few days I was nearly bedridden, ruminating on the events of the night of the storm, Krystal, all the broken things I could not fix. Sometimes when I fell asleep I woke to frank vertigo, a terrifying phenomenon, and when Rita found me she'd have to help me walk to the bathroom. I was at her mercy.

I was wary of her. I didn't want another Ray or Krystal situation. But as the days elapsed I sensed no agenda from her. She was right, where the bullet grazed me was only a flesh wound, and she had taken it upon herself to stitch the wound shut, just to be on the safe side. I'd woken up one morning with half a tube of Neosporin slathered over my forehead. Her stitches were perfect, small and tight, a miniature train track of black thread. I started looking forward to her company there in that impersonal room, though I missed my roommates. After a few days I could at least sit upright without any major episodes, and I would stare out the front windows toward my real home. I worried about all the broken windows I remembered seeing, the puddles of water. Had they receded without me? What decay was taking hold while I was stuck here, a prisoner once again of my own body?

One afternoon, while giving myself a hand bath at the bathroom sink, a violent spinning hit me and I fell to the floor. I thought Rita had been outside somewhere, working, but somehow she heard me, came running. The panic of vertigo erased any shame I had in my nakedness, but she threw a thick towel over me anyway, and gathered me in her arms, carrying me to the bedroom and gently setting me back down in my bed. She sat beside me, making sure my pillow was straight.

By this time the spell was easing somewhat, and I was able to speak. I thanked her. She rose to go, to leave me to it, but I stopped her. Without looking at her I reached out and grabbed her wrist, which was nearest to me. "Stay," I said, surprising both of us. "I want some company."

The canary, afraid to be left alone.

The side of the bed sagged as she sat down again. "Okay, sure. You all right? Do you need anything?"

I wanted to shake my head but I couldn't. My eyes kept

pulling to the right. If I moved my eyes too much, outright vertigo threatened. "I just thought . . . we could talk." Realizing how pathetic that sounded, I amended, "It might help distract me."

"Okay. What do you want to talk about?"

"I don't know," I said to her. We both went quiet. "Why were you hunting rabbits?"

I heard her snort. "Oh. Well. I like rabbit."

"You eat rabbits?"

"I eat pheasant, squirrel, whatever I can find. I'd eat the Easter Bunny if I caught him."

My eyes were still dancing. I stared at a fixed point to steady them. Her voice was playful, yearning, as if she could have eaten a rabbit right then.

"Not much to a rabbit, though, is there?"

"You'd be surprised." She sounded amused. "Do *you* eat a lot of rabbit?"

"No," I said. "Not anymore." The dizziness was slowly abating. "My dad used to hunt."

"Ah," she said.

"I think he ate the Easter Bunny a few times."

I was quiet for a moment. I could not look at her. I kept staring at the corner of the window.

Suddenly, unexpectedly, I felt her fingers brush my neck. "What is this?" she asked.

"Nothing," I said, alarmed. I put my hand up to cover it. "A scar."

"Clearly."

I held very still.

"Sorry," she said, and immediately pulled her hand away.

I closed my eyes. "Where are you from?" I asked lamely. "How did you learn, you know, how to do all the mechanical stuff?"

She sighed. "I'm not from around here. I kind of found myself here." A pause. "I think I used to be a mechanic in a past life. I think I travel around a lot."

"You 'think'? You don't know?" I felt her looking at me.

"Do you know how you got your scar?" she said.

I could finally look at her. Slowly I sat up.

"I think I do," I said. And we both smiled.

•••••••••••

Slowly, over a couple of weeks' time, the dizziness grew less intense and I could get around on my own. I found that I missed Rita visiting me in my room, and, not having much else to do, I began following her around as she fixed the generator and replaced broken lights and wires. Her knowledge of machines seemed mystical to me. Where I was stymied by anything more complex than a screw, and might have stood around for a whole hour, mealy-mouthing about next steps before ransacking drawers for an instruction manual, she would take a wrench and start twisting and yanking with full enthusiasm.

She had a sudden, unexpected sense of humor, her face a mask of guarded solemnity one second, her lip wryly curling with a blunt joke the next. Sometimes her humor was mysterious; I often felt like she was sharing an inside joke with me I didn't fully understand, but felt privileged to be let in on.

Like me in a past life, she did not like to be surprised. Once, when I visited her in the outbuilding where she was working on the generator, I must have entered too quietly. She was hunched over something, fully absorbed. Metal parts clacked, and for a moment I watched as she ran her hand over her face. It was warm in the room.

"Hey there," I said.

She jumped, frightening both of us, but when she turned to face me, the look in her eyes—

Murder.

I stuttered an apology, backing out of the door, running the rest of the way back to the house, my head swimming.

That night, I didn't see her. I kept listening for my truck engine, waiting for her to drive away forever. Maybe she would walk back into the woods the way she'd come.

The next morning, though, she was downstairs, sitting on the kitchen floor near the fireplace, opening a can of beans. I heard her rattling around before I saw her, so I made sure to clomp in noisily. I sat down six feet away from her and concentrated on opening a can of beans for myself.

After a minute she said, "I don't like being scared." Her voice was matter-of-fact.

"I understand," I said.

"No." She stood up and looked down at me. I gripped the can opener and looked back, thinking she was going to say something, but she started pacing instead. She went over to the window overlooking the porch and the field beyond. "I was in prison, see."

I only nodded. Living the sheltered life that I had, I had never known anyone in prison. In the show, I would not have met anyone else who was in prison, either, until Season 6.

"I don't know why I'm telling you this." She started gnawing at a thumbnail as she stared out the window. "I got out and now I'm here."

"What did you do?"

She looked back at me and spit out her hangnail. "To get in or get out?"

I shrugged.

"Whatever they said I did, I did it a long time ago. I wasn't in my right mind back then. Just a kid. But then I got better. I worked on machines while I was there. I learned a trade. I used to be on pills, I used to smoke cigarettes," she said, and rubbed her eyes, her whole face, "I used to do so many things. But now I'm out and now I'm here."

Not knowing what to say, I just kept nodding.

She let out a short, bitter laugh. "That was a long time ago. I've been traveling around, looking for somewhere that feels right. I looked and looked and I never fit in, you know? I keep wandering around, seems like forever."

She suddenly dropped down and sat in front of me on her knees. "But here feels right. I can't explain it. Something feels right up here, on this mountain." I stared at her. She took my hands. I was still holding the can of beans and can opener. "Don't worry, though. I promise no one will bother us while I'm here."

I stared at her. "How can you promise that?"

"I promise, I won't let them ruin it. I will kill them if it comes to that."

The thought of Krystal returning occurred to me. I looked into Rita's eyes, and darkness floated there, an abyss. I believed her.

"Okay," I said.

And we resumed our breakfast like nothing had happened.

This new information, along with the general crisis of the larger situation, helped distract me from my usual paranoia. Part of me still felt like I had felt the morning after the storm—that I was being borne along on a wave of uncertainty, each day a widening hole in the reality I had spent three years creating, and Rita was just another part of the scenery I had to give myself over to for the duration. If she could protect me from intruders, from Krystal, so be it. Still, I hesitated to show her my project. I didn't even risk sneaking off by myself to visit it, in order to avoid the possibility of her discovering my absence—for so long I had been so adamant about protecting it from others, it was my natural instinct to resist sharing it. The more time I spent with her, though, the more the possibility opened, like a pinhole in a camera.

Something about her quieted something inside me, as if she had answered a question I'd never heard spoken aloud.

I still didn't know where she slept. Twelve days after her arrival, the first time I could get out of bed without feeling like falling, I couldn't sleep. I sneaked down the back steps, wondering what I would find. There, on the living room floor, in the corner furthest from the front window, lay Rita, curled up, using her pack as a pillow. She looked like every sleeping creature looks, stupid and defenseless, maybe dead, and her mouth was open and I detected a small line of drool. She was still dressed in her camo gear and boots. From the doorway I studied her. I stood there for a few minutes, listening to her breathe, then tiptoed upstairs.

In the morning I casually asked where she slept. She looked at me with that smile and said, "Oh, I think you know."

"What?" Then I realized she'd caught me. My face tingled with shame. I tried to play it cool. "You can sleep on a bed, you know. This house is full of them."

She never took her eyes off me. Her gaze was relentless, amused, calculating. She swallowed the piece of bread she'd been chewing and took a drink of bottled water. "I don't know," she said. "I wouldn't want to be too needy." And she smiled her smile at me, another mysterious inside joke between us.

On the afternoon the generator was fixed, I was feeling better and puttering around indoors, looking out the windows of the main house toward Apartment 201 and daydreaming, when the back door slammed. It was just Rita, rosy-cheeked from the cold that had settled into the landscape in the last week, and her face was happier than usual. I knew what that meant, and I smiled back. She beckoned me outside, and I followed her to the outbuilding where the generator was housed.

As I stood at the open door, I watched as she pushed the button to fire it up. I could sense us both tensing up and holding our breath at the same time, as if we were operating the same body.

When the machine slowly ground to life and then settled into a comfortable hum, we both breathed out air with a whoosh, and she let out a whoop, turned, and picked me up off the ground and swung me around. The sudden movement startled me, and I pushed her away reflexively, which caused her to lose her grip and drop me, and then I was sitting on my ass.

"Oh god, are you okay?" she said, immediately reaching out to help me up. Embarrassed, I took her hand and stood. She looked at me with a worried look on her face mixed with curiosity. Like she had recognized something in me. "Listen, sorry about that. Just got excited there."

I shrugged. "It's okay."

We walked back to the main house in silence. Once there we wandered around, flipping on switches and stoves, seeing if everything worked. In the living room, when I flipped on the light, I noticed her pack was still leaning against the wall near the fireplace. She had not moved it since she arrived. It contained everything she owned—a change of clothes, rations, a flashlight, a first-aid kit. Once she showed me these tiny tablets that, when mixed with water, became toilet paper. We had a big laugh over that, my first real laugh with another fleshed person in a long time.

I was standing there looking at her pack when she came into the room. "Everything looks good," she said. She was wearing the same outfit she had first arrived in. It occurred to me that all of her clothes were different shades of camo. They were baggy, as if they were a size too big. The sleeves of her shirts were always rolled up.

"Thank you so much for doing all this," I said. I hesitated, then said, "I can pay you." Immediately I wished I hadn't said it.

But she only laughed. "Nah. I *shot* you. I owed you one. And anyway," she added, "that'll all probably be over with soon." By "that" I think she meant the economic construct of money, but she also might have meant the world in general. "But, I gotta ask. What are you doing up here?"

I cocked my head in surprise. "What?"

She crossed her arms. "Look, you seem pretty uptight about stuff, and that's cool. I'm not here to pry, and I've enjoyed the food and all . . ." Her eyes went to the floor and her voice trailed off, leg jiggling in agitation. I think it was the first time I had seen her not completely sure of herself. "I just see all those buildings and have wondered. Do you prep, too?"

For a moment I stared at her, honestly at a loss. Then I laughed. And again I realized how good it felt to laugh, a real unexpected pleasure.

Why yes, I wanted to say, I was prepping for the end. The end of my life, hopefully, which would take place right here, on this property. Inside my dream. Whether I'd be myself at that point was yet to be determined. I shook my head. "Not the way you mean."

"Really? Then in what way?"

I didn't say anything. She shrugged. "Oh well. It's your business. I was just passing through, anyway." I detected a hint of disappointment and—hurt?—in her voice. Something shifted inside me.

She picked up her pack and slung it over her shoulder. "Guess I'll be heading out now."

"Wait," I said, surprising myself. "What if, instead of telling you, I just showed you?"

The furious arithmetic of my brain was happening just like it had with Geannie and Jim, just like it had back a million years ago before it all went wrong. I could feel Rita getting close, and I wanted her to be close. Oh, I tried to justify asking her to stay as purely practical—having someone around who could fix things would definitely be helpful. I still wasn't sure of the extent of the damage on the rest of the property. But something else, deeper, tidal, pulled me toward her.

Since our conversation on the kitchen floor, Rita had not mentioned anything else about her past, and I had not asked. I wasn't sure if the prison story was true or not, but I sensed that whatever her life had been before, she had abandoned it much like I had abandoned my own life. With Rita I had never felt, as I had felt with Krystal and pretty much every other human on earth before I left civilization, that I wanted to be rid of her. Instead of sucking the energy out of me the way most people did by merely existing, her presence gave me a second breath.

My suggestion to show her around caught her by surprise, I could tell. Her eyebrows lifted. "Okay," she said fast, as if she sensed my inner doubt and didn't want to give me an opportunity to take it back.

I took a deep breath. "Come on," I said, and we walked out of the house and toward the city's hidden entrance.

As I walked, my legs felt like lead. She would not understand, and I did not want to explain it to her.

But when we reached the edge of the city I had built, and I opened the secret door that led inside, she only looked around and said, "Whoa." Her mouth hung open. An expression crossed her face that I hadn't seen in ages, one of pure wonder, of delight.

After we stood still for several awed seconds, I guided her to the front of my apartment building and up the stairs to Apartment 201. "This is where I live," I said, "usually." Catching sight of the birdcage on the balcony as I crested the stairs, I positioned myself between it and her so as to shield it from her view. I unlocked the door, motioning for her to step inside first. I stepped in after her, breathing in the air I'd been missing.

For a moment I was nervous, my stomach fluttering over the next sentence, but then my heart clenched when I saw that many of my plants were suffering, and a few of them had died back. Without thinking, I dodged around Rita and rushed into the kitchen. I got a large water glass and began watering them, starting with the small ones in the kitchen. After a minute or two, Rita poked her head into the kitchen and, when she saw what I was up to, got herself a glass, too, and started on the plants on the other side of the living room. Quietly we tended to them, pulling out the yellowed leaves beyond saving. The plant that sat near the telephone in the living room, a large schefflera, was bone dry, and Rita carried it into the kitchen to sit in the sink. She held it while I took the sprayer to it, and each of us took a moistened paper towel and gently wiped down its leaves. When we were finished, I put it back out on the side table and stepped back to admire it, and I looked up at Rita and nodded, saying, "Looks good," and she smiled back.

I resisted the urge to take her hand. Tending to this plant was, perhaps, the most intimate thing I had ever done with someone.

As it turns out, I didn't have to explain to Rita. There were a great many things that passed between us that needed no explanation.

At first, she slept on the couch, but as the days and weeks wore on, and as time did its thing of abstracting itself, stretching into infinity between the passing hours, she took the girls' bedroom and slept in Janet's bed.

I was still Jack. Despite the interruption, I slipped back into it as if I'd never left. And I admit, Rita presented somewhat of a problem when it came to sustaining my full mirage—I eventually began treating her like Janet here and there. Oh, at first it was fairly subtle, but one day I said something rather suggestive, flirtatious, as Jack would have done, and Rita smirked at me. "Excuse me?" she said, and I flushed.

"Sorry," I said. We were having breakfast in the kitchen. I was reading my morning paper—the date on it was December 16, 1979. Burning with embarrassment, I looked down at it as if it held the secrets of life, my nose inches from the print.

"I've seen the show, you know," she said, and took a drink of orange juice. She was matter-of-fact. "I know what's going on. The basic idea."

"You do," I said. I felt that old hot-cold prickly feeling grab at me, and I resisted the urge to take a butcher knife, plunge it into myself, plunge it into her. "What do you think it is," I said.

She leaned back and looked toward the ceiling, mulling it over. "Well, at first I figured you just really liked the show, but now . . ." Her eyes squinted in a thoughtful way. "Now I understand that you want to be these people," she said simply. "You're playing them. You're the guy right now—what was his name? Jack?"

"And?" I said. I sat extremely still.

"And . . ." She paused for what felt like a lifetime before letting out a small sigh that ended in a burp. "And I think it's pretty freaking impressive, if you ask me." Sitting back in her chair, she waved her hand around. "Just look at all this. You have it down to the last detail. I gotta hand it to you. I mean, I found all the clothes in the drawers and closets in my room, but there's nobody else here . . ." She shrugged. "I knew something was up. At first I thought you were a little crazy, but you seem pretty normal." Then she leaned forward. "*Are* you crazy?" Her voice was soft, mischievous.

I gave a weak laugh. "I sort of have to be, to do it all."

Rita nodded. "So, what do you do during the day? When you disappear?"

So she had noticed. Of course she had noticed. Calmly, slowly, stuttering at first, I explained to her the basic gist of what my days were like. What my plan was. The project on a macro level. It didn't feel so terrible now that we had been living in this peaceful arrangement for a few weeks, though part of me still balked at this betrayal of myself. I still wasn't sure why I trusted Rita. I could have been ending it all, right then and there.

When I finished, she sat back. She sat like a man, knees spread casually, one arm slung over the back of the chair. Her eyes sort of narrowed and she said, "You don't act rich."

I didn't know what to say to that. We hadn't been talking about money. Though maybe, in a way, we had.

Sitting up straight, she put both forearms on the table and

smoothed the yellow place mat with her hands. "I want in," she said.

"What?"

"I want in. I want to try it. What do you think? Can two be company?"

My face must have betrayed my horror, because she put her hands up and backtracked. "Hey, sorry. I just thought, you know, it might be fun."

I was speechless. Though an idea was forming.

My term as Jack Tripper was coming to a close. In a couple of weeks I would move on to my next iteration, but which one?

I had decided, months before the storm, before Rita, that I would be Mr. Roper next.

I told her this slowly, the idea gaining power as I spoke the words, but she caught on right away. "Yes! I'll be Mrs. Roper!"

"But you have to commit completely," I said. My voice was so stern that it didn't betray my manic heart that beat *NoNoNo* into my ears as I spoke. "You can't laugh at the premise of it, not even once. You wouldn't be acting, you would be *living* as Mrs. Roper. So you can't go in and out of it like it's all an act, because it's not."

Her face became serious. She said, "Hey, cross my heart."

....

Down in Apartment 101, I began the preparations for moving. There was very little to do in the way of actual moving—all the clothes had been waiting for me all this time, hung in the Ropers' closets in vacuum-sealed bags, and the food could easily be carried down from upstairs in an hour. Otherwise, everything that was needed to become the Ropers was there, down to the toothpaste in the bathroom.

I tried calling Bernie to reinstate the food deliveries. After the storm interruption I'd discovered enough canned food to last for several months, but to be on the safe side I figured I would resume deliveries. Nobody picked up when I called Bernie's phone, so I went through the backup list. No answer, no answer.

Finally, I called Mr. Larwin's private line. He picked up on the first ring. "Miss Lincoln!" he exclaimed. "I've been *trying* to get in touch with you! I even thought about coming to see you, but"—his voice lowered—"it was against the contract, and you *explicitly* stated to stay away, no matter *what* . . ."

I assured him I was fine, relieved to hear his voice, my only arm to the outside world. I instructed him, however, to ask Bernie to return, to pay him whatever it took to get him back. "If his family needs money after the storm, see that he's taken care of. And tell him not to come find me again."

Larwin sounded surprised but said, "Oh yes, oh yes, that can be arranged. No problem at all! Now, Miss Lincoln, I just want to make sure you're all right . . ."

"I am fine, Mr. Larwin, and that will be all. Thank you." I hung up.

A week later, right on schedule, Bernie returned. Rita and I hid from sight and watched him come and go, just to be sure. I was worried that my generosity might somehow pique Bernie's curiosity, or encourage him to enter the city as before, even against the instructions. However, he showed zero interest in his surroundings, not even a head swing around when he first emerged from his car. As far as I could tell, he resumed his duties as if he'd never left them. I was relieved.

Soon it was New Year's Eve. By that time Rita had repaired most of the electronics we used, though some, like the portable radio and the TV in 201, were fried beyond repair. Luckily I had extra DVD players that still worked. Imagine my pleasure when I discovered this—it prompted a six-hour binge of us sitting and eating ourselves fat on the couch. I didn't even bother going to 205; with Rita's help I dragged the newer TV from 205 to 201, and we watched it there, the old TV pushed aside for the occasion. Somehow Rita's presence had a way of relaxing my rules.

New Year's Eve fell on a Tuesday evening, and all that day I had been dyeing and trimming myself into Mr. Roper, and I donned the ugly cardigans and polyester pants he wore. When I finally emerged from the bathroom of 201, Rita, still wearing her usual clothes, jumped off the couch. "Oh, Stanley!" she said.

I gave a Stanley snort, though inside I was utterly delighted. "I think it's time to change locations, what do you think?" I asked her. "I have something for you."

After turning off everything in the apartment and locking the door behind me, I led the way downstairs, to the front door of Apartment 101. The air outside was bitter cold and felt like snow, the clouds a thick, gray mask above us. The silence was absolute. Our breath smoked as I unlocked the door.

We went in and turned on the lights. Rita found a record player in the living room and put on an album of romantic standards while I checked the kitchen to make sure everything was in order. It was.

"Now," I said, returning to her. I crooked my finger and beckoned her down the short hallway. In the cloyingly pink bedroom I opened the wardrobe and showed her Mrs. Roper's muumuus. I laid a pink one out on the bed, the same one Mrs. Roper had worn in the pilot of the series. Beside it lay the red, curly-haired wig and heavy costume jewelry, a ring for every finger and two necklaces. "What do you think?" I said. My stomach was knotted up. This would be the test.

She smiled. She smiled!

She scooped up everything and went into the bathroom.

I waited on the bed and then, realizing the error, darted to the bench at the foot of the bed. Staid Stanley would not be caught dead on the bed. After a few minutes I felt restless and began pacing. Why didn't I go out to the living room? I wondered. I could leave this room at any time.

Just as I was about to follow my Stanley instincts, the bathroom door opened.

Helen Roper emerged. Tall, dazzling Helen. The wig complemented Rita's face, made her look daring and jaunty somehow, and the jewelry sparkled around her as if emitting its own light. She looked as if she were more three-dimensional than anything else in the room. The bottom hem of her muumuu was a little short.

"Oh, Stanley!" she said again in an exaggerated tone, and I laughed. I was standing by the bureau near the bedroom window. "What do you think?" she asked, twirling around.

I stood there like a brick. "I don't know what to say."

"Oh yeah?" She came closer to me so we were standing face to face. I looked and looked at her. Every time I saw her I felt like something was being smoothed within me, a rough patch I forgot I had until I laid eyes on her again.

In the living room, the record reached the end of the side and turned itself over automatically. We both heard it click, and listened to the first notes of the second side begin to play. It was a slow song full of longing.

"And what now?" she said. "What are we supposed to do now?"

We were standing very close. At some point she was touching my arm. She was leaning down and kissing me, her tongue slipping past my lips, her hands on my face, then my neck, and her arms were gathering me to her. And then I truly was Mr. Roper, unable or unwilling to comprehend love, or what it was to receive love—any kind of love—and scared of being subsumed by a body, or by desire. But I also wanted it, my insides now one fiery, throbbing mess. And though I was afraid of wanting it, there I was, getting it.

Outside, beyond the window, night was falling, hurrying itself into a new year. Tomorrow the newspapers would start over again in 1977.

Rita took me by the hand and led me to the bed. I sat down, and she stood before me, holding both of my hands. "What do you say," she said softly. "Is this okay?"

I nodded and swallowed. My eyes were closed, and then I opened them.

We lived life as the Ropers for a year, and then another and another, losing track of the days except when the seasons told us it was too hot or too cold, or when it snowed and we had to suit up as our old, original selves and shovel and salt the stairs and walkways. Time passed smoothly. The days flowed in and out of one another like a thread being woven in an infinite cloth.

We rewrote history when it came to the original characters. I cannot say we hated one another, not even sometimes, and we rarely fought. Sometimes we forgot about being the Ropers entirely and lapsed into our other selves, laughing and helping one another, avoiding discord. Some days I wondered where this gift had come from. It hadn't seemed possible at that point in my life, that luck would come again so completely. I wondered who Rita was, where she'd come from, what her full backstory was beyond the few things she had shared, but I kept the questions at a minimum. It was a kindness I was returning. She never asked and I never told her about the robbery, or about Geannie or Jim or Hernan, or Krystal, or the lottery. Miraculously, she had never even asked where the money came from. Where would I have even started had I told that story? And what did it matter now?

The truth was, at the bottom of everything, I had succeeded. I had achieved my dream. I had muscled my way out of my old life, wrapped myself in a new cocoon, and wriggled out born anew. I had jumped timelines, and I had even brought someone with me, and together we lived on an alternate plane, inside

another time. People who declare things impossible lack a ruth-
less imagination.

Each day was a gift. As Mr. Roper I made the rounds on the
apartment building every morning. I kept the plants in 201 thriv-
ing. Jack and Janet and Chrissy came back to me, and I went to
see them regularly, though I never stayed long. Sometimes Helen
came with me, having more mechanical experience than I had,
and took care of anything that went awry. She was very handy.
In the evenings I would cook, or she would make us peanut but-
ter sandwiches, her nails black with grease from whatever she
had been doing with one of the vehicles she drove around the
property to keep herself entertained. It felt rather wicked and
delicious to subvert things this way. In the bedroom, too, we
reversed the narrative. Instead of running away from Helen, I
ran toward her. I was unafraid.

The days were round and full and sweet. It was an era of
golden light and gentle breezes, of falling asleep holding hands.
No dread and no fear entered in. We did not have to practice our
parts. For once I lived effortlessly, my mind as clean as a tooth-
pick pulled from a fully baked cake, and there was no record, no
history, no memory, no larger world to which I had to answer. I
was free.

But good things can never last, can they. This is the nature of good things. And finally, one afternoon in March, the phone rang.

I was checking on Apartment 301 when I heard it. At first it sounded far away, across the sea. Then its clear bell seemed to vibrate up three flights until it reached my ears, my stomach slicing at me.

Helen was downstairs washing dishes, and I envisioned her pausing, drying her hands. I could almost hear her footsteps as she moved toward it.

Earlier that morning we'd had an argument. It was about keeping pets. On a recent binge we had watched the Season 1 episode "No Children, No.Dogs," again, and in the week since then she had become fixated on getting a puppy. Several times she had broached the subject, but I always found a way to steer the conversation in a different direction.

And when she suggested it again over breakfast that morning, I had said, again, "No."

Because we were Stanley and Helen, I had never explained to her my own brief foray into pet ownership, but I was determined to dissuade her of this notion. I tried to conjure a sad scenario of pet loss I could say I didn't want to repeat, a white lie about my past that would pull at her heartstrings, thus closing the matter. But as hard as I tried I could not come up with a suitable sob story on the spot.

"I'm not an animal person," I told her as I salted and peppered each individual bite of my eggs. "And besides, a puppy would only get bigger."

"Well, of course it would, that's what puppies do," she said. She leaned forward and copped her singsong Helen voice. "Come on, Stanley, wouldn't it be nice? A dog is easier than a baby."

Uneasy, I laughed. I decided to bring out the big guns. Any hint of going off the property would hint at the outside world just enough to finally put the issue to rest. Neither of us had ventured off the property in years.

"Where would we get it, though?" I chewed my food and looked at her meaningfully. "I don't know of any nearby pet places in town."

She caught my meaning. She said, "True," and for a few seconds continued cutting her pancakes. The fingers of relief massaged me.

But then, unbelievably, she said: "I could go get one. I could take your truck."

I sat up and swallowed, the food suddenly tasting like ashes. "No way," I finally said. "No. I thought I made that clear. No leaving the property." I looked at her, mildly disturbed. In that second we were no longer talking as the Ropers. We had slipped back into our other selves. "I would have thought you, of all people, wouldn't want to go back out there for anything."

We never referred to the larger world other than as "out there." We never mentioned any familiar town names or nearby roads.

She just waved me away. "Maybe I've changed." She took a sip of coffee. "Helen wouldn't be afraid to go to ——" And here she mentioned the name of the town at the foot of the mountain.

I sat back, my alarm increasing by the second, and looked at her, but she only shrugged and made a face like, *What do you want from me?*

Breakfast was finished in silence.

Since then I'd been too upset to speak to her. I had busied myself with minor projects in the upstairs apartments instead, trying to put the troubling conversation out of my mind. I told myself I would put my foot down next time we saw each other, really let her hear my disapproval. The thing that perhaps most greatly upset me was that she was right—Mrs. Roper *wouldn't* have been afraid of the outside world. To refute her statement would, in part, be refuting the whole premise of my project. And the fact that she said it out loud—"Helen wouldn't be afraid to go to ——"—reminded me of a new, terrifying possibility: by design the characters would act upon their natural impulses, but by doing so within a constructed world whose construction they were aware of, they could transform themselves into alien versions of themselves, doing and saying and wanting things beyond these walls, these streets, this timeline.

But wasn't that what we had been doing, Helen and I, Rita and Bonnie, ever since she'd arrived? For the past two years we had been warping the Ropers into the version that we most enjoyed for the sake of our own vanity, our own quest for love and comfort, tranquillity. Sometimes for hours, sometimes for days, we flouted the rules of this reality, the ones I myself had created, and though we dressed as the Ropers and lived in the Ropers' apartment, we often spoke and interacted with one another as our other selves, the ones we had met after the storm, the selves that had arrived from a bleaker reality I had spent a lifetime yearning to escape. I had not been as strong as I'd thought, after all.

These thoughts presented a knot I had trouble untangling, and over the course of the morning it had settled in my stomach, slowly tying itself into more impossible convolutions. The ringing telephone seemed like an auditory extension of my anxiety. Upon hearing it I ran out and down the first flight of stairs, toward 101, where the door was open on account of it being a beautiful day, blue and green and warm, one of the first days of spring, but by the time I got to the second-floor landing I could tell I was too late.

Too late. The ringing stopped and Rita's voice replaced it. "Hello," she said.

By the time I clattered into the doorway, startling her, I caught the tail end of the conversation. "—let her know you called. Goodbye," I heard her say. She hung up and turned to me. I was panting, doubled over. "Why," I said. "Why did you pick it up."

She tilted her head, observing the state I was in. "I'm sorry," she said, "but it seemed like the natural thing to do. She said she was your lawyer and was going over the files, the old lawyer had died—" I stood there staring at her. "What is wrong with you?" She looked concerned and reached for me.

I waved her hand away. "What did you tell that person?"

Rita shrugged. "I didn't tell her anything. I thought it was weird. I told her I would tell you she called."

I didn't hear any more. I stumbled into the living room and sank into the couch. "We're done. We're done."

She tittered. She thought it was a joke. "What? Oh, now really, Stanley." I didn't respond. "Really, Stanley," she repeated, sounding more serious now. "What do you mean, 'We're done'?"

The flop sweat that predicted a fainting spell was coming on again. I lay down flat. "That wasn't the lawyer, Rita! I know it wasn't!" I put my feet straight up in the air.

She shook her head and walked over to the couch. All pretense of her being Helen was dropped. The knot tightened. "Calm down," she said. "I didn't tell her anything. And why would you say that? Who would it be?" When I didn't answer, her voice took on a more soothing tone. "I mean, she sounded official. I think you should calm down. The lawyer was old, right?"

I thought about Mr. Larwin. Rita knew about him, and she had witnessed the rare occasions I had spoken with him on the phone. He was old but not at death's door. He still had a decade left before total breakdown, maybe, and another decade of life after that. He was rich, the type of guy who could afford doctors.

I just shook my head, and in a hoarse voice said, "What kind of survivalist *are* you? Giving things away?"

It was maybe the meanest thing I had said to her in the entire time we'd known each other. Her face hardened and she left, slamming the door so hard it banged itself open again. I might have been crying. I covered my face with my arm. For the rest of the day, I didn't move. I dozed.

Around 6 p.m., I heard a sound from the driveway. A car.

Cars never came around here, except for deliveries, and this wasn't the day for it. From where I was I couldn't tell if it was arriving or leaving. If Rita was leaving, I didn't want it to be like this. I dragged myself off the couch and went out the door, down the street to the city exit door, and looked toward the main house.

As I realized what I was looking at, every happy year I had known drained out of me, becoming a puddle of dead, scummy water at my feet.

Krystal.

She didn't see me. It was just like before, when she came during the storm. From where I was, peering through a crack in the door, there was no way she would notice me observing her, and I watched as she swung herself out of the car and knocked on the front door of the main house.

Just like she'd done the night of the storm.

I couldn't help but try to see if she had a smirk on her face as she waited on the porch. I imagined her smirking. Bamboozling Rita with the lawyer talk, ever the proficient liar.

She knocked again.

This is it, I thought to myself. She will get back in her car and leave. Just like before. I outlined the speech I would give to Larwin afterward, how I would instruct him to get people to build a gate at the end of the lane. Or get a restraining order against Krystal. How had I neglected to do that before? It must have slipped my mind in the aftermath of the storm.

She knocked a third time. She had the look of someone about to turn around and leave, and I sucked in a slow, deep breath through my teeth, sure it was about to be over.

Then, the front door of the main house opened.

My mouth fell open. Rita, who had changed into her old clothes at some point—the outfit she had worn on the first day we met, in fact—stood in the open doorway.

Stunned, I watched as they exchanged greetings.

I watched as Rita shook Krystal's hand.

I watched as Krystal disappeared *inside the main house.*

She had been invited in. Rita had invited Krystal inside.

My brain couldn't handle it. The meaning of it. All sound faded.

After I stood still for what seemed like several minutes, my hearing came back to me. The birds were singing their last songs. The sun was setting. The dew was gathering, and the grass smelled sweet, that early springtime smell. Everything felt false.

Keeping to the side so I wouldn't be seen, I left the city and crept around to the side of the main house. I passed each window until I came to the kitchen, where a light was on. It was a high window, so I stood on my tiptoes.

Inside the kitchen, Rita and Krystal stood together at the counter, their figures distorted by the old, wavy glass. I watched as Rita moved to the fridge and removed the ingredients for a sandwich. Confused, I wondered why Rita would be eating dinner so late, and in here, but as the minutes passed I realized she was not making it for herself.

She was making it for Krystal.

To my further surprise, Krystal took the sandwich and ate it with gusto. It was gone within minutes, even the crusts.

And Rita. I couldn't hear what they were saying, but Krystal became more animated the longer Rita talked. They laughed together.

I could not believe what I was seeing. I wanted to peel away the glass to see it more clearly, to make sure it was real. They behaved like real people doing real things. Rita took away Krystal's plate when she was finished and rinsed it off in the sink, still talking.

Krystal giggled again.

Shaking, I fell back onto my heels and braced myself against the wall. I was breathing hard.

Not knowing where else to go, I walked back into the city. I went straight to the Ropers' apartment and locked the door behind me. I drew the curtains.

My mind was buzzing; I couldn't think. Outside, full dark was descending.

I didn't have to wait long. Soon there was a knock. Someone tried the knob. Then I heard voices, and a key was in the lock. Panicked, I wondered why I had never installed a dead bolt, but remembered that that would not have been accurate to the Ropers' apartment.

For the first time, I cursed my own project.

At the last moment, I threw myself against the door, holding it shut.

It was a vain attempt. Rita was bigger and stronger.

"No!" I yelled. "I won't let you in." But it was too late, the door was already opening.

Rita stood before me. Krystal stood right behind her.

The skeleton I had left screeching in the front yard of Geannie's house was gone. In the past six years she had plumped out, and it looked good on her. She looked younger. I could almost remember this Krystal fondly.

Then she opened her mouth and sound came out.

The sound was: "Bonnie?"

I felt dizzy, my body weakening.

"Bonnie?" she repeated. "I'm sorry."

She stepped toward me, raising her arms, her palms up. As if to hug me.

"Don't call me that," I said. "Get out of here." My voice was shaky, faint. I wanted to clear my throat.

Now Rita stepped toward me. "Come on now, Stanley," she

said. "It's Helen, remember? It's okay." I glared at her, thinking she was mocking me, but her voice was sweet, cajoling, and she looked at me kindly. Somehow that made everything worse.

I stared at her, her camouflage and boots. My face felt frozen in a scowl. How dare she step foot in this apartment dressed like that.

She saw me looking. "Oh, the clothes, I was going to do some maintenance work and—"

I cut her off. "I don't want you here. Either of you. I don't!" Stumbling backward, away from these two strangers, I turned and ran into the kitchen, seeking an exit. Due to fire codes there was a back door in the kitchen, god bless fire codes, and I slammed out of it, grateful for the fresh air. My knees felt a little stronger. I started walking. I went around the back of the building and waited, plotting my next hiding place in case they came after me.

After about fifteen minutes I could hear them talking, and I crept further along the wall to listen. I saw them as they passed by. Rita was apologizing for me, spilling her guts about me, about my "project," how I was "working through things" by being here. Like she had any idea! Krystal was bobbing her head, eating up every morsel of information about batshit Bonnie. As usual, she disgusted me. Nothing had changed there.

But Rita! The betrayal was breathtaking. Making sandwiches. Laughing.

When I heard their voices moving away, exiting the city, I stole back upstairs, to Apartment 201. I alone had that key.

Unlocking the upstairs apartment door, I felt total relief as I slipped inside and shut it against the terrible world. For the moment, I felt safe.

Two days went by. Three. I was under siege. In the kitchen I found four stray cans of food I had left in the cupboards three years ago upon moving downstairs, and I began rationing them.

I felt feverish, wired. Sleep didn't help or didn't come. At least the door to Apartment 201 had a security chain lock, unlike the Ropers' apartment, but it was laughably flimsy, so for extra protection I shoved furniture against the door. Each day I piled more furniture there until, on the fifth day, the door was completely obscured.

At different times throughout each day Rita would knock, begging me to open the door. At first she was beseeching. "She just wants to talk to you. Please come out," she said on the second day. "Please?"

"You don't know who she is," I said through the door. "I saw you making sandwiches." I paused. She didn't reply. I got angry. "This is *my* thing, Rita! I told you I didn't want anyone else here. Why aren't you listening?"

She may have sighed. "Come on, she just wants to talk. She seems nice. And she's worried about you. She wants to know if you're coming home. She needs you."

When I didn't reply further, Rita lightly knocked again. "She says you're a relative? Her sister?"

After that I stopped responding to her appeals.

On the seventh day she tried to get wily, told me, "She's gone, Bonnie." Called me by my old name!

And she was lying. I had heard Krystal's laugh earlier from somewhere in the distance, I knew I had. Maybe Rita had her downstairs in our apartment—what had once been *our* apartment, anyway—drinking tea and eating cookies. God only knew.

Now, there is an argument to be made here for Rita. Being Mrs. Roper had warped her somehow. It was the only explanation I could think of as to why she had abandoned all semblance of her formerly paranoid, prepper self and was now serving crumpets to my enemies and trying to wheedle me into peace talks. Helen Roper was, after all, a courteous host, a loving soul. She believed there was good in everyone, even me, crusty old Stanley.

Even Krystal.

The previous morning's nightmares were coming true. It made me sick to think my beloved characters had turned against me, were the very thing that let Krystal back in. Though it was my own mistake, letting someone else in on this project in such intimate ways. The very word "intimate" now made my face burn hot with melting regret and shame, which reflexively turned to the surest cure: anger. Holed up and desperate, my truest Stanley Roper self was realized.

If only they would leave! I would have done anything just to have them leave.

Apartment 201 was dark and remained dark. When the power surged the night of the storm, it had taken the television with it, and all that magical computer programming had been wiped from its innards. Rita had tried to fix it but failed. I could turn it on but there was only static now. Before Rita and I moved down to the Ropers' place, we had carried the other television, the one compatible with the DVD player, back to 205. All of the chairs and dressers and bookcases populating the bedrooms and kitchen had gone toward the barricading of the door, and the empty spaces they left were full of desolation. Jack, Janet, and Chrissy had left the premises. They were out wandering in the dark, haunting some other place I couldn't reach.

The dream was mortal. It was all coming apart, little by little, and me with it. Each evening during my siege I fell asleep on the couch, a guest, and the television was turned on, its snow the only thing keeping me company.

In the middle of the night on the eleventh day, the static woke me, until I realized it wasn't the television, it was a whisper.

"Bonnie!" it said. Krystal.

She was speaking to me through the front window. I had the curtains drawn, but the panes were so thin and the night so quiet that I could hear her clearly.

I crept toward her voice. I also whispered, but it was angrier, more like a hiss. "What the fuck do you want?" I said to her. "I don't know what Rita's told you, but I want you gone."

"You can come back now," she said. "I miss you."

When I didn't reply, she said my name again.

And then, in an even lower, meaningful tone, she whispered, "They're all dead, you know."

I knew something like this was coming, but my breath caught, anyway. A flash of floor tile, of a coffeepot shattering. I snorted, trying to shake it off. "No shit, Krystal," I said. I thought around the memory, concentrating on my anger. "I was there, remember? I should have grabbed the pickle jar? We've been over this." I actually rolled my eyes, annoyed. She had come all this way, and she couldn't come up with some original material? "I think I made myself clear. I want you G-O-N-E."

For a moment all I heard was the white noise on the TV behind me. A headache was forming at the top of my head. I waited for her response, anxiety building. After several moments of silence I felt a second of relief, that she had given up and gone away.

But no.

She said, "I'm not talking about the robbery, though."

One by one she named the surviving members of the main *Three's Company* cast.

"They're all dead now," she repeated. "That's what I mean."

She continued on, like a news broadcast, informing me of their illnesses, or in one case a car accident, and the ages they were when they perished.

I had not expected this tactic. At first I was shocked. I almost said, *Really?* I stopped myself at the last second.

It very well might have been true. Years had passed on the outside, and no one was getting any younger. But then I remembered who I was talking to, and I was so taken aback at the grossness of it, the sheer lengths she was willing to go to drag me back into the shit puddle with her, that I was struck dumb. I couldn't help but admire the cruelty of it. It reminded me of me. Could it mean, in these intervening years, that she had finally grown a backbone?

"I don't believe you," I said. I tried to keep my tone aloof, scornful.

"You better believe it. You've been out of the world for a while."

We were both silent for what seemed like full minutes. I prayed that this was it, that she would go away.

But she said, "Everyone back home misses you, too. Your neighbors. People you used to know at the market, your warehouse coworkers. They all ask about you."

I actually laughed out loud at that. "Get the hell off my property, Krystal."

She continued, still whispering, as if I hadn't said anything. "The thirteenth anniversary of the robbery is coming up, Bonnie. The town is doing a memorial service for Geannie, Jim, and Hernan in front of the market. They're going to raze it to build a Walmart next year. I just thought you might want to be there."

"Go *away*," I told her.

"And Geannie and Jim's house is gone, too." She paused, letting that sink in. "You'll be happy to know I never bought it. You were right, Bonnie, I had to move on, and I did. I have a good life now. But I miss you. I want you to come back with me." When I didn't answer, she said, "Look, I'm sorry about the actors, and I'm sorry for coming here, but I told you that for your own good, Bonnie." She sounded remorseful. "Because it's over now. You can come out. Move on."

She paused and said, "I don't think this is good for you."

My own words echoed back at me from a long time ago. From a past life.

"Please leave," I said again, done with this exchange. "Please." I crawled back to the couch and put pillows over my ears.

Minutes passed. Maybe hours. I didn't dare look out the window to see if she'd gone. My heart thumped in my head, fear and pain and loathing swirling together. I watched the static on the TV screen throb and bubble until I finally fell into a dead, bottomless sleep.

I woke to Rita pounding on the door again. I had stopped responding to these knocks a while ago, but she was more insistent this time, though it was muffled through the tower of furniture I had moved in front of the door.

Then glass was breaking. A crowbar dropped onto the carpet inside. I jumped to my feet, dazed, Krystal's words from the night before still rebounding in my skull.

The picture window was large, and its panes shattering sounded like water falling. I stood by the couch taking all of this in as Rita's arm snaked inside to unlock the casement before raising the window. She climbed inside, pushing the curtains away, and stood up. "There you are!" she said when she saw me. "Are you all right?"

She was still dressed in her camouflage clothes. Not my Helen anymore.

She was not a small woman, but I charged at her like a bull. She was so surprised that she did nothing, which allowed me to plow right through her, it seemed, throw her to one side, before I vaulted out the window and landed on the terrace.

The sun was so bright, another beautiful day, but the days would be beautiful no longer, I thought, until these bitches cleared off. "What's *wrong* with you?" I heard her disbelieving voice say from inside. "I didn't know if you were alive or dead! I had to do it!" Then, "I cut myself. Shit. Bonnie!"

I was already racing down the stairs and heading up the

street. The physical fact of the buildings, the street, encouraged me. I could still save this. If only everyone would leave.

Slamming through the city door and heading toward the main house at a dead run, I felt more energized than I'd ever felt in my life. I had spoiled love and rage and the shining day's sun thrumming in me, giving me power. When I reached the main house I could see Krystal inside, in the main kitchen usurping what was rightfully mine, opening my fridge, pouring a glass of fucking tea, whatever. She looked like she was making herself right at home. She was now wearing a faded sweater that had dingy yellow ruffles at the neck. I squinted. Not a sweater. Geannie's housecoat.

I threw the front door open and it slammed against the wall. She jumped.

I must have looked like I had come there for exactly what I had come there for, because she bolted. Blindly she ran through the house, but she was new here, wasn't she, and I had been here my whole life. My whole *real* life. The one that I was meant to live from the beginning. It is only through great sacrifice that great blessings can be bestowed. *Pain is weakness leaving the body! No pain, no gain!* Old clichés from fitness commercials blazed through my head. Their message was clear: *I am here to kick ass and chew bubblegum, and I am all out of bubblegum.*

I caught up with her as she spied the back door in the smaller kitchen at the other end of the house. My eyes were her eyes, I could see what she saw—escape! Salvation! And somehow I melded with her in a way that either slowed her down or sped me up, flew me to where she was, and then I overtook her and we both fell down, and I got hold of her throat and sat on top of her, but she was like an animal, wriggling, but I felt like the bigger animal, the kind that wins in these fights, and there was a full certainty in me, a total and complete surety, that I would win, this time I would win.

But I was wrong. Suddenly she jerked away and I lost my grip, and then she was on top of me. Screaming at me. Slapping me. Telling me that I had failed her, that I'd abandoned her and she had lost everything, and soon after I'd left she had developed a drug habit, and had lost several jobs, floating from place to place, and it was all my fault, all my fault—and as she screamed at me I noticed that her face had shrunk, and now she was the Krystal I remembered from that last night I had seen her, the Krystal with the fever eyes and bobblehead.

She had me by the collar and kept slapping me, words falling out of her in spit-riddled fits, and though I kept trying to get out from under her, her knees locked me in tight. I could see the sky outside the window above the sink. Her words fell out in a dense rush I could not stop, no matter how I tried to interrupt and take over. I recalled all the times I had made my case to the invisible Krystal, how I, too, would go, go, go, yet try as I did, I could not get one word in. My rage built as I listened. But at some point I started laughing. It seemed so ridiculous, her being there. Out of a television show, even. She looked at me with contempt, and I took this pause in her monologue to throw her off of me and roll beyond her reach. I tensed, waiting for her to come after me, but she stayed crouched on the floor where I had pushed her. Her shoulders sagged. She looked emptied of everything.

"Why?" she asked. "Why do you hate me so much? I loved you? We were family?"

These statements were phrased as uncertainties, which I thought more than answered her questions. Still, I decided to take the bait. "I don't hate you, Krystal," I told her. "I love you." I ran my hand through my hair, my poor Mr. Roper hair. My eyes had returned to brown. "But love don't mean a thing." I singsonged it, jerking my shoulders in time with imaginary music.

I stood up but she remained on the floor. Crying, of course. Nothing but weakness. For a moment it looked like we had both exhausted whatever energy we had just expelled, and for a second I even saw her whole body relax. But I had other ideas.

A butcher knife, waiting patiently in its dusty butcher block for years and years, left by the last owner, made itself known to me, and now I grabbed its handle. She heard its small *ting* when I drew it out of its slot. She looked at me. When she understood what was on my mind, she stood up and faced me, shaking. She kept staring at the knife as if unable to comprehend its meaning. "What—" she said. "What—" She could not finish the sentence.

She shook her head at me. "No, Bonnie. No. I told other people, you know. I told everyone. They'll—they'll know where to look. They'll come find you . . ." Her voice stuttered off, her face pale and waxy.

"Why can't you leave me *alone!*" I said in a crescendo-ing scream—again, I heard it happen outside myself, inside a movie—and I rushed at her, and the knife ran into her belly, and it wasn't nearly as difficult as I had imagined it, the clothes and flesh giving way under the blade with a satisfying, wet sound, the sound of steel meeting soft sponge, so I drew it out and did it again, both of us falling forward, hunching over, and the hot blood ran over my hand, making the knife slippery, but I kept at it, and I was on the fourth jab when she slumped to her knees and fell to the floor, grabbing at my arms as she went, and then she was yelping, hollering, but it was coming from another place, somewhere behind me.

Rita was standing in the doorway of the kitchen, looking

down on it, my work. Her forearm was in a thick white bandage, wrapped neat as a pin. She was back in Mrs. Roper clothes, a blue muumuu and beads, the red curly wig sitting atop her head.

I dropped the knife when I saw her. "You," I said. And then I blacked out.

When I came to, I was in the bedroom of Apartment 101. I had been bathed, and I was wearing Stanley Roper's pajamas. Outside it was nighttime. The air in the room was chilly and stale, like a tomb. I was alone.

I winced as I climbed out of bed—I had a cut or abrasion on my rib cage that had been bandaged—and limped first into the bathroom and then out to the living room. I expected to find Rita, but each room was dark. Everything was still arranged as I remembered.

The kitchen of the apartment yawned in front of me. No one there, either. I flipped on the light and got a saucepan down from the cupboard. I pulled milk from the fridge and made myself a cup of hot cocoa. As I poured it into a mug, I saw that my fingernails were stained brown underneath, and I picked at them. Sienna flakes dropped all over the counter. I stood there, spaced out, digging for a while.

As I finished my cocoa and went to wash the mug in the sink, I saw the note on the counter. *Dear Stanley*, it started.

I'm leaving you. I hope you understand. Fridge
is stocked and the window is fixed upstairs.
I cleaned up the kitchen in the other house.
I don't think I will come back but who knows.
Don't worry, I won't tell anyone.
Goodbye now.

Love, Helen

I let my empty mug clatter into the sink. Though it was the middle of the night, I went outside in my pajamas and half walked, half ran to the main house, the wound in my middle hurting every step of the way. Outside, the world was quiet. My house shoes were soaked with dew. I turned on all the lights when I arrived, and moved toward the smaller kitchen at the back of the house.

Nothing seemed disturbed. On the floor a long, thin stain led to the back door. It had a smeared look to it, as if something had been dragged out. It didn't look big enough for what I'd done. I remembered her blood gushing over my hands, the heat of it. I closed my eyes.

I went to the door, which was unlocked and ajar, the screen door unlatched, lazily billowing in the breeze.

The night was as dark as a well. I switched on the back porch light. At the tree line, a small white form stood looking at me, meeting my eyes, before it limped away.

*L*ife without Rita was strange. For one, I thought of her as Rita, not Helen. Which troubled me. And I missed her.

The other thing that troubled me, and something I had not expected, was being afraid. Fear was the price of love. I had come to rely on her help, and her sturdy presence had bolstered me. Now that she was gone, her absence glared at me from every second, every surface, and I became fearful of something breaking down, of a random catastrophe. Ever since the storm I had been on edge, which Rita's presence mitigated. Now my paranoia returned with a vengeance. Once the worst became possible, disaster lurked everywhere, shrouding my mind. Before, my dream had been a paradise, a playground, a place where minor things went wrong all the time in a reassuring, everyday manner that kept larger calamities at bay. Now I lived in a wonderland of failing machines and fragile buildings, just waiting for their moment to die.

And I was no exception. My body was also a machine, and after Rita left I found myself susceptible to illness, suffering from random headaches and the occasional cold, fits of diarrhea and nausea that would come over me without warning, no matter how much I watched my diet or exercised. My joints ached. My back hurt even after I took several aspirin, washing them down with a beer. I started to wonder if Mr. Roper was somehow manifesting himself in a corporeal way, my aging process accelerated to that of a late-middle-aged man's.

Still, I soldiered on. I double-checked the upstairs window like a good landlord, oiling the stiff casement lock Rita had over-looked in her window repair. I sorted out the furniture pieces piled against the door, fixing what was broken before returning them to their proper places. Apartment 201 went back to its old self. Each day I returned to the rooms downstairs and moped over my lousy life, flipping through *Plumber's Digest* and dozing off, or morosely studying girlie magazines, full of desire and sadness. My only saviors from complete despair were *Name That Tune* and *The Gong Show*, which shepherded me through the end of each passing day, and *Charlie's Angels*, which sent me into an erotic reverie that made my loins ache with grief.

At the end of the year I decided it was time to graduate to Cindy, the second blonde roommate who replaced Chrissy. Cindy was Chrissy's cousin. I couldn't bear to be Mrs. Roper after Rita's departure, and I wanted to reclaim the solace of Apartment 201, where my real heart lay. So as the year got on I let my hair grow out a little, and by December it was long enough to attach extensions to it, and on New Year's Eve I bleached it all out and dyed it a warm blonde color, and I traded my cardigans and khakis for kneesocks and short shorts and crop tops. I stopped taking the birth control pills, which relieved me of the horrible fits it gave me, but overall I found it difficult to go back to being so radically feminine—within a matter of weeks I had returned to gazing in the mirror, arranging my hair and face into pleasing contours, and I could find no joy in it.

Before I went upstairs for good, I emptied the downstairs apartment of anything perishable. I stood in the open doorway and said goodbye to what had once been such a happy place, now turned sour. Then I shut the door and pulled the lever the way Ray had shown me, switching it over to Furley's place, saying goodbye to the Ropers once and for all. Behind the shut door the gears ground as I listened. I inwardly prayed that nothing would go wrong. I had no cause for worry, though. I opened the door to Apartment 101 and it was new again. For a while, my heart was lighter.

Cindy was the shortest-lived of the roommates on the show, irrepressibly young and sweet. She was not as empty-headed as Chrissy but she was clumsy, and I adopted her way of moving through the world, which was disaster personified, slamming open doors, knocking things over, a walking accident.

I had been Cindy for nearly two months before I saw the first intruder. It was one of my off days, the days I did the restocking and necessary chores. I was walking toward the main house to retrieve the groceries (a phone call to Larwin had fixed the business about Bernie, the fink, just in case Krystal's story was true) when I noticed movement in my peripheral vision. When I turned around, I saw two young men standing at the tree line. Both of them were peering into a camera in their hands. When they saw me, they turned and ran.

In a few seconds I was alone again, stock-still, staring at the tree line. I walked to where they had been standing but saw no one. It was late February and the air was still biting, and a light snow had fallen the week before. I could see their footprints where they'd run into the woods.

What did it mean? I remembered Krystal saying she had told people where she was going. But why had they come now, why so much later? Nearly a year had passed since her visit. If police were going to come, they would have come by now.

Two weeks later, performing the same task, I saw them again. The same two men, I thought, at least they looked the same to me, standing at the tree line and taking pictures. This time they had a tripod set up. A third person was with them, a woman.

I decided to run toward them. Adrenaline shot through my limbs and I charged headlong at them, never taking my eyes off their faces. They scrambled to collect their equipment, and then they vanished. I could see the bright colors of their winter jackets retreating over the hill from where they had been standing. The three indentations the tripod had made in the scrappy snow looked like bullet holes.

Around this same time I was losing it a little, losing the thread of my original project; it started in earnest when I tried moving Mr. Furley's television up to Apartment 201. Moving the TV was purely an indulgence. Miraculously, the programming on Furley's TV had not been damaged by the fried generator, perhaps because it had been hidden inside Ray's secret compartment at the time, and my yearning to set everything in 201 right again, even if it was a terrible patch job, overwhelmed my previous adherence to keeping everything in its place.

The only snag was that Furley's television was a giant floor model, with a heavy, ornate casing that made transporting it nearly impossible. I tried not to think about Rita, or her strong arms. On my own, I had loaded it onto a dolly, and was slowly pulling it up the steps, grunting with every tug, when my Roper back pain flared up and my grip loosened for a second.

I watched, horrified, as the dolly and the TV tumbled down the steps, end over end, until it landed on the first-floor concrete with a spectacular crash, and broke into little pieces.

That loss disheartened me in a way I never fully recovered from. I had no one to blame but myself. And what was with my back? I was supposed to be Cindy, the effervescent athlete. Clumsiness aside, I should have been able to hoist that up by myself, no problem. It seemed as if the ghost of Mr. Roper had possessed me, had resurrected himself at the worst possible moment.

And where was Jack? Where was Janet? I hadn't seen either of them since Rita had left.

I let it get to me. Instead of going out to my day job as I should have done, there were dreary afternoons I sat around the apartment unbathed and unfed, moping and staring at where the useless television sat, my eyes inevitably drifting upward, drawn to the wall beyond, where the director of *Three's Company* would have stood with his cameras aimed right at me. The fourth wall.

What did this wall look like? The at-home television audience, of course, never saw it on the real show. In fact, there were a total of five walls in Apartment 201 that were completely unknown to me, one for each room that appeared on-screen. Everything in the show—every line of dialogue, every tape date and trivia tidbit, every plant, every wall hanging, every stick of furniture—all of it was knowable to me but this.

The mystery began to eat at me. For several years now, each of these walls had been decorated with wall hangings that fit with the rest of the décor, and the long-gone caseworkers had furnished these mysterious areas according to my own imagination and suggestions. Furniture that was occasionally glimpsed on-screen sat in these areas. I'd reasoned that these items had to have lived against the fourth wall when they were out of sight of the camera, *but I could never know for sure.*

That was the thing. There were so many uncertain elements of this world I had dared to improvise or change according to my selfish whim—Furley's TV was proof of that—and the guilt and uncertainty suffocated me and filled me with total desolation. How could we ever know another person's life? All the tiny details that are never relayed to us, that are kept hidden. Sloppy guesswork is as close as one can come to the truth. So who was I to say what was on these fourth walls?

The whole enterprise started feeling like a sham. A fraud. If one thing was wrong, it was all wrong. Punishment for trying to build it at all, for my own hubris, seemed nigh.

Sometimes, if I stared long enough, I could see things in the wall. Its stucco and wallpaper would rearrange itself into the shapes of childhood memories, shadows of my father. His coat that hung on the basement door in the home I grew up in, clotted with dust, until the day I sold the house.

Sometimes my mother would make an appearance, me reading to her in the hospital.

Sometimes Geannie and Jim. Sometimes Hernan. Chilly autumnal evenings would come back to me, the smell of rot and earth. I dozed and slept for most of the days, always between consciousness, watching as reality became a wavy afterimage of itself.

By then I rarely thought about Krystal's demise. Time was a river that carried me away from events in the recent past that I had not yet assimilated as reality, and in its waters these memories could easily drown, sucked under by the current of repeating days, seasons, weeks, routines. I've often wondered if it's the same in a convent, or a prison.

Midway through a March day of sulking on the couch while contemplating the wall, the phone rang. Its noise made me jerk so hard I bit my lip, but I walked over and picked up the receiver casually, as if I had been answering the phone every day for the past six years.

It was Larwin. "I've had a heart attack," he said. His voice sounded weak, the bluster gone. I believed him. He took it as a sign to retire, he said, and since I was one of his only clients, he wanted to let me know. "My younger partner Morris is taking over. I'm sending him out to meet you."

"Meet me?" I panicked. "What? No."

"Yes, he'll have to meet you," Larwin's breath was so short and shallow he was nearly panting. I wondered if he was calling me from his hospital bed. I tried to hear the beeps of heart monitors, or other indications of his location, but I couldn't make anything out. "Don't you want to know if you can trust him? You can't do that over the phone."

"I trust him, I trust him," I started to say, but Larwin cut me off. "Look, young lady, he's coming out to see you. You must sign things. I can't do it. It's a changing of the guard, you see. Even your contracts can't get you out of it." He coughed a phlegm-rich cough. It occurred to me he was probably dying. "Signatures are needed. You understand. It's all formality. He won't bother you, you can meet him in the middle of the driveway if that's what you want, and then he can turn around and go. But you must see him if you want someone minding the store."

"Fine," I told him. He gave me a date and time I forgot as soon as I hung up, the numbers meaningless.

I went outside and walked around. The weather was still cold, but with each passing day there came another few minutes of warmth, glimmers of spring. The snow had melted. I had seen the intruders three times since February, but even when I called to them in what I thought was a friendly voice, they turned and ran. And each time I ran after them, they disappeared into the woods and down the mountain.

I walked behind the perimeter of the city on the side abutting the forest. Only ten or twenty yards of grass lay between the line of trees and the backdrop that marked the city's border. I rarely walked there, as it showed the whole ass of the operation—walking on this side exposed the back of the canvas, which in some places had been torn and frayed by weather. But I craved something new. The fourth walls were demoralizing me again, mocking me with their unfinished business. I missed television. I kept thinking, If only I could be Furley! Or Terri! Terri had a definite job, bleak as it was—emergency room nurse. But it would get me out of that apartment, away from those walls! Oh, how I yearned to switch over. My plan, though, was a commitment, and the only thing I was hanging on to at that point, so I would remain Cindy for the remaining nine months.

My drudgery brought up so many questions, though. At what point does it stop being a dream when you're dreaming other dreams? Can a person strangle a fantasy with rules carried over from another place? If one constructs a separate reality, should not that reality dictate its own rules? On and on. All of these philosophical quandaries nauseated me. I felt adrift, no longer in the safe harbor of nostalgia that was the early 1980s, busied with everyday concerns. I was sinking in the sallow current year of myself, anxiety-ridden Bonnie Lincoln.

A clatter sounded to my left, near the trees. At first I thought it was an animal breaking through the brush, but the steps were heavier. More regular, more menacing. And there was more than one of whatever it was.

I stopped and waited. I could hear murmuring. Human voices. Then, up ahead of me, a group of maybe five or six people emerged from the trees.

"Come 'ere!" I heard one of them call entreatingly, as if to an animal. "Come 'ere!"

Were they speaking to me? I was too far away to tell.

"Hello?" I called, wanting to make sure they were real. Some of them looked like they were carrying camera equipment, but two of them looked like they were holding weapons. I froze.

Upon seeing me they also paused, and we looked at each other.

"Hello!" a male voice said, in a tone I took to mean he was the leader. "We didn't mean to scare you." He came toward me, hand outstretched.

Did he want me to *shake* it?

"Is that your dog?" he asked.

When I didn't answer, he gestured behind him. I thought I saw a white tail amid the brown, dead brush. It wagged and disappeared.

I stared after it, willing it to come back.

The man shrugged at my silence, bravely moving onward. "My name is ——" and he murmured a name and the name of a film company I don't remember, have blocked out. "We're just here to take some pics and video, if that's okay?"

I didn't know what to say. I stood staring for a few more

seconds. I had forgotten how large people were, how much space they took up. "Go away," I said finally. I felt weakened, drained. "You're trespassing."

Then, feeling inspired, I said, more forcefully, "Trespassers will be shot."

He kept trying to introduce himself. His tone was condescending. Each sentence involved more and more soothing words, as if he were talking down a spooked horse, and he moved closer, his hand again stretching out toward me. He was finally standing within a few feet of me. I resisted the urge to step backward, to run away.

Instead, I swiped at his hand. I raised my voice. "Go away. I have a gun. I'll shoot!"

Instantly his demeanor changed. "Jesus," he muttered. "Calm down, lady. We're leaving," he said, and turned away. He sounded offended. Most of the group were already hustling into the forest when he turned back. "Please, can we get some pictures? I can give you credit."

Something inside me reared up. It was like old times. Another male face came to mind—what was his name, Patrick? He, too, had wanted something from me.

"How did you find this place?" I demanded. "Have you been here before?" I walked toward the stranger, my anger suppressing my fear. When I came close I could see he was much younger than me, and fairly small-statured. I had a good three inches on him.

"No, ma'am," he said. And he looked me up and down in a way that felt physical.

For the first time in several years, I saw myself through an outsider's eyes. A forty-something woman, dressed in kneesocks and tight shorts. A sporty crop top spilling flesh, in March. Bleached and dyed hair, curled haphazardly, and heavy makeup.

I was no Cindy. I was dumpy Bonnie Lincoln trying to be Cindy. That's all I was to him, anyway, and who the hell was he? But my mental attempt to shrink his judgment from mattering to me didn't work.

To my horror, it mattered very much.

I remembered now. This was what happened when other people got their hands on the things I loved—my eyes inevitably became their eyes. I would see everything from outside myself, from a distant perspective, and whatever I had loved would be ruined. I would see that it was not what I had imagined at all, and it never had been. It never would be again, either. Not as long as others laid eyes on it. Their mere *existence* took it away from me.

Was there nothing in this world that couldn't be mine alone?

I ran at him, a move that had worked for me before and seemed to come naturally. Surprising him totally, I took him to the ground. He struggled but I was bigger, and I ripped the camera off his neck. I stood up and steadied myself, and then, using the long strap like a sling, whipped the camera into the dirt that was still hard from frost. It exploded, pieces of it bouncing in all directions. I stomped on what was left for good measure, crushing the lens with my heel.

Some of the others in the group had rushed toward us, and I could tell they were contemplating coming to his rescue, but a look from me stopped them. The broken camera hung from the strap in my hands, shards of glass or plastic clinging to what was left of the lens, and I was prepared to use it. They stood a few yards behind their leader, who was crab-crawling away from me, looking ashen. "Do you know how much that *cost*?!" he squeaked out.

I could now see that they were not carrying weapons—it was sound or camera equipment. A boom mic?

What did they think they were going to do out here?

"You're gonna pay for that!" the twerp on the ground shouted. With some swaying he finally got back on his feet. "You're gonna pay for that!" he repeated.

I took a big step forward and shoved him. "Get out of here! I have a gun! I'll call the police!" I gestured toward all of them. "Trespassers!"

He staggered back, blinking and bending over, his hands on his knees as he caught his breath. He was looking at me again, and I saw something click in his face. His eyebrows lifted. "Hey, you're the lady, the one from—" Straightening, he finished his sentence. "You won the lottery, right? The woman who was in that robbery?" He said the name of my hometown. "At a market?"

He was looking away from me now and toward the sky, as if plucking the memory out of the air. "A family was shot. And you were . . ." His eyes fixed on me again and I watched him doing the mental math, calculating the events he assumed added up to the creature who stood before him. "Scheele's Market?"

"Get off my property, you fucking asshole," I said, his words shrinking me down into one tiny, shuddering locus, my imagination forsaking me. The past rushed back at me like a fist, the force of it taking my breath away, stinging my eyes. This is all I was to him, to every one of them. A girl who was raped in a news story, who won money. An object of pity. Of contempt.

For all my ambition, for all my imagination, for all the lives I had lived after that event—and had lived happily—for all of that, I was small.

And then, through my haze of anger, I noticed him glancing back over his shoulder and imperceptibly nodding, as if to say, *Are you getting this?*

A few of the people standing behind him had their screens

out. They were recording this, had possibly recorded everything, the whole exchange.

Shoving him out of the way, I ran toward them with a mind to knock the things from their hands, dispatch them the way I had his camera, but everyone scattered and ran into the trees. I followed, fury shooting through me like the purest drug. I pursued the fastest of the bunch, the ones I had seen recording. I ignored the voices of those who lagged behind me, yelling at me to stop, they didn't want to hurt me, but then I felt something shove me hard, a flash of pain as I fell forward, then nothing.

When I woke it was dark and everything smelled like an earthy basement full of water. I was outside, in the woods, and there was no moon or stars, and rain had turned the ground to mud. Thankfully I was close enough to the tree line that the streetlights from my makeshift city shone a beacon above the canvas, guiding me back home, but even that felt far away. I lay there and kept thinking about drowning in a teaspoon. *Drowning in a teaspoon, drowning in a teaspoon.* My brain whirled and the world whirled, and I went to sleep again. Drowning in a teaspoon.

• • • • • • • • • • • •

Somehow, the next morning, I dragged myself back to Apartment 201, though I admit I had to crawl up the final few stairs on all fours. My head felt like it was a million pounds, and each of them was alive, rioting, roiling inside my skull. Once inside I collapsed in the bathroom—another blackout, but when I woke again I at least had the firm, man-made floor to greet me, and hot water in the bath. Unconsciousness had done its healing work, I determined, as after I bathed and changed I felt less frayed, but after putting on my Cindy getup I planted myself on the couch and did not move. For two days I watched shadows scan the walls as a day and a night passed and another day came. As the dawn light wormed its way toward late morning on the third day, a knock on the door broke my reverie.

Fear registered within me, dully, the only emotion in three days that rose above the physical headache and emotional resignation that had infiltrated every second since the confrontation. The intruders. I figured they had come knocking on my door now, the last show of politeness before ransacking everything. But when I dragged myself to the door and peeped out the peephole, I saw a strange man in a light gray suit and thick black-rimmed glasses. He carried a briefcase and looked official. "Who are you?" I said through the closed door.

I saw him jump. "It's Mr. Morris? Ms. Lincoln? Mr. Larwin sent me?"

I rested my forehead against the door's cool, sturdy planks and closed my eyes. Life had certainly not gone the way I had wanted. Somewhere, the path had taken a turn.

I opened the door. "Mr. Morris," I said.

He seemed surprised. "H-hello, Ms. Lincoln?" His face registered concern as he took in the person before him, and possibly pity. "Are you all right? You look . . ."

"Yes, I know how I look," I said wearily. "I had a run-in with some trespassers." At his expression, I hastily added, "They're gone now."

This flabbergasted Morris. "I knew that they—but! They beat you? We must call the police!"

"No!" I snapped at him. "No police." I gestured for him to come inside and, hesitantly, he followed. I shut the door. "What do you mean, you knew? Knew about what?" My voice was monotone.

Morris sat down on the couch. I almost vomited. Strange people outside, strange ass on the couch. This was how dreams were broken. Every part of me hurt.

"Oh, well it's all over the internet, you know. 'Crazy Woman in Woods.'" His face fell when he realized I didn't understand. "Someone filmed you crushing the camera of a famous urban explorer. The video went viral, as they say." He paused. "He hadn't realized who you were until he met you. You've been quite the mystery, you know. Local legend. For years now."

I sat on the other end of the couch in a low slouch, leaned my head back, and closed my eyes. "Krystal," I murmured.

"Excuse me?"

"Oh, nothing," I said. "So these people are after me."

"Yes, I think so. Not after *you*, I don't think, but this thing you have going here"—Morris looked around, indicating the apartment and everything around it—"well, it's quite the sensation. People love classic television, you know." When I said nothing he continued. "It's hard to keep a secret these days. Everyone has to know about everything. No mystery left in the world, no privacy." He paused and looked worried. "If I were you I would hire a security detail. Two men at the end of the—"

"No," I said, opening my eyes. The curtness of my reply must have surprised him. He sat up straight, as if surprised I could speak at all. "No security. No police. If someone tries anything, I will kill them."

Morris started playing with his hands, his right hand twisting at his left thumb. "Oh dear. Well, we don't want that. No killing."

"Why not?" I said without conviction. "They're killing me. They're killing this." I leaned my head back again and weakly gestured at the room.

He turned to his briefcase and opened it. Took out some file folders. "I have some papers for you to sign. Mr. Larwin mentioned them to you, I think . . . ?" He set them down on the rattan coffee table in front of me.

So Krystal had told someone, and that person had told

someone. Now they had found me. Now, with the video, there would only be more coming. One thing I had not anticipated was that such a large property left me open to attacks from all sides. Lonely terrain lay the whole way around—anyone could come and go unseen. There could be people in the streets out-side, hiding in the various buildings—in *this* building—at this very moment.

I groaned and sat up, put my head in my hands. How could I know where the infiltrators were? There was only one of me but several of them, probably, and only more to come. Faces from long ago floated past my vision. Who was to say it wasn't people from my past? Or strangers? What did it matter? Everything I thought I had escaped was coming back now. And what would keep the hundreds of caseworkers silent now that this video had gone viral? They could disclose everything—the project, their work, the location, even my name. No one would be able to trace it back to them. I realized how meaningless the NDAs had been, how stupid I'd been. All of my precautions had been for nothing.

I signed the papers in front of me without reading them. My head throbbed, and I was finished trying to understand anything anymore. He said they transitioned the power of attorney over to him, Mr. Morris. As soon as I signed, his demeanor changed. He seemed much surer of himself, calmer. Ingratiating. In the old days I would have despised him, but in that moment I could see he was my only ally.

"Morris," I said. "How much money do I have now? Can you give me a figure?"

He did, and when he said the number out loud we both leaned backward a little in its wake. "That much?" I asked, and he nodded. "Mr. Larwin made some very sound investments for you," he said.

"I guess so." The day was still young. Not even lunchtime. I could hear the birds outside. "Do you want something to eat?" I asked him, and stood up.

There was nothing in 201's kitchen in the way of food. Recent events being what they'd been, I'd allowed my restocking days to slide. My hunger had disappeared, anyway. I indicated that we should go to the main house to eat, and said "You first" as I opened the front door. After he exited the apartment I followed, but not before turning and looking back. The place needed to be cleaned but I felt a pang of affection nonetheless, and the feeling that an era was over, of sand rushing through my fingers, passed through me. I touched my neck, the ridge of the scar still there. I closed and locked the door, then caught up to Morris and led the way.

The day was clear, perhaps the first real day of spring. The sun fell from the sky in a harsh, unpleasant way. The rain had put a hard varnish on everything.

As we exited the city, on my right, in the trees, I caught sight of unnatural colors. The intruders were back, though whether they were the same ones, I couldn't tell. The lenses of their cameras flashed in the sun. I looked back at Morris, but he had not noticed them.

Inside the main house I took him to the big kitchen where the food was stocked, and he seated himself at the counter like a patron waiting to be served. It had been a long time since I had made a sandwich for another living human. Robotically I spread the mustard on the bread and placed the cheese just so, and though a memory of the supermarket deli, the one with the bitchy boss who yelled at me to hurry up, whooshed through me for the first time in ten years like an electric shock, I remained cool, calm. I could also remember the market before that, my days behind the counter with Jim, sometimes Hernan, listening to them joke around with the customers, the smell of the soup of the day wafting up, making my stomach rumble, happy hours long gone. Morris noticed nothing, and from a distance I could hear him prattling on about futures or stocks, something boring and safe.

Outside, I thought I could hear the intruders coming closer, the clicks of their cameras, the rustle of their excited chatter, their profane feet crunching across my grass. I should have known. Escape would not be allowed. There is no escape from other humans, from being human.

Handing Morris the sandwich, I turned and left the kitchen, grabbing some large trash bags on the way out. "Stay here," I said. Like a child, he watched me leave but stayed put, chewing, too polite to follow me.

Walking out of the house, I went to the garage where my old truck was parked. There, on a far wall, were several full gasoline cans. Next to them were a variety of unopened kerosene cans.

I stuffed several of them into a trash bag and walked out. The bag was so heavy that after a few steps I began dragging it behind me, heading toward my beloved buildings, listening to the sloshing metal cans make their music.

Morris had ventured out of the front doorway of the house by this time, still holding half his sandwich at his side, when he saw me passing by. "M-Miss Lincoln?" he called from the porch. "Aren't you going to have some lunch?"

I ignored him and continued my trek. Something was breaking loose inside me. Finally! After months and months of being dead, of mind-melding with the maddening wall. After months of my roommates' stubborn silence.

Morris followed me at a distance. I could hear the city door squeak when he came through it behind me.

When I arrived in front of my apartment building, I stopped, and he stopped, too, but did not come any closer. "Miss Lincoln?" he asked. I unlocked the door to Apartment 101.

Standing in the doorway, I took one of the gas cans out of the bag and started splashing it around the living room.

From the street Morris let out a little gasp of horror. His sandwich was still in his hand but splayed out like a deck of cards because he was gripping it so tightly. He asked me what I was doing but again I did not reply, though when I made to come outside again he immediately stepped backward, frightened.

I passed by him and walked to the other side of the street, splashing gasoline on the false-front buildings.

"Miss Lincoln! Bonnie! Please stop this! Are you all right?"

I snapped around and pointed at him. "EAT YOUR SAND-WICH, YA BIG TURKEY!" For the first time since Rita had left, I was getting into the spirit of the show again. I remembered epithets that Janet had used. "GO HOME, FINK!" Janet, my favorite. I began laughing. My face was wet with tears or sweat, I couldn't tell. I swiped at it with the back of my hand.

He was pale and his tie was askew, and my words, like magic, seemed to knock his sandwich out of his hand, its limp contents dropping to the ground. I continued along the street and turned down another block, and he trailed me all the way, helplessly, like a zombie.

After a few more minutes of walking I stood in front of my precious Arcade Florists, Janet's old workplace that had been such a refuge for me during my first year here. For a moment I stared at it, remembering my days there. Then I picked up the gas can I'd just emptied at Furley's and threw it toward the window, and it was like listening to one of my own bones break. The hysteria that had been building inside me mushroomed, and

I started howling obscenities until my throat bled. Somehow knowing I had an audience made it that much worse, and it was like the old days after I had just won the lottery, when I wished only to shock everyone, to watch their faces turn to ash and vanish in the wind.

I took one of the smaller kerosene bottles out of the bag, the squeeze kind used to start up a grill. I held it at hip level in front of me. *"Let's give 'em a show, Morris!"* I hollered, lasciviously squirting kerosene over the doorstep, onto the door's lintel.

This, out of everything he had just witnessed—the window breaking, the gas on the Furley's carpet, the demented yelling—at last offended him into action. Shakily he drew a phone out of one of his pockets and began texting, and seeing this one motion—something I had forgotten in the intervening years but was still familiar to me, the meaning of it—had me at his throat in a flash, so fast I didn't even recall moving, and then I was thwapping it out of his hands, crushing its screen under my heel.

Morris turned and fled. I chased after him, reeking of kerosene, but he was surprisingly quick, and when we reached the edge of the city I stopped and watched as he ran toward the main house, where his car was parked. Within seconds he was peeling out of the driveway, but as he sped off I saw him holding something to his ear—another phone? His lips were moving. Calling the authorities?

The "authorities."

I was alone again, but nothing was mine any longer. And now I had started something that I could not stop. The living room in Apartment 101 had been desecrated, Janet's workplace had been vandalized; there was no turning back. I knew that I didn't have much time in case Morris had sounded an alarm.

The day was clouding up and rain threatened. It was the time of year when things could turn from sunny to black in minutes. I had to get going. Turning back toward my project, my heart, I began laughing again, realizing at some point that I was sobbing.

The dream was over. Now it was known, now it had been witnessed, now it was a termite-ridden structure with damage beyond repair. I had tried, and I had succeeded, but my success was mortal, like all things. I could not, as I'd hoped, transcend time, or my own body, or this ugly human plane while alive.

There was only one future for me now. The one that had always waited patiently in the shadows. In my own blood.

I retraced my steps back to the flower shop and kept walking, and began the benediction at the far end of the city, where Jack's technical college was, where Terri's emergency room had been. I spread gasoline and lit a match. As I walked back toward Apartment 201, I destroyed each building I passed. Arcade Florists, in flames. The Regal Beagle, gone. God. I stood and watched each place burn. With each match I struck and threw I felt as if I were ripping off a hunk of my own flesh, my own spirit, paring myself back down to drab Bonnie Lincoln, a stranger I no longer knew.

By the time I returned to my beloved Apartment 201, I was exhausted and high on gas fumes. An indeterminate amount of time had passed. The light seemed different. Destruction takes a while. I climbed the stairs for the last time, smelling the distant fires. I looked up at the sky, and for the first time it felt like a California afternoon: warm and smoggy, far-off burning hills making themselves known, and I willed myself into Cindy, Terri, Janet, Chrissy, Jack, Larry, the Ropers, Furley. I gripped the balcony railing and shut my swollen eyes with satisfaction, my final happy moment.

Inside the apartment, I took my last gas can and spilled it over the carpet, across the bedrooms, my precious kitchen. All the good times I had had there. The defunct TV, the kitchen table. In the far corner of the fourth wall, the dog's auto-feeder full of petrified kibble still sat, and the empty birdcage lay stashed somewhere in a closet. I had never gotten rid of these trappings, maybe my first mistake.

In Jack's bedroom, as the smoke from outside clouded up outside his window, I soaked his bed in gasoline. I struck a match and held it aloft, remembering the smell of birthday cakes and romantic dinners, better times.

I thought of Rita, those first days together, the way she would light a campfire. For a moment, I wanted to see her. I squinted my eyes to see her, trying to will her into existence again, to say hello again, to see my Helen again—but the match burned my fingers and I dropped it, a reflex, and I watched it drop the same way I had watched Furley's television fall, every second suspended.

The fire was instant and huge, its whooshing, scalloped beauty near incomprehensible. Stumbling backward, my face seared, I felt my way toward the living room couch and collapsed. I took a throw pillow into my arms and wept into its rough fabric, curling myself up into a fetal position, grateful to die inside my own womb.

The smoke was tremendous. It thickened until my surroundings were obscured and I was floating in a void. Heat was my whole body, the pain not registering at first, and when the first flame licked me I swear I felt cold, a white, brutal cold, like an ice cube on an unsuspecting neck.

Then a tugging. I was almost there, now. In the elapsing seconds that taffied into minutes, hours, I suppressed my panic and resisted running, embracing my doom instead. I tried to make myself breathe in the fumes to bring it faster, but my body resisted, and I settled for the choking cough, the manic thrashing my arms did, trying to clear the air in front of my face. I may have been hollering in outrage at the injustice of it, the end I was forced into; I may have been crying and gagging from the smoke and fear. But I definitely wanted to die.

The tugging on my arm continued, strengthened. Then my shoulders felt as if they were being lifted and shifted sideways, and I experienced a disorienting vertigo, as if my body was being moved or turned over without any reference point. "Rita," I gasped, trying one last time to see her, or maybe the dumb dog, my roommates, anything to comfort me in this final, terrifying moment.

Something was coming closer, a demon, sprouting arms that began reaching for me, grabbing at me, pulling me. My body was being dragged down stairs, over burning macadam, crisped grass, the noise of fire roaring around me, orange and black boiling overhead like a living Halloween. The demon's mouth was moving, and slowly I realized it was making sounds. It was willing me to live. Yelling it at me. Saying my name. And though I yowled and writhed in opposition, yanking myself away, kicking and slapping at its hands, it was unstoppable, a riptide that kept sucking me out to sea, trying to drown me with life. For a moment in the struggle I extracted myself and stood up, but a second after that I crumpled and fell face-first on the ground and began crawling back toward the heat, trying to get back to the fire, to find the steps up to 201, the place I belonged. But even this failed. I felt something tighten around my ankles and pull. And with my arms flailing, trying to grab hold of something, anything, the ground rushing away from me, shearing off the skin of my palms and my fingernails as they scrabbled for purchase, I was dragged by my feet, shrieking blood, out of the fire.

When the movement stopped, and I felt cool grass beneath me, cradling my cheeks, I looked deeply into the dirt, trying to X-ray it, wanting to find a home with the worms and bones and roots under it. I think I was moaning, gasping, still weakly trying to crawl away. But again I was stopped. Against my will I was turned over onto my back. The big sky above me was still there, clotted with smoke and ash. Beyond my feet was an inferno.

And above me was a familiar face. One I knew was coming.

"Don't fight me, Bonnie," Krystal said, gripping my shoulders and staring down at me. "I'm trying to help you."

Three

I have entered a new way of life now, one that smells like canned green beans and disinfectant. I live in a hospital masquerading as something else, something homey and intimate, and it is populated with doctors masquerading as regular people, dressed in jeans and casual wear. It is a large, echoing place that's always chilly and endlessly white. When I close my eyes, I can imagine snow.

Each morning I wake and a nurse attends to me. They help me into a sitting position, dress me, wheel me out to the dining room for breakfast. I am a compliant guest. I sit at a table with four strangers near the kitchen door, and as we all stare at our morning mush I listen to the industrial blender that sounds like a buzz saw. I find it comforting. I envision myself as the morning fruit being pureed to a smooth, easy consistency, the world passing in the same way fruit pulp passes over the blades, my brain holding loosely to everything. This is the only version of consciousness I can bear.

From the tiny stones of reality that refuse to pass smoothly, though, I've gathered that I'm back to the name "Bonnie." I am no longer allowed to wear proper shoes, or watch *Three's Company*, or see many visitors. And Krystal, with Morris's help, put me in this place using my own money. I've been told it's for my own good, my own safety. Here it is hard to do what you want, like hang yourself with a bedsheet, or stow away pills, or drown in a sink full of water, without a jean-clad someone politely stopping you. Outside my room is a number, 205, a cosmic joke to be macerated right along with all the other small insults of being alive.

The end of my world was all over the news, the nurses have told me, though I don't want to hear it. They tell me how they valiantly fended off reporters who'd tried to see me at the time. I listen, their kindness exhausting. The reporters couldn't have gotten to me, anyway; for two months after the whole mess, after I was first transported here, I was placed in a medically induced coma on account of my burns, and by the time I woke up, the news cycle had long forgotten my name.

I get few visitors now, but the ones who do venture in are either photo- or money-seekers, and the nurses don't stop them anymore. The photo people get their money's worth. The burns on what they say is my skin were extensive and required skin grafts that may or may not have made things better. Whenever the doctors talk I let their updates wash over me as I adhere to the old rules of chaos, trying to uninvite whatever misfortune was visited upon me, and wait for them to leave. I nod at anything they say, because compliance is painless. I have little idea what is going on with this husk they seem to think is my body.

Though I am sure none of this will last. I am sure that I'm just playing a part for now, biding my time until the next phase. I made the mistake of saying this out loud once or twice, that the universe would not leave me this way. That I was destined for greater things, or that I was destined for death. Soon afterward they put me on medication that made me crave sweets and blew me up like a balloon. I've come not to mind it, however. Now when I look in the mirror, or when someone shows me the photo they just took, I look like no one I know.

Every week Krystal comes to visit me. I torture her with silence, one of my few remaining pleasures. I haven't forgiven her for saving me. She wasn't the one who pulled me from the fire, but she had arrived with the paramedics. She has a nursing license now. If it even is the "real" Krystal. I have my doubts. She has a kid now, though it's no surprise that she's never brought the rug rat in to see me, his fat, extra crispy Aunt Bonnie. Sometimes Krystal talks about him, how he's changed her life, made her see things differently. And she's married. Married! Three years, she told me dreamily, to a man who owns a house-painting business. She has been very lucky, she tells me, but other than her outer trappings I see no sign of the Krystal I knew. The girl who sweated inside Geannie's housecoat and begged me for money, the person I was ninety percent sure would succumb to emotional delusions and eventual drug addiction, now has her hair professionally dyed every fourth Tuesday.

She's shown me her ID to pacify me, but I remain uncertain. Plunging the knife into her guts is still pretty vivid, let me tell you. But over the year I've been here, on two separate occasions, she's pulled down her Spanx to show me her stomach, and though it wasn't a pretty sight, it wasn't marked with knife wounds, either.

"See?" she said then. "You never killed me. You never even hurt me."

I took this as a challenge, but when I checked her face for a smirk, none was there. Her eyes were hopeful, entreating me to believe her.

I don't know what to make of it.

"I only ever wanted to help you, Bonnie," she said. "Not hurt you. Not sabotage you." She paused. "I was worried about you."

I was quiet for several moments. I let them think I had fallen asleep. "I wish you'd died of sadness," I finally told her.

To my surprise, she's never broken down into tears. Not when she saw me unbandaged for the first time, not when I deliver any of my cutting remarks. She's different somehow, stronger. Something about her newfound strength chips away at the ground of my being, hinting at something that lies underneath everything here, an unpleasant and volcanic underworld I can feel at all hours threatening to overpower the medications, the bland white halls, my pureed smoothie of a life. All I want now is to see her cry. To get back the Krystal of yesteryear, the one I hated but the one that was familiar, not this stoic stranger who sits across from me every week and holds my hands. How's the snow village? I want to ask her. I imagine her face crumpling. I wonder if that would do it, reminding her of all that she's lost, of what a deluded fool she was. But I have to bide my time. Our little scenes, when I'm brave enough to try them, usually land me in some form of sedation for a while, and the nurses take away my pens and paper.

None of what I say is taken seriously, anyway. The doctors like to dwell on my fantasy life. After I first confessed to murdering Krystal in hopes of getting the electric chair, they suggested I imagined it. Most of them have seen the viral video of me raging as Cindy Snow, crushing a stranger's camera. But they ignore my violence and concentrate on my "costume," as they call it. They pathologize my imaginative powers. They say it's therapeutic if I don't watch television for a while, especially not my favorite show, and I go to art therapy twice a week to fingerpaint. This, they say, should be the extent of my imagination. For now, they say. Until I get control of it. So I paint trees, I paint blue skies. At the end of the session a counselor congratulates me on my use of color, my composition, and she hangs the picture up to dry with a clothespin. I close my eyes.

I've never mentioned Rita to anyone here. I want to believe she's out there somewhere living her life. Surviving.

Lately they've been probing my past, the robbery, Geannie and Jim and Hernan, all of that. It's become kind of a game. At first I was reticent, mistrustful—I had always assumed therapy was for weak, attention-seeking whiners or for the truly damaged—but I've since succumbed to its charms. It's a pretender's paradise. Now I look forward to my sessions, where I feign epiphany and confession, all the roller-coaster emotions of someone as disturbed as their version of Bonnie Lincoln.

I demand their opinions on things. "Don't you think we become other people every day?" I ask.

Or, "Don't you think that who we are is determined by who we love?" I really want to know. "Isn't love a form of impersonation?"

No one wants to answer.

Whenever I go for a really deep moment, I glance at the therapist's face, watching their intensity grow with my near-breakthroughs and honesty, and it's beautiful, almost moving. It's like witnessing someone on the brink of orgasm. I feel like I'm doing good work, giving them the gift of doctoring, but I am getting tired. I wonder where all my games are getting me. If they are really games at all.

They say I am making great progress. They say I am on my way to recovery.

Mostly I sit in my room and stare out the window and long for an end. For release, for freedom. The final credits. My father was onto something, that's for sure. I envy his access to a shotgun. Those were the good old days. I've been writing my own history, my weak attempt not to forget, to try to form a wormhole to the past, to get back to all that I've lost, but I fear the more I write about it the more I destroy it, the essence of it. I find my descriptions have not served my memory at all. If anything, my inadequacies as a storyteller are hastening the end, proving how far out of my hands my life has fallen. Writing it down has been like trying to capture the colors and flavors of a dream upon waking. The meaning and the body of it fade away.

I have a nice writing desk. My money has paid for a fancy room that mimics a hotel suite, except the mirror over the bureau is bendable, and the bed has tasteful, foldaway restraints. There's plenty of space, at least. The windows in my room are large and double-paned, and I have a fabulous view. From my bed I can see water. I've been told that it was by my own request, before I was put into the coma, that I'd be shipped off to a hospital in California. Practical Krystal vetoed it, thinking it would be better if I stayed near her, the closest thing I had to family. And besides, California is burning, I've been told.

The place I'm in now is an hour's drive away from my hometown. It faces a large lake that extends almost to the horizon, and each evening, as the sun sets, I sit and gaze out the window. The medicine kicks in. I doze. I can see Santa Monica beaches, the palm trees, the Pacific.

In the end, we all go west.

•••••••••••••

Yesterday, after lunch, a man came to see me. He was bald and thin and carried a large shopping bag, and when he said his name, he spoke so softly I didn't hear him. When I asked him to repeat it, he said, "Ray."

Since the fire it has taken a lot to rouse me, to make me feel anything, but I was shocked, both at his arrival and at his appearance, and I was also shocked at how, in a moment, all of my previous suspicion and paranoia ran away from me. I felt so tenderly toward him that I could have cried if my tear ducts still worked normally. Instead I grunted and snorted a little and stood up out of my wheelchair, wobbling on my bum leg that's going to heal any day now, and I held out my arms, and we hugged.

He was surprised. Neither of us had ever been too affectionate. I was a little embarrassed. Either medication or time's attrition had worn down my hard defenses. But he was clearly moved, too, and he sat down on the nearest chair as I practically fell back into my wheelchair, both of us thrown off-balance by emotion. Our knees were almost touching.

An hour earlier the medication had been passed out and already it had started clouding my brain, so the finer details of our conversation now elude me. I do remember him telling me he had lung cancer, had been fighting it for a year now, longer than most, but he was worried the end was coming. He was afraid of death. I could see it in his eyes when he spoke. Part of me felt so sorry for him, such empathy, that I wished I could euthanize him right then and there. His head and face were veiny and hairless, victims of a cure that wasn't curing him, and his arms were covered in blood bruises. As for me, I was dressed in my daily pajamas and socks and orthopedic braces, and most of my hair, where it had been able to grow back, was wild, untamable. To any onlooker we would have made an ugly, sorry pair.

But he looked me in the eyes, and he seemed so warm that my heart loved him for the hour he sat with me, someone who had known me in my glory years.

"I have something for you," he said, and picked up his shopping bag. He looked around and dipped his head closer. "I thought I'd slip you some contraband."

Inside the bag was a large stuffed bear. Ray pointed out a near-invisible seam in its torso, and once he made sure no one in the hallway was watching, he unzipped the seam and slipped out a tiny screen and headphones. "I've loaded it with all the seasons. I know they said no 3C stuff, but what do I care, I'm a dying man."

I stared at it. Surreptitiously he showed me how to use it, how to put the earbuds into my scarred-over ears, how to adjust the volume, how to charge it.

We quietly giggled together, partners in crime. As he placed everything back inside the bear and zipped it up, I noticed he was wearing one of the same flannel shirts he'd worn years ago. Under it he wore a faded T-shirt that said *The Outer Banks*. Below the words was a man walking along a beach near a lighthouse, and behind him trailed a white dog.

"Ray," I said suddenly, placing my hand on his forearm, and he looked at me. I wanted to apologize to him. I had thought so badly of him all these years, and here he had been on my side all along. I wanted to confess, to beg forgiveness. I wanted to tell him about the dog. The poor canary. I wanted to share my memory of Rita, those happy days long gone.

But I couldn't. Instead, I grunt-snorted, choking up again. He seemed to understand. He held my other hand and squeezed it.

When it came time to leave, he folded the shopping bag neatly and placed it under his flanneled arm. "My ray of sunshine," I said softly, squeezing his hand, and he smiled at me. We both knew it was probably the last time we'd be seeing each other.

As I watched him disappear into the hall, I felt myself already falling away. Sleep enveloped me, the bear clutched to my chest.

⋯⋯⋯⋯⋯

Today was a Tuesday, a Krystal day. She showed up at my doorway in her scrubs and looked tired. Coming off her shift, I supposed. It was mid-afternoon. I was dressed and in my wheelchair by this time, looking out the window. I hadn't taken my meds yet. The teddy bear sat on my pillow, where I had left it that morning after I woke.

Krystal took notice of it right away. "Where'd this come from?" she asked. I was afraid she would go over and touch it, or pick it up, but she didn't move, still slouching against the doorjamb.

"From a friend," I said.

She brightened. "A friend, huh?" She came in and set down her bag, pulling up a chair close to me. "Anyone I know?"

I shook my head. "No, someone from the 3C days." This was how we referred to those years.

"Ah," she said. She ran her hands through her hair. It had one giant crimp in it that made it lie funny, as if it had been up in a ponytail for hours. "I'm glad to hear you have a friend."

I studied her face for signs of sarcasm, idly wondering if this would be the day she'd finally break and cry, or even fight back. But there was nothing.

She was looking out the window, a long day etched in her face, and in the afternoon light I saw for the first time how much she had aged. She had the beginnings of crow's-feet near her eyes, very faint, feathering out in fine creases. A small vertical line near her eyebrow that I remembered from our childhood was also visible, the one where her forehead would scrunch while she was concentrating, or casting me a funny scowl at one of my more outrageous remarks. *Yeah right, Bonnie.* It never unfolded now.

In my mind, even now, she was still her sweet and timid teenage self who had followed me around, or the grief-ravaged Krystal I had left behind on that December night. I realized that this new version had graduated all of them. Those people didn't exist anymore. Time had passed, after all.

I thought of Ray, of all the time I had wasted, assuming the worst.

The longer I looked at her, the more my mind wandered. I thought back to that fight, the one we'd had before I left. Her angry, desperate words, the ones I had been afraid of for so long. I could barely recall them now. How long had I been filling in the blank spaces, nursing my anger? Those days were so far behind me now, in another life. The fight felt like a bruise, something that might fade if I just let it be.

"Krystal," I said. I reached out my hand.

I saw her stiffen before she turned toward me, bracing herself for another one of my smartass jabs. But then she saw my blistered, trembling hand. She looked at me, really looked at me, beyond the burns, beyond our fractured past. I hoped that she saw that I was finished hurting her. Her whole body relaxed and her face sagged. She took my hand.

"Bonnie," she said, and stopped. Her voice choked up. "I'm so sorry," she said.

I grunt-snorted. I took her other hand. We sat there for a while in silence. The lowering sun dodged in and out of clouds, the light in the room waxing and waning.

She sniffled and said, "You can come home with me, you know. We would be happy to have you." She wiped at her face with her hand. "You could have your own room and everything. Whatever you wanted."

I imagined the life she was suggesting, of going back to the places of my youth, of seeing the people I used to know, the old landscape. I pictured holidays together with Krystal and her new family, Christmases, the new traditions they had formed, the routine of her days, the smiling face of her kid. My own room, my own window. I remembered the smell of Geannie's house when Krystal and I were younger, remembered how she used to stand in the kitchen, urging us to go outside. *Go get some sun on your face*, she'd say.

A normal life. I wanted to want it.

The ground inside me broke wide open and I fell into it. All this lost time, all these lost people. I buried my face in her hands and shook.

I was sorry, too.

•••••••••••

After Krystal left, I sat at my window for a while until someone came and got me, wheeled me to a late dinner. The autumn season was coming on, and the dining room was adorned in all the trappings—red and gold paper leaves, white fairy lights, fake plastic gourds. Outside the weather has turned cold, the nurses say. I heard them talking about corn mazes, about carving pumpkins. "And did you know the original jack-o'-lanterns were turnips?" one of them said tonight. She was standing behind me, chatting with one of the more talkative patients.

I could almost hear Rita chime in. *A light carried in such an ugly vessel? Can you imagine?* Her laugh.

Krystal had stayed for another hour after I wept into her hands. She took it as my assent to go live with her, and maybe it was. She patted my back as I cried. I had been wrong about everything.

When the time came for her to leave, we both stood. I hugged her goodbye. She squeezed my hands, promising that she would be back, that all would be made right. She would talk to the doctors. I would go home with her, and I could see her new house, her new life. We would start our new lives together. Her face was shining, hopeful. She looked like a real person now, the one I might have become had I gone a different way. The way I wanted to remember her.

When dinner was served I sat at my table quietly. I took in my surroundings. The sun was low in the sky, nearing the golden hour. People moved and talked around me, and I felt the river of time pull at me once more. I thought of Krystal and my father, my mother, of Hernan. Of Geannie and of Jim. Of Rita. They were all there with me. I closed my eyes. I had reached my destination.

Now there's only a short way to go. A hallway with one door at the end. And if I try, I can see the room on the other side, the version of Bonnie Lincoln that waits there. It is my future and my past; it has already happened and will happen again. I move toward it slowly, wanting to reach it before it shuts forever.

On the other side, in my room, in a state of neurotic agitation, I wait for sunset. I turn onto my side and gather Ray's teddy bear into my arms, his final animal gift. In front of me, the window glows. Behind me, footsteps in the hallway are fading, fading.

From the belly of the bear I extract the screen with shaking hands, and I make sure the earplugs are firmly in place. I press Play. When the music hits I grunt-snort to myself, breathing through my mouth. Outside, the last of the sun sinks into the sea.

My dearest friends walk across the screen and I see all the dead alive again, in all the old places in the old days, all the sleepless, grieving nights and sad, angry hours erased. Inside their rooms my existence is cradled, its rough corners sanded down into one fond longing. Everyone looks so young and happy, good people on the brink of good things, and I recall being born again within each of them, unaware of any past or future, borrowing their freedom, their open arms. Such beautiful, deathless characters!

Was I not them for a time? Did they not live in me still?

Darkness falls. The room, and the past, and the pain, recede. I shut my eyes. One episode ends its journey and another begins, and in my chest my living heart beats. I dream.

Acknowledgments

Many thanks go to my literary agent, Zoe Sandler; to Drew Weitman, my editor; to Amy Robbins, my copy editor; and to everyone at Norton.

And to *Three's Company*—thank you.